Love, Secrets, and Sacrifice

Penelope Ohmann Lindblom

DEDICATION

As a young girl growing up in the nineteen fifties, my father used to regale me with stories that his mother told him about her growing up years in Germany. I never met my grandmother, as she died in her middle forties from complications of rheumatoid arthritis. It is believed that this developed as a result of malnutrition during World War I. My grandfather never spoke of his time during the war, but the stories my father used to tell made me laugh and cry. I never forgot those stories and they are what eventually inspired me to write this book. Without those family tales, this book would not have been possible. I want to thank my father, Ernest August Wilhelm (William) Ohmann and dedicate this book to him.

ACKNOWLEDGEMENTS

I want to thank all those who have put up with my talk about this book for years. I could not have done this without my critique group, especially Jerri McCloud, and all their help and advice. I appreciate that they told me what I needed to know and not just what I wanted to hear. I want to thank my professor and friend Dr. Robert Billinger, his comments and encouragements were a great help. To my friend and editor Liz Washburn for spending a summer reading, editing and commenting. Your work improved mine so much. To my friend Elizabeth Williamson, who, when I was tired, encouraged me to go on, I couldn't have done it without you. I especially want to thank my husband Charles Lindblom, who has read every chapter nearly as many times as I have. He always seems to know just what I need at the time is always encouraging and proud of my achievements.

Table of Contents

Table of Contents (continued)

All of the characters in this story are fictional. If you know my family, however, you may recognize traits and attitudes. Many of the happenings are real though: Elsa and Georg's trip to Germany in the summer of 1914 and what happened afterwards, as well as, the daily trolley ride over the Rhine river and the mysterious need to stop in the middle of the bridge, and Paul's internship at the Schoenbrunn Castle, to name a few. The historical events are as close to actual as my research allowed.

Love, Secrets and Sacrifice is a story that takes place during World War I in Germany and from the German point of view. This is a story about war, but not battles. Rather, it is a story about what happens to the families left behind when husbands, fathers, sons, and brothers go off to fight the battles.

I hope you enjoy this story. My friend Elizabeth once told me that we never think about our enemies having families. This is that story.

July 23, 1914 Austria issues ultimatum to Serbia

Kaiser Wilhelm declares: As soon as the period allowed
Serbia to reply has elapsed, or in case she does not accept all
the conditions without reservations, mobilization will be
ordered. The note has been drafted in such a way that it will
be practically impossible for Serbia to accept it.

"Now we can no longer hold back. It will be a terrible war."
(Emperor Franz Josef (Austria) upon hearing of the Kaiser
'Wilhelm's (Germany) support.)

Chapter 1
Düsseldorf, Germany
Morning of July 24, 1914

The newspaper headlines seemed to scream at Hedwig. What did it all mean?

"Momma, they're here, finally here," Hannah shouted as she ran down the stairs, taking them three at a time.

Hedwig quickly folded the newspaper and slipped it under a dishtowel.

"Momma, did you hear me? They're here. I just saw Papa's auto turn onto Dorfstrasse." Hannah ran into the kitchen throwing her arms around her mother. Soon they will be here in this house."

Hedwig gently removed Hannah's arms. "Yes, Liepchen, I heard you."

"You don't look excited. Is something wrong?"

"No, of course not." Hedwig smiled at her youngest child. "You go on and meet them. I will be there very soon."

"Are you sure? Do you need some help?"

"I am just waiting for the last loaf of bread to finish." Hedwig brushed at her hair. "Go and meet your sister."

Hannah smiled, waved to her mother and nearly flew out the front door. "Be careful not to slam the doo...." Too late. The screen door banged against the frame and Hannah was gone.

Now? Why did they come now? Hedwig wondered. She extracted the paper from under the towel. Emotions in turmoil, she pushed back her chair, and stood up. The mother and grandmother in her urged her to run, just as Hannah had with joyful abandon. Her more pragmatic side held her back. What secrets did the future hold?

Hedwig glanced around. Everything was ready. She had prepared for this day for weeks. Hannah helped her wash all the windows until they squeaked. They laughed at the memory of so many family occasions this house had seen as they washed, starched, ironed and put the curtains back up on the windows. Otto, after helping polish what seemed like acres of wood, commented that the floors sparkled and looked clean enough to be a dinner plate.

After careful consideration of all the flowers in the yard, Hedwig had filled every room with iris, phlox, and roses of every color. Then she had flung open the windows, to allow the curtains gently flutter in the breeze as the fragrance of flowers filled the house with the perfume of her love.

She walked to the stove to take the final loaf of her darkest pumpernickel bread from the oven and place it on the counter next the loaves of her lightest rye. Hedwig thought of all the planning she had done for this very special meal and smiled as she remembered starting the lebkuchen, Elsa's favorite Christmas cookie, in June to be ready for July. It did feel like Christmas in July. The Sauerbraten started last week so it would be perfect for today. Then there was the wonderful sauerkraut the boys made last year. Everyone said it is the best they had ever made. The strudel cooled on the counter and the spatzel sat in the bowl ready to fix. Yes, everything would be perfect for this wonderful homecoming.

Against her will, she seemed drawn by an invisible force to look at the newspaper one more time. There it was again, Will there be War in Europe this Summer? She picked it up and stuffed it into a drawer, determined not to let anything ruin this day and walked to the front door.

Hedwig reached down to straighten the rug Hannah had kicked up on her way out, an errant wisp of graying hair fell across her face. She stood up and caught sight of herself in the mirror by the door. Her once beautiful auburn hair was now peppered with gray. She stiffened her back but somehow felt shorter than her former five feet. She certainly was rounder than she was four years ago. She tucked the wayward hair back into the bun at the nape of her neck.

Would her daughter think she had become an old woman, she wondered? Tears welled in her eyes at the thought. She stepped out the front door just in time to see Hannah climb onto the running board of the still moving vehicle. The isinglass shades hid the passengers. She knew that Elsa and Gus were there, just beyond view.

At last, the vehicle came to a halt and Hannah opened the door. There sat Elsa, Hedwig's elder daughter, elegant in azure silk, her flaxen hair piled high, pins of lapis cut in tiny overlapping pairs of hearts, completed her traveling costume. On her lap a blanket that held the sleeping child was a perfect match to her outfit.

Hedwig's tears now threatened to overflow. It had been four long years since Elsa and Georg left to make a new life in America. Now they had come home for a visit to introduce little Gus to his family.

Hannah sounded breathless as the words tumbled from her mouth, "Elsa you're here! I can't believe it. Oh, I see Gus. Please, may I hold him?"

Elsa sat on the rich leather seat of her father's 1912 Mercedes taxi, laughter in her voice, "Hannah, your enthusiasm hasn't changed one bit, still full of fun and excitement. However, you must slow down before I can give little Gus to you."

"Oh, Elsa, I missed you so much." Hannah nearly crushed her sister with a hug. Hedwig felt the lump in her throat grow as she watched her daughters laughing together.

Elsa kissed Hannah's cheek and then held her at arm's length. "How beautiful you are. I would hardly recognize you. My goodness you're not a little girl anymore."

"Of course I'm not a little girl. I just turned sixteen," Hannah spouted with indignity.

"I bet Papa has a hard time keeping the boys away."

"I don't care about boys. All they ever want to talk about is the war, guns, and Wilhelm and…and… I don't know." Hannah shook her head, mahogany curls sprinkled with cinnamon bouncing in unruly tendrils. "I just won't listen to them anymore."

"You had better be careful what you say. You might be surprised someday."

"Well, maybe someday I'll meet a boy like Georg who doesn't care about war, who just wants to be a husband and a father. But I really doubt it; all the boys I know are just so stupid."

Georg stepped down from the front of the vehicle. "Not so fast, you'll have lots of time to find the perfect man, just like me." He gently lifted the sleeping baby from his wife's arms and turned to Hannah. "Do you think you can carry this precious child to his grandmomma waiting so patiently by the door?"

Hedwig clutched her chest when Georg called her grandmomma.

"I'm his Tanta; of course I'll be very careful." She turned to start up the walk then looked back. "Georg, I'm glad you're home too."

Hedwig watched Hannah cautiously carry the baby, her own excitement barely contained. She saw Otto come around the vehicle and take his daughter's hand helping her to the ground. How exquisite Elsa looked, tall and statuesque, standing next to her father, with those stunning soft features that melted men's hearts. The sheer look of joy on Otto's face assured Hedwig that Elsa and Georg's homecoming was just as important to him as it was to her.

Otto never said, in so many words, how much he missed Elsa, but Hedwig knew. He had spent weeks working on the old half-timbered house, patching the stucco, refinishing the timbers, checking every tile on the roof, making sure theirs was the best on the block. Moreover, this morning he left at least an hour earlier necessary to get to the train station. Yes, he was just as anxious as she.

Hannah slowly made her way toward the house, her petite frame with sharp angular features such a contrast to Elsa's classic German look. After what seemed a lifetime, she finally reached her mother.

"Momma, look who I brought you," Hannah shouted as she got near.

Gus began to fuss just as Hedwig took him. Tenderly she opened the blue blanket to see her grandson for the first time. She leaned against the rail on the stoop to keep her balance, the rush of emotion overwhelming. She had no idea that this child of her child would grab her heart and soul so completely in just one moment. She bent her head, kissed his little nose, and buried her face in his soft sweet neck. She had forgotten aroma of sweetness and soft skin only babies have. Was there ever a child as perfect as this?

Gus' fuss continued to grow in intensity. Hedwig laughed, "Ah, so you greet your grandmomma with a cry, do you? Welcome home little one, welcome home."

Chapter 2
Düsseldorf, Germany
Later that same day

Hedwig was enjoying a few minutes of quiet in the house. She had been so busy the last few days that this short respite was welcome. Soon the house would be full of noise again because August and his wife Louisa were coming for dinner. How wonderful it would be to have her whole family around the table for the first time in four years.

Opening a drawer to get a ladle, she discovered the newspaper lying where she shoved it that morning. Quickly, she turned it over, afraid the awful news that filled the paper would suck her in one more time. She knew it was better she just ignore it, refusing to let the rest of the world spoil her day.

"I'm back, Momma. I didn't mean to be gone so long." The screen door closed with a bang behind Hannah.

"Hannah, will you ever learn to enter a house without slamming the doors?"

"Sorry, I'll be more careful next time. Greta and Ingrid were at the market and they wanted to know all about Gus and Elsa and I guess I just talked too long." Hannah had to stop talking to catch her breath as she put the packages on the table.

"Were you able to get everything on my list?" Hedwig asked.

"I got everything but the blue tulips. Herr Vander Linden only had yellow and red today. So I got yellow. I hope that is alright with you."

"Of course, yellow will be fine."

"Where is everyone?" Hannah bounced passed her mother and into the parlor.

"Please, Hannah slow down, you make me tired just watching you."

"Yes, Momma, I'll try. Everything is just so exciting with Elsa home. Where is she?"

"She is upstairs with Gus, trying to get him to take a nap. Georg and your father are in the barn."

"I was upstairs," Elsa countered as she entered the kitchen. "The little mausi has finally fallen asleep. He seems to have gotten his days and nights mixed up on this long trip."

"I am not surprised," Hedwig said, "so many days of traveling had to be difficult for all of you."

"Both Georg and I enjoy traveling, especially by ship."

"I don't think that I would like to travel on a ship. All that water must be scary," Hannah shivered at the thought.

"Not really. You get used to it pretty quickly."

"Hannah, someone is at the door, will you get it, please," Hedwig asked.

"I'll get it, Momma," Elsa said. "It's probably August and Louisa."

Before Elsa could get across the room, the door swung open and there stood her only brother August with his wife, Louisa. "Welcome home Little Sister!" August threw his arms around his Elsa, picked her up and twirled her around the room. "It is wonderful to see you." Setting her back down, he said "Let me look at you. Somehow, you are even more beautiful then you were when you left. How is that possible?"

"It must be the glow of motherhood," Elsa laughed and kissed her brother, a mirror image of herself with the blond hair and soft features that made him almost too pretty to be a man.

"Speaking of motherhood, where is my little namesake?" August asked.

"He is upstairs asleep and if you dare try to wake him up, you will have to be the one to change and feed him."

"I am not at all sure he is equipped to do that," Louisa chimed in. "I will do my best to keep him under wraps until little Gus wakes up." Louisa gave August a punch on the shoulder. Turning back to Elsa she continued, "I can't remember when I last saw him as excited as when we got your telegram telling us that you had named your baby after August."

Elsa wrapped her arms around her sister-in-law. "Louisa, it is so good to see you too. I have really missed the time we spent together. Remember how we used to talk until the middle of the night? I am sure your mother believed I was never going to go home."

"I've missed you, too. I love your brother. He is my best friend but I can't talk to him like I could you."

Hedwig watched as the young women embraced. They were so very different, Elsa flamboyant and inclined to act without thinking while Louisa was the quiet, steady, almost shy one, and yet they had been best friends since childhood.

"Where are Papa and Georg?" August inquired.

"Out in the barn," Hannah answered. "Where else would they be?"

"I think I will go and join them before I get myself in more trouble here in the house. Is there anything you need help with, Momma?"

"I do not think so. Go and enjoy whatever it is that you men talk about. We will call you when dinner is ready."

***

August exited the house through the kitchen and back door as quickly as he could. Following the path through Momma's garden he could see the wide open door of the barn, that grand old structure that used to house Papa's horses and coach. The horses were gone now, replaced by the Mercedes taxi that Papa drove every day. The coach, however, still sat in its special space at the front of the building.

There in the barn door stood Georg an imposing figure at more than six feet tall, dark hair with tanned skin and muscular arms. He had the body of the mechanic he was. One look into his eyes and you knew behind all that brawn lived a very intelligent man. He may claim to be just a mechanic but August knew he was truly a gifted engineer.

"Well there he is, my long lost brother-in-law," Georg grinned a slapped August on the back.

"Look who's talking. I'm not the one who just up and left for America." August responded shaking Georg's hand with genuine pleasure.

"I bet you have thought of it, though. We have some very good universities in America. I am sure they would jump at the chance to have wonderful Professor of Literature, Herr August Kruger on faculty."

"I have thought of it, Louisa will never leave Germany as long as her mother is still alive. She is Genevieve's only family."

"Perhaps we will see you, then, in thirty years, in the 'New World'."

"Well, that is good to hear," Otto said. "I would hate to think that all of my family had gone across the ocean. Someone has to stay here to take care of Momma and me. We are getting quite old, you know."

"You are much too pessimistic Papa. You and Momma will live a very long time! Don't worry, though, we will take care of you when you really do get old," grinned August.

Otto got his pipe from his pocket, tapped it lightly against the barn door, dipped it into his tobacco pouch and carefully pushed just the right amount of tobacco into the bowl. He retrieved his tamper from another pocket and tamped the tobacco just so. Next, he put the pipe in his mouth and tilted it to the right as he struck the match and held it over the tobacco. Ever so gently Papa drew in air and breathed it out. The bowl of tobacco soon had the perfect glow.

"I swear, Papa, you have that down to an art. I much prefer my American cigarettes." Georg pulled a pack from his pocket. "Would you like to try one, August?"

"I don't mind if I do." August accepted the proffered pack. "Tell me, Georg, was there any talk of war in America before you left?"

"All the newspapers were full of it. The talk was only of Europe, nothing about America. I don't believe what happens here in Europe will make much difference in America." Georg ventured. "Do you think that Germany will become involved, Otto?"

Georg noticed that Otto lovingly caressed the bowl of his pipe as he pondered the question. Some things never change, he thought with pleasure, as he watched this man he loved as his own father.

"I certainly hope that Germany stays out of this mess. Regretfully, I fear that will not happen. You may remember that the Pan-German League said back in April that both France and Russia are preparing for war with us and with Austria-Hungary. Now the Kaiser seems determined to goad both countries on with decrees to support the Austrians on all fronts."

Otto paused to relight his pipe more from habit then necessity. "Fighting a two front war could be very dangerous. I do not like the sound of it."

"I agree," August sat on a bail of straw next to his father. "But, do you really think the Kaiser would be brazen enough to get us into something like that?"

"Oh, I definitely think that he would," Georg took a drag on his cigarette. "Wilhelm thinks his Germany can do anything."

"You are so right, Georg; I am glad that you and Elsa will be in America. I almost wonder if it was safe for you to come at such a time as this," Otto said.

"Otto, you worry too much. Elsa and I would not have missed this trip for anything. Nothing will happen to any of us." He took one final drag and ground out the cigarette on the bottom of his shoe. "I am sure that this will all be over soon, even before anything really happens. You know these rulers. They are all talk."

"Georg, I would not be so certain of all that," August leaned his chin on his fist in a thoughtful manner. "I am not sure that Russia and France will give in to us Germans. They are both very powerful nations and really do not like us. They never have."

"Yes but Kaiser Wilhelm, Czar Nicholas and King George are first cousins," Georg countered. "Surely they will not fight against each other."

"I'm glad to see that you know your rulers, Georg," August laughed, "I would have to give you a top grade in my history class."

Georg frowned and pretended to be hurt, "I may be just a mechanic but I did study some history."

"I'll take that into consideration," August smiled. "Think about this, though, who is Wilhelm, II, to tell other countries what to do?"

"What do you mean?" Georg asked.

"Perhaps things would have been better if the Kaiser had stayed out of it. I think that he really wants to go to war, to prove how powerful he actually is. After all, he claims that Germany now has the most powerful navy in the world. Great Britain is not very happy about that," mused August.

"You may be right about that, August," said Otto. "However, I still do not think he will take us into war. In general, the economy is good. The great citizens of this country are content. War is expensive. Why would Wilhelm throw his people into turmoil that war inevitably presents without just cause?"

"Because he wants to prove again just how powerful he is, that's why. It is all about power. Just power," argued August clearly agitated. "Just power!"

"Papa, August, Georg, dinner is ready", Hannah shouted from the back porch.

"Come, enough talk of war, let us go and see what wondrous treats the ladies have prepared for us." said Otto as he got up from an old pile of hay and knocked the tobacco out of his pipe onto the old clay floor. "I will have none of this of talk of war inside my house."

Otto, a big bear of a man, pushed his chair back and surveyed the scene that played out before him. He had despaired of ever having his whole family around his table again. He could not help but look at each one with pride; August, a successful and much respected history and literature professor and his lovely wife, Louisa, sat to his left, the capricious Hannah next to Louisa. On his right sat Elsa, elegant as always, next to Georg, so strong and handsome. His wonderful Hedwig sat opposite him with precious little Gus on her lap. What man could ask for more? He was content, as he had not been for many years.

No one not even Hedwig, knew how much he had missed Elsa. He always thought giving his daughter away in marriage was the hardest thing a man would ever have to do. He never dreamed that it would be even harder to have them move an ocean away to another world. He had tried, but could never understand the pull of America that had worked its magic on Georg. Why would a person want to live anywhere but Germany? For him, this was the perfect place. Rubbing his stomach, Otto looked at the table still so full of food. "Hedwig, you have outdone yourself this evening. I do believe that was the best sauerbraten that you have ever made." He watched his wife blush, as he knew she would.

"Thank you, Otto. The sauerkraut you and August made last year certainly helped make it perfect." Hedwig smiled looked down and blew little kisses at the sleeping baby.

Elsa carefully wiped the corner of her mouth with her napkin. "I think the bread is the best part. It has been so very long since I had homemade bread. Momma, no one makes bread better than you."

"What do you mean you haven't had homemade bread? What kind of bread do you eat?" Hannah had a look of true concern on her face as she tickled little Gus's feet.

Georg laughed aloud at Hannah's remark, "We buy our bread at the store along with all of our other food. Life is very different in America."

"Bread from a store?" Hannah seemed very surprised. "You must live in a very strange place."

Louisa chuckled and gently shook her lovely brown curls, "Elsa, what is your house like in this strange place, America?"

Elsa, caught up in the conversation now looked at Louisa and then Hannah. "Well, America is indeed, very strange, actually we don't live in houses we live in holes in the ground."

Everyone at the table chuckled except Hannah. "Elsa, that is not nice. You are no different than you ever were." Hannah looked to Hedwig. "Momma, she's picking on me."

Elsa quickly realized she had gone too far. "I am sorry dear Hannah. Let me tell you what our house truly is like. We have three bedrooms upstairs and a parlor, dining room and kitchen downstairs very much like this house. The biggest difference is that I have a very modern kitchen with a gas stove, an icebox and running water."

It was Hedwig's turn to be surprised. She gasped, "A gas stove and running water. What do you do if you run out of gas? Can you still burn wood?"

"Oh, Momma, you are so silly. We do not run out of gas. It comes in a pipe directly to our house so there is no need for wood. We have a furnace that uses gas, too. It is much smaller than the monster that lives in your basement, gobbles up coal and belches out smoke."

The family once again erupted in laughter all except Hedwig whose face showed more fear than frivolity.

"I am sure that I would be afraid with so much gas floating around. Is it safe, Georg?" Hedwig sounded truly worried.

"Of course it is safe. There are many new and modern conveniences in America that are not here yet, but they will come." Georg assured her.

Louisa looked awestruck, "I think that I would like the running water best. Sometimes the pumping makes me so tired. How nice to just turn a knob and the water would come out."

"Everything makes you tired these days, Louisa. I worry that something is wrong." August squeezed her hand.

"She just has to work so hard to take care of you, big brother," Elsa said with a mischievous twinkle in her eye.

"No, seriously, I am worried about her. She is always tired and she does not want to eat. Some days she says, just the thought of food makes her sick. I keep telling her we should call Dr. Ostermann, but she refuses." August shook his head.

"I am fine, really I am. I am just a little tired and feel sick in the morning once in a while," Louisa protested. "Oh my, Louisa, are you expecting a baby?" Elsa asked with excitement. "I was just like that when I was first expecting little Gus. You must do as August says and see the Dr. Ostermann at once." She turned to look at her mother, "This is so exciting. Momma, I do believe that you will be a grandmother again."

"And I will be Tanta Hannah again. This is wonderful, two babies in our family. I am lucky to be part of the best family in the world."

Otto soon wearied of all the woman talk and looked at Georg, "Tell us about that wonderful job you have in America. I am sure that it must be grand if you can afford to leave for three months on a little vacation."

"I do have a wonderful job, Otto. I am working for the railroad, building new and rebuilding old engines. You know that I have always loved working with my hands and this job allows me to do just that. It is very dirty work though." He held up his hands. "Elsa worries that I don't always look like a gentleman with my dirty hands." He grinned at his wife. "However, I do make a good living."

Elsa looked at her husband with love in her eyes, "When we knew we were going to have little Gus, Georg promised me that we could come home for a visit. He knew how homesick I was. Sometimes I would cry myself to sleep at night because I missed all of you so very much." Elsa looked uncharacteristically depressed. "Then, after Gus was born, it just got worse. Georg worked many extra hours to make this trip possible." She smiled at Georg, "Thank you, Darling, for bringing me home." Elsa's eyes filled with tears as she looked at her husband and her son who sat on Grandmother's lap.

"Elsa, tell me, little sister, what is it like to live in Toledo, America?" August inquired.

"It is Toledo, Ohio, in the United States of America. You know that Mister very smart brother of mine." Elsa reached across the table and cuffed her brother on the shoulder. "It is wonderful. We live just down the street from two other families who speak German. Of course, we speak English most of the time, though it is nice to hear German occasionally."

"I do not think that I would ever be able to speak English every day. Especially if I could speak German," Hannah said.

"One of the most exciting things is," Elsa continued with pride in her voice, "because Gus was born in America, he is an American citizen. Georg and I have been going to classes and have applied for American citizenship, but we have to live there for one more year before we can become citizens.

"Why would you want to become American citizens? Is Germany no longer good enough for you?" Otto's voice sounded gruffer than he intended.

"Papa, do not be upset with us. We are still German citizens; in fact, we traveled on our German passports for this trip. Next time we visit, though, we will be American citizens."

"Otto," Georg nearly stepped on Elsa's voice as he tried to sooth ruffled feelings. "Please understand that Elsa and I will always be German at heart, but now that we live in America and Gus is an American citizen by birth, it makes sense that his parents should be American citizens as well."

"Well perhaps you are right, when you put it that way." That was as close as Otto would ever get to an apology.

Chapter 4
Düsseldorf, Germany
July 31, 1914

"Georg, it has been wonderful having you ride with me these last few days. Not only have you made my work easier, it has been grand to share my views of the world with you. As you know, I will not speak of war, nor will I discuss politics at home. I fear that it will frighten the women." Otto pulled his pipe from his pocket, pondered lighting it.

"I understand, Otto. I, too, feel the women must be sheltered from all possible worry and harm. Still, I'm very concerned when I read the papers."

Otto and Georg were leaning against the side of the taxi, waiting at the train station. Neither man seemed aware of the perfect summer weather. Otto did notice that the travelers seemed more serious than usual, most faces wearing a frown rather than the smiles of summer revelers. They appeared to greet each other less and move about the station with purpose, rather than with the joy of a summer holiday.

"The paper today says that Kaiser Wilhelm is still in Norway on holiday. Surely Germany cannot be preparing for war with the Kaiser away," injected a passenger as he climbed into the taxi. "It also says that the English fleet is discharging its reservists and giving crews leave according to their schedule. I submit that there will be no war this summer, gentlemen."

Georg walked around the vehicle as Otto got behind the wheel of his luxury auto. "That may be true. However, there is a feeling in the very air that seems to be whispering war, war, war." Otto tapped the steering wheel for emphasis.

The passenger agreed, "I wish I could reach out and grab that menacing feeling right out of the air. My heart aches with the thought war. I fear that leaders of this great country are not all in accord concerning the realities of possible war with Russia."

"I have to agree with you, Russia cannot stand idly by and let Austria mobilize against Serbia," Georg added.

"Georg, I worry about you and Elsa and the baby. Perhaps you should leave very soon. I know that you have only been here a short time, but each day this concerns me more. You must consider changing your plans."

"I'll think about what you say. However, I won't mention it to Elsa just yet. She is enjoying her visit so much. She mentioned only this morning that she was looking forward to going to market. Something that she always hated when she was younger," mused Georg.

"True, true, she certainly does seem to be enjoying your visit. I, too, am reveling in the role of grandpapa. I had no idea I would ever be so captivated by such a small child.

"Otto, I believe that you are turning soft in your later years. You're a much gentler man than the one I knew as a boy growing up."

"I do not know about that, but I do know my concern is great for your safe return to America."

"Did you say that you are from America, young man?" asked the fare. "Tell me is there talk of war there as well?"

"Well Sir, when we left a month ago now, the papers spoke of the conflicts in Europe. However, of America, they spoke only that it was going to be a beautiful summer and the economy was good. The people like President Wilson, because they have jobs. In America, there are jobs for all who are willing to work. Why would they want to go to war?" asked Georg.

"If there is war, it will be a European war. America will stay out. They are an ocean away and have no fight with any European nation. The American policy is one of isolationism. We'll stay on our side of the big pond if Europe stays on hers."

"I agree with you, young man. I hope we are both right. This is my stop. Enjoy the rest of your visit and do not listen to your Papa here. He worries too much."

Otto laughed as he took the man's Marks. "Georg, what do you say we call it a day and go home to the ladies? I think this would be a wonderful afternoon to stroll down to the Hagen Brau and enjoy our family and friends. I am sure there must be at least one neighbor who has not seen little Gus yet."

* * *

"Hello, we came home early so we could spend some time with our lovely ladies," boomed Otto as he entered the house.

"Quiet, the baby is sleeping," Hedwig whispered testily. "What nonsense brings you home so early? Were there no fares today?"

"What is wrong, Hedwig? We came home to spend time with you, the girls and the baby"

"There is nothing wrong. The baby has been fussy all day and now is finally sleeping. We are all just a little tired," Hedwig replied, wiped the perspiration from her forehead with the back of her hand, and sat on one of the big ladder back chairs at the old trestle table.

"No, there is more than that. I have spent too many years with you. I know when something is wrong. What has happened?"

"There on the table, a letter from Ernst."

"Letters from your brother, officer in the Imperial Navy, usually bring a smile to your face."

"You will see."

Otto sat down at the table and picked up the familiar envelope with the symbol of the Imperial Navy on it. It was with a feeling of trepidation that he removed the folded sheets of stationary.

July 26, 1914
My Dear Sister Hedwig,

I hope that you are enjoying your much-anticipated visit from Elsa and Georg. It is with confidence that I say I am sure you have become the world's proudest grandmother. How is that old stuffed shirt Otto going about being a grandpapa? I wonder if even the baby can get a smile from him.

I fear that I will not be able to join all of you for this festive time. It is with great sadness that I realize I will miss meeting little August and telling him all of my stories about life in the navy. I will look forward to their next visit. Please give my beautiful Elsa a kiss for me. You know that she has always been my favorite. August is a good solid man and Hannah puts a smile on my face, but Elsa, my sweet Elsa, has always held a special place in my heart.

We have been cruising in the Norwegian fjords with the Kaiser's fleet. We are all speculating about the possibility of war, but hear very little from our superiors. We stopped in Balholm recently and the Norwegian newspapers gave the impression that the situation was growing worse.

An order has just been issued to report to the Captain's office. I fear I must finish this letter later.

I have just returned from a meeting of all

officers. We learned that the English fleet has not dispersed as we had been led to believe, but may have left secretly for Norway in order to find and capture the Kaiser. We were also told of the Austrian ultimatum to Serbia and the Serbian response to Austria.

I must make this letter very brief so to get it into the Post before we leave port. Kaiser Wilhelm has ordered the fleet to sail for Wilhelmshaven immediately.

Give my love to all of the family.

> Fondly,
> Your loving brother
> Ernst

Otto read and then reread the letter. This was ominous news indeed. Why was the Kaiser cutting his holiday short and returning for Wilhelmshaven? He seldom acted on rumor alone. There must be some evidence that the English fleet was searching for him. First, the Russians and now the English, European matters were grim, indeed.

Otto, got up, walked over and leaned casually on the sink. "My Dear Hedwig, you put too much stock in a letter from your brother." He commented trying to keep the growing alarm out of his voice. "This is all rumors. Perhaps the Kaiser has just changed his plans and is tired of cruising,"

"Otto, do not pretend that I know nothing about what is going on in the world. I know what you men talk about. You leave the newspapers on the kitchen table every morning. I do know how to read, you know. We are going to war of that I am convinced."

"This is nothing for ladies to be concerned about. War is for men. Women are not involved. Please do not dwell on such things. Elsa, Georg, and little Gus are here. Just enjoy their visit and do not fret about world affairs. Let us men take care of that." He turned to walk from the room.

"Do not turn your back on me, Herr Kruger." Hedwig stood up and faced her husband. "How can you be so blind? Do you not realize that if there is a war we will all be involved? August might have to fight, he and Louisa are expecting a baby." Anger or perhaps fear growing in her voice with each word. "Ernst is in the Imperial navy, he would certainly be in danger. How can you say that we women would not be involved? War affects us all. Can you not understand that? It affects us all… every one."

Otto looked at his wife with a new understanding, "At least Elsa and Georg will not be involved. They will go back to America, "

Hedwig moved closer to her husband, he put his arm around her. With a sense of imploring she said, "I know that you think that you can protect the women from this threat of war. However, you cannot. If there is to be war, we are all going to experience it together. We must talk and share all of our concerns. It will be so much better if we can do that. Promise me, Otto, that you will keep no secrets from me."

"Papa, it's a beautiful evening for a walk." Hannah pushed the baby carriage in front of the rest of the family group. Otto and Hedwig walked close beside each other. They decided that they would not share Ernst's letter with everyone else just yet. They would just enjoy the rest of the day. Now that they had made their pact to keep no secrets from each other, they saw no need to worry the rest of the family

"I agree with Hannah, the weather is perfect and a special Hagen Brew will taste wonderful," Elsa added. It has been so long since we enjoyed anything like Hagen Brau. Don't you agree, Georg?"

"Yes, there is nothing really equal to the typical German beer garden in Toledo. We have some restaurants that serve German food but nowhere that we can sit outside under the trees all afternoon or evening.

Elsa continued, "What I like about German beer gardens is that whole families can spend time together and even bring their own food. Of course, no one makes pretzels and breadsticks with caraway seeds like Hagen Brau does."

"I think what I like best," Georg added, "is that in Germany the beer is served at just the right temperature. It is always so cold in America."

Otto had a look of shock on his face. "Cold beer! Whoever heard of such a thing? Why there would be no wonderful aroma and certainly no taste if beer were served cold."

"I have to agree, Otto." Georg patted his father-in-law on the back. "There is nothing to equal a good warm brew."

"Hannah slow down," Elsa cautioned. "Your friends will still be there when we get there."

Petra, one of the servers, greeted the family as they entered the garden. "There is a table over there on the left that looks perfect for your group. Shall I bring refreshments for you?'

"That would be lovely, thank you Petra." Otto began moving toward the table.

"Hannah, over here. Hannah!"

"Papa," Hannah asked excitedly. "Ingrid and Greta are at that table by the band. Can I sit with them please?"
Papa looked at Momma who nodded her approval. "Yes, but please leave Gus with us."

"Here, Elsa, you take him now." Hannah practically fell in her rush to join her friends.

"Sometimes I think that she is truly growing up, and then I see her like this and I wonder if she will ever grow up." Elsa laughed. "I know one thing for sure, though. Papa, you will soon have more boys than you can count knocking on the door to court your Hannah."

"Yes, my little girl is growing up. Please do not encourage her. Surely she is too young to be thinking about boys yet!" replied the doting father.

"Oh, Papa, don't you remember me at that age."

"I certainly do." Otto screwed up his face in a frown.

"Thank goodness Hannah is very different. I do not think that I could live through another one like you."

Hedwig grinned at Elsa and then her husband. "Otto, you best be quiet, you will find yourself in trouble with Elsa, once again."

"Oh no, I do not want that!" Otto mockingly covered his face with his hands. "You are right as always, Momma. I will just drink my brew in silence."

"That will be the day." Hedwig picked Gus from his carriage and took a seat next to her husband.

"Momma, who is the little girl with the short curly blond hair? She looks like an adorable elf." Elsa asked as Hannah sat down at the table with her friends.

"That is Ingrid. She is one of Hannah's best friends. The other one is Greta. The three of them are inseparable."

"Greta is beautiful, that long wavy hair and statuesque figure. She could be a model. I wager that the boys are all after her. Papa, you should be very happy that one is not your daughter."

"Yes, Greta is much like you were at that age."

"Otto..." Hedwig's voice was threatening.

"Yes, I know, just drink my brew."

Everyone at the table laughed at the thought of Otto being contrite.

* * *

"Hannah, I'm surprised that you could leave that nephew of yours long enough to spend time with us," Greta laughingly chided her. "We are having great fun. Sit there across from me."

Hannah greeted everyone at the table and found her seat.

"Have you met Anna's cousin yet? He is so cute," Greta asked.

"No. You know that I do not care about boys."

"This one is different. You will see," Greta smiled.

"Cute or not, I really am not interested in any boy," replied Hannah.

"Oh, I think you will like this one." Greta winked. "Here he comes now."

Hannah turned her back, "Ingrid, are you looking forward to school starting."

Ingrid laughed. "Hannah, you know that you can't ignore Greta."

"I can try."

"You had better look soon, Hannah. He is the one in the uniform over there coming with the beer."

Hannah kept her back turned.

"Isn't he just the most marvelous thing you have ever seen? I just love men in uniforms. It makes them all look so handsome," swooned Greta.

Hannah sneaked a look. "Greta, you think every man is heavenly. I don't see anything that makes this one any different from all the others you think so wonderful," replied Hannah.

"There, I knew you would look. You just can't help it."

"Greta, that's not fair." Hannah harrumphed.

"Fair or not, I made you look. See, you really are curious." Greta had a look of triumph on her face.

Hannah turned back to Ingrid. "Is he really your cousin?"

"Yes he is. Let me introduce you." Ingrid stood up and very formally began, "Hannah Kruger, I want you to meet my cousin, Paul Ulhman.

Greta jumped in even before Ingrid could finish, "He has been working at the Schonbrunn Palace, in Vienna, for the last three years and he met lots of very important people." Greta waved her arms as if introducing him to a large audience. Now her voice became solemn. "He has just joined Kaiser Wilhelm's Imperial army." Then the teenage girl that she was, showed through, swooning, "Doesn't he look divine in his uniform?"

"You are too kind, Greta. All men look good in uniforms. That is why we wear them just to attract women." Paul turned then to Hannah, "It is very nice to meet you Fraulein Kruger."

He doffed his hat and executed a perfect court bow for her benefit.

Hannah, somewhat taken aback by this, but never one to be outdone stood and curtsied back. "It is a great pleasure to meet you, as well, Herr Ulhman. However, I am not just any woman and it will take much more than a uniform to attract me."

"My, my, what have we here, a woman with spirit, how refreshing." Paul's laugh was infectious.

Turning away, Hannah felt her face growing red and realized she was enjoying this young man's taunts. She had to admit to herself that he was very handsome in his uniform and he seemed to be so sophisticated. Surely, he will fall all over Greta just as all the other boys do, she thought. Greta is so beautiful.

Paul joined the group and sat down opposite Hannah, next to Greta. There, just as I thought, Hannah sighed to herself. Her friends continued their conversation, but she remained uncharacteristically quiet. What made this young man seem so different?

"Hannah. Where are you Hannah? Are you going to answer my question?"

"What. What did you say? Elsa and Georg? Yes, they are visiting from America." She tried to catch up with the conversation. "They live in a place called Toledo. They will be here for a few more weeks and then will be returning to America." She thought she must sound like a dunce the way she fumbled for words.

"I would like to hear more about this place called Toledo. In what part of America is it? I have heard of many places but not this Toledo," questioned Paul.

Hannah was surprised by Paul's question. "I am not sure. I think I can find it on a map and it is near a great lake in the north of the country." Warming up to her subject a little, Hannah relaxed a little. "Elsa, she's my sister, says that they have lots of snow in the winter and warm weather in the summer, very much like Dusseldorf. I think that she likes it there because it reminds her of home.

"Does she speak English?" Paul wanted to know.

"She says that there are lots of people who speak German, but they usually only speak English. I don't think I would learn English. I have enough trouble with French."

"I'm studying English. I want very much to go to America." Paul spoke with great determination. "I have an English dictionary that I carry with me everywhere I go. I study it whenever I get a chance. I want to be ready when my opportunity comes,"

"You have to make your own opportunities, if you are going to get anywhere in this world." Hannah thought she sounded very wise. "I don't see how being in the Kaiser's army will give you a chance to go to America."

Ingrid jabbed Hannah in the ribs and whispered. "Why are you being so mean to him?"

"I don't think I'm being mean. What I said is true." Secretly she wondered if she had gone too far.

"I think it's time to change the subject." Paul announced to the group, then looking directly at Hannah. "Fraulein Kruger, I believe the band is playing a waltz. Would you do me the honor of a dance?" He asked.

Hannah could hardly believe her ears. He was asking her to dance, not Greta. Even after what she had said to him. She peeked at Ingrid who gave her a gentle push. Greta grinned from across the table. "I would be honored, Herr Ulhman," she replied with much more bravado than she felt.

Once they were on the dance floor Hannah closed her eyes and could not believe that this was happening. She was actually dancing with this handsome soldier. What would Papa say when he saw her, as he surely would? Would he be angry? She hoped not. She put those thoughts out of her mind and allowed herself to be caught up in the moment. She had always loved the Viennese waltzes and to be dancing with this interesting young man was beyond her wildest dreams.

Walking back to the table Hannah asked, "Were you really working at a palace in Vienna?"

"I was." Paul didn't anything further.

"It must have been very exciting. What were you doing there?"

"I just completed my apprenticeship as a landscape gardener with the Obergartner. He is one of the master landscape gardeners of the world. It was a wonderful opportunity and I hope to someday find a job in America doing the same thing."

"Well if you like gardening so much, why did you join the Imperial Army?"

"It is my duty. I believe that Germany will soon be at war and I must defend my country." Paul's voice had a note of reverence Hannah had not heard before. "My country has given me, a poor boy from Leipzig, a grand opportunity and I must repay the fatherland."

"Why are you here in Dusseldorf?"
My assignment is here in Dusseldorf for now. I am a motorcycle courier and it is my responsibility to carry messages between units."

Back at the table, Paul sat beside Hannah this time. He leaned over and whispered in her ear, "Do you think that I could call on you sometime?"

"Oh," Hannah felt herself blushing again, "I would like that very much."

Hannah rolled over and struggled to open her eyes. How could it be time to get up? She had slept so little, the excitement of the evening at Hagen Brau and then the worry about what Papa would do when he found out, had kept her awake most of the night.

She listened for the sounds of the city going back to work. She could hear the traffic on the Rhine River, lifeline of the entire country, coming awake. The tug horns bellowed as she imagined Papa was going to bellow at her. She heard the trains rattle across the tracks to the ironworks and the autos honking on the bridge over the river and wondered if Papa's taxi was amongst the fray. The clock tower tolled the hour as the cuckoo clock in the parlor echoed its response. She must get up, the hour was late and that was just going to make things worse.

She closed her eyes for just a few minutes more to savor her dream of last night, for a dream it must be. Was it real? Did I really dance with the handsome young soldier, Paul Ulhman? Did I float across the dance floor my feet barely touching the ground? Yes, she really had danced, and laughed, and carried on like all of the other girls. That wonderful evening was all too real and now she had to deal with the wrath of Papa.

Hannah shook off her dreams and got out of bed but could not shake off her thoughts of last night. Corporal Ulhman, Paul, he seemed so different from the boys she knew, perhaps because he was older. He must be at least nineteen or twenty. His manners were so sophisticated, probably a result of his time working at the palace in Vienna. Still, he sounded almost shy. Had he actually asked if he could call on her, or had she dreamed that too? No, he had asked, she remembered his words, the sound of his voice, the look in his eyes.

Oh dear, what would Papa say? Why did he always have to be so gruff? She could still hear his terrible explosions when Elsa was young. All that yelling, she wanted no part of it. Oh my, what should I do? I want to tell the whole world about Paul. How am I ever going to do that without Papa knowing? I just know he will be so angry with me. Thank goodness, Elsa is here, maybe she will know what to do.

Quickly Hannah got dressed and ran down the stairs to find her older sister.

* * *

Across the city, Paul had been up for many hours. Germany and Russia were on the brink of war. The dispatches were flying almost as fast as the generals could write them. Paul had already delivered six messages and the clock had not yet struck 8:00 a.m. He sat outside General Weisinger's office now waiting for a reply to a dispatch he had just delivered. The only other person in this outer office was the general's clerk.

His mind wandered to last evening and the lovely Hannah Kruger. What an interesting person. Their verbal sparring had been so exhilarating, and yet her shyness on the dance floor seemed to contradict the stinging retorts to his comments. He could not remember ever meeting anyone quite like her before.

"Excuse me, Corporal, didn't I see you at Hagen's last night?" the clerk asked.

"Yes, I was there with some friends,"

"I think I saw you dancing with Hannah Kruger. I never considered asking her to dance. She's a little too mousy for me," the clerk said.

"Yes, I was dancing with Fraulein Kruger." Paul replied a little taken aback. "I found her to be a most interesting companion. I am looking forward to seeing her again."

"You want interesting you should try dancing with her friend Greta, now there is a beautiful girl. I would give my eye teeth to get a dance with her just one ti…."

Paul would have none of that kind of talk. "She is not my type. I met many girls like her when I worked at the palace in Vienna. They just flirt with you and get you into all kinds of trouble. I have no time for that. No, Hannah is much more my type, witty and funny, at the same time very serious and thoughtful."

The sound of a door opening ended the conversation. A young officer stepped out of the office and handed Paul an envelope. "Corporal Ulhman, please see that this message gets to General Von Kleinhoffer with all possible haste." Paul closed his mind to frivolous thoughts of lovely young women and raced for his motorcycle to deliver the dispatch.

* * *

"Well, will you look at who finally decided to grace us with her presence." Elsa laughed. "Did you sleep well?"

"Yes, just fine, thank you. Where is Momma?"

"She's still out in the garden. I expect that she'll be in soon. She has been working for some time now." Elsa moved the squirming baby from her lap to her shoulder. "There's still breakfast on the stove. You certainly slept in this morning. I guess you had quite an exciting night."

Hannah walked to the stove and turned her head away from Elsa before speaking, "Did you see me dancing?"

"Of course I did. You looked like you were having a wonderful time."

"It was fun." Hanna said scooping some warm oatmeal into a bowl.

"I want to hear all about this handsome young soldier with whom you were dancing"

Hannah walked to the table and sat down. "There is nothing much to tell. I danced once or twice that is all."

"Hannah Kruger, I can see the look on your face there is so much more to tell."

"No, Elsa, really there is not."

"Hannah, remember I was young once. Now I want to hear it all."

"Oh, I want to tell you everything, but I am so afraid of what Papa will say."

"Quiet, I hear Momma coming in. I have an idea," Elsa said. "Just follow my lead."

Elsa got up and opened the door for her mother, "Good morning Momma, you were up very early this morning. It looks like you have a large harvest this fine day."

"I have been in the garden since about 6:00. I like to get done before it gets too warm."

"I was wondering. Would you like Hannah and me to do your marketing today? It's such a glorious day and I do believe that my sister and I would enjoy a walk to market."

"That would be wonderful. Leave dear Little Gus here with me. I love spending time with him." Hedwig said smiling at her grandson.

"That's a wonderful idea Momma. Give Hannah the list while I will run up and get my bag."

Momma looked a Hannah, "I can hardly believe my ears, Elsa volunteering to go to market. Being a mother has certainly changed her."

"Yes, I can remember her telling you one time that going to market was beneath her. All her friends had maids to do marketing and we should have a maid too."

"I remember that day. I was not very happy with her."

"Well, I also remember you putting her in her place with just one look. I may have only been eight years old but I decided right then that I never wanted to see that look."

"Somehow marrying Georg has been good for her. He is such a fine solid man and has loved Elsa since boyhood."

"Did he really love her that long?"

"Oh, yes. It never ceased to amaze me that he steadfastly persisted, even though Elsa turned him down, over and over again, and in such mean ways."

"I'm sure that I would have given up."

"I am very glad that he did not. He somehow prevailed and won her heart."

The sound of footsteps on the stairs alerted Hannah,

"Here she comes now. May I have the list and we'll be on our way?"

The July sun shone with such flawlessness that the flowers in the yards seemed alive with color. Hannah thought she must be the happiest girl in all of Dusseldorf. She was walking to market with her big sister and today she had the exciting story to tell. Yet Hannah was a jumble of nerves. She could hardly keep her thoughts straight. Oh, why did she have to be so terrified of what Papa would say?

"Now, tell me little sister, just who is this man and how did you meet him?" Elsa asked.

"He's Ingrid Schneider's cousin and his name is Paul Ulhman. He has been working at a palace in Austria and now is a motorcycle courier in the Imperial Army, and he is studying English so he can move to America and..."

"Slow down! One thing at a time. I can't take all of this in at once." Elsa laughed.

"Oh look, there's Ingrid now. She can tell you all about him."

"Ingrid, hello," Hannah waved for her friend to join them. "Will you tell Elsa about Corporal Ulhman? I told her that he's your cousin." Hannah talked so fast she had to catch her breath. "Please tell Elsa that he is a nice person?"

"Hannah, you are so silly. You are the one who always says that boys are just boring and you want nothing to do with them."

"I know, but Corporal Ulhman is different," Hannah sighed.

Ingrid turned to Elsa, "Paul's father is my mother's brother, Onkel Dieter. They live in Leipzig and he has twelve brothers and sisters.

"My, that is a big family." Elsa looked amazed.

"When Cousin Paul was only thirteen, my Onkel Dieter made arrangements for him to live and work at the local nursery in Leipzig. Paul seemed to have an understanding and love for plants, so my Onkel thought that nursery work would be good for him...."

Elsa interrupted, "It is always good to have a career that matches your interests."

"After several years, Herr Hessel, the owner of the nursery, made arrangements for Paul to do an apprenticeship at the Schönbrunn Palace in Vienna with one of the greatest obergartners in the world," Ingrid explained.

"Now he is in the Army?" Elsa asked.

"He volunteered for the army because, in his words, he felt the need to serve his country as payment for all the opportunities he has been given in his life."

Elsa looked at Hannah, "Papa will appreciate his sense of responsibility."

"He is a very responsible person." Ingrid said. Looking directly at Hannah, "he told me last night that he found you to be fascinating."

Hannah could not believe her ears. She could feel her face getting red again and turned away so that Elsa would not see.

"Why, Hannah, I do believe you're blushing," her sister teased. "This Paul sounds like a very likeable person."

Hannah looked at her shoes. "He is."

"I can understand why you might be intrigued by him."

"Really"

"Of course. I think if we do this right, Papa could learn to like him as well."

"Oh, I hope so." Hannah was now all smiles. "Can you believe he asked if he could call on me?"

Elsa laughed, "Why wouldn't he ask. You are a fascinating woman to use his words."

"I told him yes, but ever since I have been worrying about what Papa would say. What am I going to do? Papa used to get so angry with you."

"Don't remind me. We had some very difficult years."

"I do want Paul to make a good impression on him." Hannah was very serious again. "He may be my Georg."

"I don't believe you need to be so worried. Let me think about this. I'm sure we can find a way to introduce the idea to our 'very mean old papa." Elsa said, grinning.

"Oh, I do hope so."

"We had better get started on the marketing for Momma; I miss my Little Gus already."

They said good-bye to Ingrid and went about getting the things on Momma's list, speaking no more of Corporal Ulhman until they were on their way back to the house.

They turned the corner onto their street when Elsa brought up the subject of Paul again. "I think that I have an idea that will help introduce Corporal Ulhman to Papa. I will speak first to Georg and tell him about this cousin of Ingrid's."

"How will that help?" Hannah sounded worried.

"Papa will get interested in the conversation and perhaps even suggest that we invite him to dinner. You just watch me and learn. Don't say anything unless I ask you. Papa will like him when I am through. But more than that, he will think he was the one to introduce Paul to you. That will make him feel that it was all his idea and everything will be fine."

"Do you think it will really work?" Hannah couldn't shake the worry. "Papa can be so protective sometimes. I am not at all sure that he will ever let someone call on me."

"Everything will be fine." Elsa laughed at her sister's concern. "Just let me take care of it." She stopped and looked very serious. "I do think that we should let Momma in on our little secret though. Is that alright with you?"

"Of course. I don't like to keep secrets from Momma." Hannah began jumping up and down. "I want to tell everyone about Corporal Ulhman."

"Otto, you look very tired this evening," Hedwig commented as the men came in from their day of work.

"Look at this." Otto threw the newspaper on the table and nearly fell into the big ladder- backed kitchen chair, heaving an enormous sigh.

> Saturday, August 1, 1914
> RHEINSCHE POST
> Berlin 5:00 p.m.
> GERMANY DECLARES WAR ON RUSSIA!

At noon today, Czar Nicholas, II ordered a general mobilization of Russian troops in direct opposition to Germany's attempts to maintain peace.

Germany having no further options to maintain peace in Europe ordered a general mobilization of troops at 5:00 p.m. today.

The German Ambassador to St Petersburg presented the following declaration of war to the Russian Government:

"The Imperial German Government have used every effort since the beginning of the crisis to bring about a peaceful settlement....

I have the honour, on the instructions of my Government, to inform your Excellency as follows. — His Majesty the Emperor, my august Sovereign, in the name of the German Empire, accepts the challenge, and considers himself at war with Russia."

> Hail to the Fatherland
> May God be with us all!"

Hedwig stifled a gasp as she read the headlines. What lay ahead for them. She had feared this since it all began back in June. She must do what she could to keep her spirits up and maintain normalcy for her family. She looked first at her husband as he sat so dejected in his chair and then to her son-in-law who stood stoically by the door. She said nothing listening to the stillness in the room.

At last Otto broke the silence. "It is like dominoes falling, first Austria and Serbia and now Germany and Russia. England and France are allies of Russia. Germany is the ally of Austria. Soon we will all be involved. I can feel it in my bones. There is going to be a European war that could be avoided with just a little common sense. However, none of the leaders are listening to each other, let alone listening to their advisors. Hedwig we are heading for disaster. I just know it.

Hedwig set aside her own fears. She knew what she had to do. "Otto, sometimes I think you pay too much attention to those beloved newspapers of yours. I am sure that if the leaders of Europe would just consult you, they could solve all their problems and the world could live in peace and harmony," Hedwig admonished.

Kissing her husband on the cheek she smiled a smile she did not feel. "Come, get cleaned up for dinner. Let us enjoy our children while they are here. August and Louisa, and her mother Genevieve, will be here for dinner tonight, so we will once again have our whole family at our table."

** *

Dinner was nearly finished. George had just drained the last of his glass of ale. Hedwig watched as Elsa put her own glass down and turned to her husband. She knew what was coming and marveled at how her daughter knew just the right time to approach a delicate subject.

"Georg," Elsa started sweetly, "when Hannah and I went to market today we ran into her friend Ingrid Schneider." She dabbed at her mouth ever so gently. "You remember her brother Heinrich? He was in the same class in school as you and August."

George grinned, "Heinrich, yes, I remember; he was one of the star football players at school. I always liked him. He was good at everything that he did, and very nice too. I wonder what is he doing now?"

"He's a banker," interjected August. "I ran into him just last week getting into a new Mercedes auto so he must be doing quite well for himself."

"Yes, well, that is wonderful for him," Elsa, said not to be distracted from her point. "As I was saying, Hannah's friend Ingrid was telling us about her cousin who is here in Düsseldorf. His name is Paul Ulhman and he is a corporal in the Imperial Army. What did she say he did, Hannah, do you remember?"

"Yes, she said that he's a motorcycle courier," Hannah's voice sounded timid.

"That's right. She also said he just finished an apprenticeship at the Schönbrunn Palace in Vienna. I suppose he met all sorts of exciting people while he was there."

"Do you think he met Franz Josef?" Louisa asked.

"Perhaps." Elsa looked at Louisa and then smiled sweetly at her husband. "Ingrid said that he is somewhat lonely here in Düsseldorf. He doesn't know anyone except his cousins."

"He sounds like he would be a very interesting person to get to know. I imagine that he would have many good tales to tell about his work at the Palace." Georg picked up as if on cue.

"I think that we should invite him to join us for dinner one evening." Hedwig joined the discussion. "I would very much like to hear this young man's stories. If he is Ingrid and Heinrich's cousin, I am sure he is a fine young man." She now turned her own charms on her husband. "What do you say, Otto, shall we invite him for dinner one night?"

"He sounds nice enough. He might be able to tell more of what is happening with this crisis. After all, you have said that he carries messages between important people." Otto looked from Elsa to Hedwig. "I am not sure why you mentioned this young man, Elsa, however I believe that I would rather enjoy meeting him. Thank you, Momma, for such a fine idea."

"Papa, what do you say to August and me joining you for a walk down to the Hagen Brau?" suggested Georg.

"Perhaps we will see Ingrid's father, Karl or her brother Heinrich. We could inquire of them how we might meet this Paul Ulhman."

"An excellent suggestion, Georg. The three of us could go while the ladies clean up after dinner," August offered. "They could join us later."

Otto pushed his chair back to get up. "Why not? It is a warm evening and a stein of Hagen's Dark would be a fine finish to this grand dinner your mother has prepared for us."

Otto smiled at his wife. "Hedwig, do you mind if we three take a walk down to Hagen Brau?"

"Of course not. We just may join you later. Genevieve, are you up to a little walk after we clean up here?" Hedwig asked Louisa's mother.

"Why yes, I think that would be very nice if Louisa is up to it." Genevieve looked at her daughter with concern.

"Mother, you worry too much. I am just fine. Now that I know why I am so tired and queasy, I am rather enjoying it. I can only hope that I will be as wonderful a mother as Elsa. I am trying to watch everything that she does and learn," replied Louisa, who wore the glow of pregnancy.

"It sounds to me as if all is settled. Come Georg and August the beer awaits. I want to hear what others have to say of the news today. Ladies, we will be anxiously anticipating your arrival," Papa laughed as they left the house.

Sure the men were out of earshot Momma grinned at Elsa. "It seems to me that your little plan worked perfectly, my dear. I knew that if anyone could convince your father that something was his idea it would be you. You have always been good at that."

"Papa is really just a pushover. You just have to know where to push."

"I do not envy poor Georg should you ever have a little girl. He will be totally controlled by the women in his life."

"He already is, and he loves every minute of it," smiled Elsa. "He knew what he was getting into when he married me. After all, he knew me from the time I was eight years old and he never gave up. He deserves just what he gets."

Louisa began picking up the dishes from the table. "Hannah, you are the quiet one this evening. Do I sense that perhaps this Corporal Ulhman means something to you and that is why we women are trying to maneuver Papa?"

Blushing, Hannah looked at her sister-in-law. "He asked me to dance last night and later asked me if he could call on me."

"My, my, our little girl is growing up right before our eyes." Louisa teased.

"I'm really not a little girl anymore you know. I am sixteen."

"Of course you are. I am sorry; I did not mean that you are still a baby. Now tell me about this oh so interesting Corporal Ulhman."

"He's very nice and so sophisticated and handsome too." Hannah almost swooned. "Can you believe that he wants to see me? I was afraid what Papa would say, so Elsa said she would help me."

"It seems like Elsa knew just what to do."

"Momma helped too. Thank you both. I just know that you will like him."

* * *

The paper lanterns that lighted the outdoor garden seemed to flicker with the energetic buzzing of conversations as men and women discussed the latest news. Here and there, someone would erupt with loud discourse on just what the Kaiser should or should not do.

"Good evening, Herr Kruger. It is good to see you and your sons again this evening. What splendid weather we are having, do you not agree?" inquired Fritz Hagen as he led them to a table.

"Ah, Herr Hagen, I do agree that we are having perfect summer weather. I only wish that the political climate was as good. I do not know if I should cringe or celebrate this news of war. I fear this smoldering ember of war will become a wildfire and where will it go next?" The worry in Otto's voice seemed to characterize the feelings of all those around the table.

"Ah but, Herr Kruger, look around you. There are uniforms everywhere. It is good for business, yes? What can I get for you this evening?"

"Bring us some of your Hagen Dark. You make the best dark beer in all of Düsseldorf, perhaps all of Germany," declared Otto.

"You are too kind. I shall pour those for you myself and send them right over."

Looking around the garden, Otto did indeed see many uniforms. Perhaps it was just his imagination. There seemed to be to be at least one uniform at every table.

"Papa." August voice brought his back to reality. "I believe that Herr Schneider has just come through the gate. Shall I ask him to join us?"

"That would be good, August, thank you."

"Papa, now that Germany has declared war on Russia, what do you think will come next?" Georg asked.

"England and France are both allies of Russia; I fear they will be tempted to follow in Russia's wake."

August, accompanied by two other men approached the table. "Papa, you remember Herr Schreiber, and his son Heinrich?"

"Of course. Sit. Sit. Join us for a stein of Hagen dark. Heinrich, you know my son-in-law Georg Mueller? He and my daughter Elsa are visiting from America."

"Yes, August, Georg, and I all went to school together. How are you doing, Georg? It is good to see you." Heinrich was dressed in a business suit while the other men all wore more casual clothing.

"I am quite well, thank you. It is good to be in Germany again. We have been gone four years. I must say, though, I miss America. Things are in much less turmoil there."

"I can only imagine." The young man settled into his chair and took a long drink of the beer placed before him. "I have been traveling in Europe and have only just arrived in Düsseldorf on business about a week ago. Things are certainly changing quickly."

"You are living in Berlin then?" inquired August.

"Yes, I went there to the university. When I finished my examinations, I went to work for Deutsche Bank in Berlin. It is a very interesting position, and I am able to travel all over Europe." A frown crossed his face. "I have wondered, however, if I will be able to continue my travel as political tensions heighten."

"Where have you been recently?" Otto asked.

"Just before I came to Düsseldorf, I was in Vienna. The mood there is one of great turmoil. I was there when Archduke Franz Ferdinand was assassinated."

"That must have been very interesting," Otto commented.

"That it was. There was an outpouring of sympathy from all of Europe, even London, Paris and St. Petersburg. However, in Vienna it seemed to be more outrage that such a thing could happen, than grief that the successor to the throne had been killed."

"How so?" Otto asked.

"The prevailing public opinion was that this is a continuation of the Albanian border crisis of last fall and that the only way to resolve this matter would be with out-and-out war."

"Tell me more. The papers did not report this." Otto took a sip of his beer.

"I am only surprised that it took Austria so long to declare war. I would have thought that it would have come much sooner."

"If I might join you, I may be able to give you some reason for that," interjected a young soldier, standing next to Heinrich.

"Please sit down, Paul." Heinrich indicated a seat next to him. "Gentlemen allow me introduce my cousin, Corporal Paul Ulhman. He has just recently come to Düsseldorf from Vienna as well. Paul spent several years in as an apprentice in the gardens of the Schönbrunn Palace. Paul please meet Herr Otto Kruger, his son August Kruger, and son-in-law Georg Mueller."

"It is an honor to meet you Herr Kruger, August, Georg."

"Please, tell us what you have to say as to why there was a delay in the declaration of war. I have assumed that Austria was trying to resolve the crisis diplomatically rather than militarily," Otto invited.

"Well, I believe that may be true, at least in part, due to the fact that many members of the Austro-Hungarian army are on leave. This is the time of year when much of the army is on leave. Harvest time requires the men be home. The Austro-Hungarian Empire is still a very agrarian society and the harvest must be in for the people to survive the winter. The monarchy would lose much of its favor with the people if they made the soldiers return before late July. In addition, to cancel the leaves would certainly be an alert to the other powers of Europe that military action against Serbia was imminent."

"You may have something there, Paul. I had not considered the agricultural implications," mused Otto. "Your background allows you to see things from a different perspective. How interesting. You may be right."

"Thank you, Herr Kruger. I know that it is true that those of us from rural areas look at things differently. I am not saying that was the sole reason for the delay, only that it may be a contributing factor."

"I appreciate your insight, young man." Otto looked around for his friend, Herr Hagen. "Bring us all another stein and one for my young friend here as well," Otto shouted over the considerable noise in the garden.

Chapter 8
Düsseldorf, Germany
August 2, 1914

General Weisinger's outer office buzzed with activity. Paul sat with several other young soldiers, all of whom seemed to be on edge, awaiting answers to dispatches they had earlier delivered.

"Corporal Ulhman, how nice to see you so early. I believe that I saw you at Hagen's again last night," General Weisinger's clerk said.

"Yes, I was there," Paul's mind wandered back to last evening.

"You were not sitting with Fraulein Kruger but her father. Very interesting, very interesting."

Paul thought he detected a smirk on the man's face. "Well, I did have a fascinating discussion with my cousin Herr Schneider and the Kruger men."

"You certainly seemed engrossed. I'd suggest that you be wary of the Fraulein's father. I've heard that one has a volatile temper, especially where his daughters are concerned."

"I'm not at all sure where I stand with Hannah. She seemed to be almost embarrassed to see me last night." Paul pictured Hannah sitting with her back to him.

Now the clerk was laughing, "Maybe she didn't want to see you."

"That's my worry. She seemed to enjoy the evening before."

"I'm sure you know that all the girls like dancing with the new soldier in town. When they think about it the next day everything looks different."

"I hope that is not so. I'm very taken with Fraulein Kruger."

"You best watch yourself. Don't get pulled into the spider's lair so easily."

"You seem to know a lot about women. I certainly don't know how to act around this one. Tell me, do you have any suggestions what I should do next?" Paul asked as another soldier came out of the General's office and placed papers on the clerk's desk.

"According to the General you need to be on your way to Bonn next. So I suggest you put the pretty little girl out of your mind for now."

"I'll take your advice. It's going to be another very long day."

***

"Momma, did you see the way the men were all talking with Corporal Ulhman when we arrived at Hagen's last evening?" Hannah asked. "It looked to me like they were having a deep discussion."

"I am quite sure that your father was intrigued with your young man. He commented that Corporal Ulhman had some very remarkable insights about the ways of war and politics for one so young."

"Momma, does that mean that Papa liked him?"

"Yes, dear. I believe your Papa liked him. Of course, he has no idea that you are interested in him and that could be an entirely different story."

"What do you mean?"

"The fact that your father finds Corporal Ulhman intelligent and well-mannered certainly may help your cause," Momma laughed.

"Momma, this isn't funny!" Hannah stamped her foot in frustration.

"I know. It is just that I have never seen you like this before."

"You surely could not say that of me at age sixteen."
Elsa walked into the kitchen, little Gus on her hip. "I was
always interested in men. Not always the best men, but
always interested."

Momma reached for the baby. "Here let me see my
little man."

Elsa kissed his cheek and handed him to his
grandmother. "I remember you saying to me, why not talk to
that nice young man, Georg Mueller? He likes you and is so
well mannered. Your father thinks much of him too."

"How well I remember. You never listened to me."
Momma bounced Gus on her knee.

"Of course not. I was sixteen and I knew everything
there was to know. I used think to myself, yes, Georg is well
mannered and Papa likes him. That is reason enough for me
not to like him."

"You were one of the most independent young girls I
ever met." Momma laughed.

"I am not sure if I was independent or just stubborn.
However, I know I was going to pick my own man. No one
was going to tell me who I should like. Certainly not my
parents and especially not my Papa," Elsa remembered
fondly.

Hannah was now very intrigued by her sister's
comments. "Did you really feel that way, Elsa? I think that it is
so important that Papa like the man I like."

Elsa laughed and hugged her little sister. "You have so
much to learn."

"I'm trying. However, I don't know what I would do if
Papa didn't like him."

"You girls are so different, Hannah." Momma smiled
watching the baby giggle. "You may be too young to
remember, there were many times that Papa was very upset
with Elsa." The baby's giggling turned to true laughter as the
women encouraged him. "You know when your papa is upset

how he tends to raise his voice and say things that he may wish later that he had not said."

"Hannah may not remember, but, I certainly do. I wonder if I did those things deliberately so Papa would get angry with me."

Momma smiled, "Perhaps you did."

"What I really remember is that after Papa raised his voice and sent me to my room, later he would come upstairs and sit on my bed and then we would talk."

"I always wondered about those times. Your papa never shared what the two of you talked about."

"We worked out many of our differences that way. It was during those times that I understood just how much Papa really loved me."

"I have always suspected that your Papa relished those times as well."

"I know he was very happy when I finally decided to marry Georg."

"There was a time I did not believe that it would ever happen."

"I am only glad that Georg was persistent enough to stay around and wait for me to grow up and understand what true love is all about." Elsa rubbed the yellow fluff on her son's head.

Hannah interrupted this memory fest, "I do not know anything about love, but I know that I felt all funny inside last night when I saw Paul, Corporal Ulhman. I could not look at him. Why am I acting so strangely around him? I have never been like this with any of the boys from school."

"I think the boys from school are too immature for you. Corporal Ulhman is a little older and he appears to be much more mature." Momma wisely commented. "I suspect that his life has not always been easy and that he has had to work very hard to accomplish what he has in such a short time. Hard work breeds maturity. I rather believe that we will see this Corporal Ulhman around for quite a while."

"I hope so," Hannah mumbled, blushing once again. A knock at the door interrupted their walk down memory lane.

"Hannah will you answer the door?"

"Of course, Momma." She skipped across the room and opened the front door to find her sister-in law there. "Louisa, how nice to see you, come in."

"Thank you. Is Hedwig here?" Louisa's voice trembled. "I really need to speak with her."

"Is something wrong? You look like you've been crying. There are red rings around your eyes."

"No, I mean yes." Louisa stumbled in the door. "Everything is falling apart."

"Louisa, what is it? Is there something wrong with the baby?" Getting up, Hedwig handed Gus back to Elsa. "Has something happened to you mother? Tell me, what is wrong?"

"Oh, Hedwig, it's awful, just awful! What am I going to do?" Louisa sobbed falling into one of the big overstuffed chairs in the parlor.

"Child, please tell me what is wrong?" Hedwig knelt in front of her daughter-in-law.

"Here read this. It will explain everything." She held out an envelope.

Hedwig took the letter. It had the official seal of the Imperial Army of Germany. She knew even before she opened the letter what it would say. August had been summoned to serve in the army. As she read the letter, her fears were confirmed. He must report for duty on Monday, August 10th.

For the second time in two days Hedwig found herself suppressing her own fears to allay those of someone else.

She took Louisa's hand and squeezed it. "Everything will be alright. We will all get through this together." She felt the unbidden tears begin to well in her eyes. "I am sure this war will not last long. August will be home again safe with you and the baby before you know it."

Hannah wondered if her mother really believed what she said. Or was she just being tough for Louisa's sake. She could almost see the foreboding on her mother's face. Louisa's sobbing was nearly uncontrollable.

Now, Hedwig had her arms around the distraught woman. "Please calm down now, it is not good for your baby or for you to be so upset. Everything will be fine. We will all be here together. You are not to worry."

"How can I not worry? August is going to war." Hedwig held her at arm's length. "It will be alright." She said with emphasis. It has to be.

"You always know what to do." Louisa dabbed at her eyes with a handkerchief Hannah handed her. "I do not know what I would do without you, Hedwig. How am I going to take care of my mother and a baby with August gone? "

"You must not concern yourself with those details now. We will all work together and take care of everyone.

"I do not know...."

"Please, promise that you will not worry about that now. You must go home and be with your husband and be there for him."

"I...."

"Do you hear me, Louisa?" Hedwig stood up, pulling Louisa with her. "You will not show any fears to August."

"How can I do...."

"Louisa, he needs you to be strong so he will not worry. He must be able to do what is required of him without concern for things at home."

"But I'm not strong like you."

"Louisa, you must listen to me." Hedwig's voice was gentle but firm. "He will need to have a clear mind to do his job well. Do you understand how very important that is? You will be strong!"

Hedwig looked pointedly at the other two in the room. "We women must bind together and put up a united front. I want all of you to listen to me." The three young women nodded. "The men, not just August, all of the men, must never know our inner feelings. They must keep their minds clear of worry to stay alive."

"You are laying a great responsibility on us women." Elsa looked at her mother then Louisa.

"You are right Elsa; however this has always been our role. Women must keep home and hearth together no matter what happens so the men will have someplace when they return.

* * *

Later that evening Otto and Hedwig, in the privacy of their bedroom, found they were whispering. "Otto, I am so worried about Louisa. She may not be able to see this through, should there be all out war. She has always seemed so fragile. I know that is one of the things that attracted August. Now with the baby coming, August gone, and the possibility of war in addition to all of her responsibilities for caring for her mother, I just do not know if she will be able to do it all."

"I am sure that Louisa will be fine. I expect that you will find she has more stamina than you know. I am most concerned about their livelihood. When her father died, he left so little to care for her mother. We may want to consider offering them a place to stay with us. I think that we could make room."

"Otto, you are such a wonderful kind man. People think of you as gruff and easy to provoke, when in reality you are such a pushover." Hedwig snuggled closer to her husband. "That is a perfect solution; of course, I would be able to help Louisa with the baby when it comes. Genevieve and I are such good friends; I know that we could help each other through this crisis."

"See, I knew I could solve all your problems." Otto kissed his wife's forehead.

"The real question is could you stand two more women in your house?" Hedwig asked with frivolity she did not feel.

"I will just have to work more hours to save my sanity. One man and four women, all my friends will think that I am a saint," Otto laughed as he embraced his wife, doing his best to hide his own concerns about the future.

Germany and France
Declare War on Each Other

Otto's heart was heavy, reading the headlines. Will my beloved Germany ever be the same? Can Europe survive these actions? I served my time in the military under Bismarck and have an understanding of the implications of war. I wonder, will my country endure this crisis? Otto decided that he simply could not pick up another fare.

He drove past the Dusseldorf Grand Hotel as if in a trance he headed for home. War is devastating to an entire generation of young men in any country. What will become of such bright and promising young men as August and Paul Ulhman? Where will this all lead and what will it take to end this madness?

Slowly, Otto became aware of the world outside his auto. The city looks imperceptibly different. This is a beautiful summer evening and yet, the flowers have less color than usual, and the trees such a brilliant green this morning have taken on a gray tint, the color of war. The usual noise of evening traffic somehow seems muted and people appear to be unusually polite in their gestures.

Otto felt a cold shiver traverse his shoulders. The flags are still for lack of an evening breeze, almost as if they are bowing their heads. Those few drops of rain on the windshield, though no cloud exists in the sky, could they be God's tears shed for the fate of Germany, Europe and world as the result of the stupidity of men?

Otto pulled his vehicle into the old barn behind the house, climbed down and gently closed the door. Home at last. Everything as always, where it belongs. My beloved coach parked at the back of the barn, the beautiful wood gleaming from my polishing last week. I wonder why I find it so difficult to give up the coach. Surely, I will never use it again in this modern age of autos. He rubbed his hand across the satin of the wood. Everything is as it should be. Yet it is not.

Leaving the barn, he stepped into Hedwig's garden so plentiful this year. Will this house, that has been in my family for generations survive a war? Will there be enough food to last the duration of a war?

Otto felt tears on his cheeks. I have lived a life of modest privilege. What will the ramifications of this war have on my life and the lives of those I love? No one must see me in such a state. Brushing the tears away, he entered his house.

There is my Hedwig at the sink washing the dishes. She works so hard to make this house a home. I cannot imagine my life without her.

"Good evening, Otto. I thought you were going to work late tonight. I saved some supper for you. It is on the table," Hedwig said, wiping her hand on her apron and giving her husband a peck on the cheek. "Is something wrong? Do you not feel well?"

"Here, this says it all," he said as he dropped the paper on the table.

***

Hedwig picked up the paper and read the headline. "Oh, my, this war is all happening much too fast. Two days ago it was Russia, then Belgium and now France." No wonder Otto is so quiet. He has been concerned about this for many days now. What will become of us all? August will be leaving for the army in a few days. My brother Ernst is already aboard a ship. Hedwig turned back to the stove. "Sit, I will fix your plate."

Otto took his usual chair at the big wood table that dominated the central part of the kitchen. "I am so glad that Elsa, Georg, and little Gus will be returning to America in a few weeks. Perhaps they can avoid all the trials of war in the United States.

"I almost regret that they came at all." Hedwig continued to prepare Otto's dinner and thought of her youngest daughter. Hannah, my sweet Hannah, what will become of her? She is too young and vulnerable to have to endure a war. Perhaps she could go to America with Elsa and Georg.

Closing her eyes, Hedwig tried to imagine what it would be like if Hannah were not there in the house. No, I cannot think of Hannah being gone, not my baby so far away. She is too young. I must keep her here, in a house where she belongs.

Walking to the table, she set a heaping plate of sausage and potatoes before her husband. "What if the war finds its way here to Düsseldorf? Even if it does not, the effects will be here."

Otto looked at plate of food. "My dear, this smells wonderful, but I am afraid that I do not have much appetite this evening."

"I understand." She took her seat across the table from him. "Otto, I need to speak to you." She could hear the concern in her own voice. "We need to make plans. I have been thinking that perhaps Hannah should go to America with Elsa and Georg."

"Hedwig, have you thought this through? I am not sure you understand what you are saying." Otto reached across the table and laid his hand atop his wife's.

"Oh, Yes, I have been thinking of this ever since Louisa was here yesterday." She looked him in the eye. "I am not at all sure I can survive the quiet of this house without her, but she must go."

"If you are sure, than we need to make arrangements right away for I fear many will want to leave the country."

***

The back door slammed and Hannah came into the kitchen to find her parents in what appeared to be a serious moment. "Momma, Papa, is something wrong?"

Momma answered, "Nothing my dear, Papa and I are just talking. Did you have fun at Greta's house?"

"Yes, Ingrid was there too. We always have fun there, but her mother is so very strange. She tries to act like one of us girls. I really like to go to Ingrid's house better."

"Hannah, you know better than to judge other people just because they are a little different." Hedwig chided her daughter.

"Yes, Momma. I will do better." She sat down next to her father at the table. "You both look so serious? What has happened?"

"Here, Schatzi, this will explain," Papa handed her the paper.

"What does it mean, Papa? I have never understood all of the excitement about war."

"It means that things may be changing soon and we have to be prepared for that."

"Changing in what way? The fighting is in Belgium, not here."

The front door opened as Elsa, Georg, and the baby returned from a visit with friends. "We are back, Momma. What a beautiful evening we had."

Hedwig got up and took the sleeping baby from Elsa's arms. "I am glad you enjoyed yourself."

Elsa put down her bag of baby things and looked at her family. "Why does everyone look so glum? You all look like someone died."

Georg picked up the paper and read the headline. "So, it has begun. I'm not surprised. I was quite sure Europe would choose the military way out rather than the diplomatic. If I were still living in Germany, I might even welcome war."

"Thank goodness, we do not still live in Germany," Elsa's voice was anxious. "So just get those thoughts out of your mind."

"Yes, you're correct of course. Still what man does not welcome the opportunity to be a hero? No matter how long I live in America, I will always be a German at heart." Georg grinned at his wife. "I love this country and would be glad to fight to protect the Fatherland.

This time Elsa's voice had the shrill note of hysteria, "You will not speak of this again, do you hear me. Never again!"

"Elsa, calm down you will wake up Gus." Georg put his arm around his wife and guided her to a chair. "You need not worry. We will return to America very soon."

August 4, 1914 –

- *Great Britain declares war on Germany.*
  The declaration is binding on all Dominions within the
  British Empire including Canada, Australia, New Zealand,
  India and South Africa.

- *Germany invades neutral Belgium.*

- *US President Woodrow Wilson declares policy of US*
  neutrality

Hannah's mood reflected the weather as she listened to the constant drone of the rain pelting the parlor window. The conditions had turned cool. What should have been the brilliant azure skies of summer were overcast, dreary gray; everything was sodden from a night and day of constant rain. The temperature, in the sixties, was raw for August. Momma and Elsa, determined to combat the doldrums, had gone shopping and left little Gus, suffering from inevitable runny nose and crankiness of two new teeth, at home with Hannah.

The immense ancient chair, inviting with its frayed striped arms and worn back, seemed to swallow her. No one in the family ever considered sitting here, this was Papa's chair. Today, however, the lure of this place was more than Hannah could ignore for she needed the calm that this cherished space promised to provide.

"What am I going to do, Gus? Yesterday, Momma and Papa told me that I am to go to America with you and your parents."

The child, sleeping on her lap, never moved.

"They told me that I could finish my schooling there and I would be much safer away from the war. How can I finish school there? I do not speak even one word of English."

Gus stretched his little legs and stirred just a bit.

"What about my friends, Ingrid and Greta? I can't leave them to deal with the war. Then there is Corporal Ulhman. I just met him, yet I feel such a connection with him." Hannah shifted in the chair and the baby let out a deep sigh. "If I leave now, I may never see him again and surely he will forget me. It's not fair, Gus, just not fair. America may be a wonderful place for you, but not for me, not now!"

The infant became more restless with each outburst.

Hannah stared at the carousel of pipes sitting on its tripod of legs that had occupied this place next to Papa's chair for as long as she could remember. Each of his many pipes had its own special resting place. There was the one with the ebony bowl encased with fine silver filigree, the meerschaum carved like a man's face distinguished by a long pointed beard. Next to the elegant white pipe was the calabash with its special curved shape. There were pipes with long stems and others with very short, briars of all shapes, some with deep round bowls and several more shallow. It was easy to distinguish the ones that Papa liked best with their stems almost chewed through.

Her fingers trailed over each of Papa's personal treasures, lingering on his favorites. She closed her eyes and pictured him with each in his mouth, or held with such love as he discussed politics with his friends. "Gus, why are they making me do this? They did not even ask me, they just told me that I must go. I had no say at all. I do not understand, if it is so important for me to leave why can they stay?"

The baby whimpered but not did wake up.

"Of course, Momma had an answer to that. She said that they must stay and help Louisa take care of her mother and the new baby while August is fighting the war. Well certainly, I could be helpful here too. I know I could. Still, I have always done as my parents asked and believed they had only my best interests in mind. This is just hard, so very hard."

She snuggled deeper into the welcoming arms of the chair, being careful not to wake the sleeping baby. Tucking her head in the corner where the wing met the back, she savored the aromas that she so associated with her father.

The fragrance of his pipe tobacco with its earthy Cavendish smell covered by just a hint of vanilla filled her with thoughts of all the good times she had shared with this man she loved and admired so much.

"I know I must do as my parents say. I may not be happy, but I will go with you, Gus, to America."

She inhaled as deeply as she could, filling her lungs and her head with the redolence of tobacco from this chair, hoping against hope that she would be able to call up these cherished scents when she longed for comfort so far away in America.

Roused from her reverie by the slamming of the back door she looked up to see her mother and sister struggling with something in the kitchen.

"What is that? I do not believe I have ever seen such a large trunk."

"I know how you love your clothes and that you would want to bring some other personal things as well to help you remember home," Elsa said.

"You must have confused me with yourself when thinking about clothes," Hannah laughed. "You're the one who always had to have a different dress for every occasion, not me."

"You may be right. However, I believe you'll fill this trunk before you leave," Elsa put her end of the trunk down on the parlor floor and reached for her sleeping baby.

"How has my sweet baby boy been behaving while we were gone?" She picked Gus up and kissed his neck to make him laugh.

"He's just waking up. I'll get his food ready. He's always hungry when he wakes up."

"I'll take care of him," offered Momma, straightening up and rubbing her back. "My, my that is a heavy trunk. I do not want to think how heavy it will be when you two are done filling it."

"Don't worry yourself, Momma . When we next move it we'll let Georg do the honors."

Momma laughed. "I suppose you are right about that. Here let me take this little bundle of joy, Elsa. You show Hannah what else we bought." She looked at Hannah. "I hope you like it."

Elsa dug around in the packages and eventually pulled out something. "Look at this beautiful coat we found for you. Momma said the one you wore last year was getting small and you have grown so much this year that she was sure you would need a new one. Isn't this just adorable?"

Elsa held up a lovely navy blue wool coat with a velvet collar and cuffs. There were two rows of gold buttons down the front. Two more gold buttons, one on each side, attached the velvet belt that draped across the back.

"Oh, Elsa, it's just beautiful. I've never had anything so grown up." Hannah slid her arms into the satiny lining, "It fits just perfectly." She danced around the room, the coat swinging out behind her.

"Wait, there's something else," Elsa pulled another package from the pile revealing the most gorgeous blue velvet muff that Hannah had ever seen. "This will keep your hands warm on even the coldest days."

"Momma, Elsa, thank you, thank you. It's wonderful. I just love it." Hannah kissed her mother and sister. "I know that it will be perfect for America."

She had made her decision. She would go to America and no one would ever suspect her secret misgivings about the decision. "I can hardly wait for Papa and Georg to get home to find out when we are leaving. Do you really think that we might be leaving sooner than the twenty-second?"

"I am not sure what kind or arrangements the men will able to make," Elsa said. "It will all depend on when the ships are sailing. I have such mixed feelings about all of this. I so love being here with my family." She stepped behind her mother and wrapped her arms around her.

"Momma, I missed you and Papa more than I can ever express these past four years."

"I know, my dear, we missed you as well."

"All this talk of war frightens me, though, and I am anxious to get back to America where I will feel safe again. I certainly do not want to expose Gus to the harm that a war may cause. He needs to be at home in his own country. And, I promise that we will keep Hannah secure as well."

"I know you will, darling. I am not sure what I will do with both my girls gone to America and my sweet baby too. You will take a part of my very soul with you. I shall not be a whole being until we are together again. Yet in my heart, I know that this is the best thing. I do not want any of you to leave. Still I want you to leave as soon as possible," Momma wiped her eyes as she kissed the top of Gus' head.

Hannah watched Momma struggling to hold in the tears. She was always such a brave woman, in charge of everything and yet today she seemed different, just a little softer. She knew her mother loved them all but to see such emotion openly expressed brought tears to her own eyes.

Soon they were all three crying as they hugged each other. Hannah could not remember when she had felt so close to both her mother and her sister. She had been so glad when Elsa came home. She had anticipated the day for months, yet; somehow, today as they prepared to separate again, the bond between them drawing them closer together was stronger than ever before.

Chapter 11
Dusseldorf, Germany
Later that same day

"Is anyone home?" bellowed Otto as he and Georg entered the house.

"Of course we are home. Why are you always so loud?" Harrumphed Hedwig, "We are all sitting right here. There is no need for so much noise."

Ignoring her testiness, Otto continued but in a quieter voice this time, "We were able to secure passage for Hannah."

"I am glad to hear that." Hedwig fidgeted with the knitting she held on her lap. "I worried if you would be successful."

Georg, who had followed Otto in, looked at his wife. "Yes, we were very lucky; in fact we were actually able to get an earlier ship. It leaves on the twelfth. We'll plan to leave by train on the tenth."

Hannah turned away to hide the look she was sure was on her face. Leaving on the tenth, she needed more time. This was too soon.

"Otto, how were you able to make those arrangements so quickly?" Hedwig asked.

"It was difficult; we had to do much cajoling. You know I have worked with the railroads and steamship lines all these many years. At least I knew the right people with whom to talk."

Oh, Georg, Papa, thank you so much," Elsa said. "I'll feel so much better when we're safely on our way back to America."

"It wasn't easy. The ships were full. I suspect that many people are fleeing the war," Georg walked over and kneeled down next to Elsa. "I'm sorry, darling , we were not able to secure a first class stateroom, but at least it isn't steerage. The room will be small but adequate," said Georg.

"It is only for ten days and then we will be back in America."

"Georg, I'm sure it will be fine," Elsa leaned her head against Georg's shoulder. I'm just relieved to be leaving before the war really starts."

"We will be on our way soon; I imagine you'll want to start your packing now. You only have a week." Georg chuckled as he hugged his wife.

* * *

Later that night Hannah lay in her bed, wiping the tears from her cheeks as she looked around her room. She was already homesick and she hadn't even left yet. In her heart, she knew she must go. She had determined to do so with a smile and enthusiasm. Momma and Papa must never know how much she wanted to stay in Germany with them. Finally, she closed her eyes and tried to clear her mind of such thoughts. She heard low voices from the next room. Listening carefully, Hannah could just make out their words.

"Georg, you are very quiet tonight. Is something wrong?" Elsa asked.

"No, it is just that sometimes I am so proud of my country, Germany. I know that we have a good life in America and I am glad to be going back to that life. Still….I do not know how to express this. I sometimes think that I should be here defending our homes and families. Fighting for Germany."

"How can you say such a thing, Georg Mueller? This is not our country any more. Yes, our family is here. But we live in America now."

"Elsa please keep your voice down, you will wake up the others."

"I don't care if the others hear me. We'll soon be American citizens. Our son is already an American citizen. I just don't understand how you can even think such a thing." Elsa sat up and began pounding on Georg's chest. "I want to leave here as soon as possible. I want to be safe. Do you understand, SAFE!

"Elsa, please stop pounding on me, I hear you and I understand. We are going home. Home to America, I promise."

So! Hannah thought, Georg wants to stay and fight for Germany too.

The sounds from the next room now much more muffled, Hannah could hear Momma and Papa talking across the hall. She pictured them lying together, Momma's head resting on Papa's chest. Papa cradling Momma in his arms. Did they really love each other so much or was this her fantasy of her parents? Was Momma crying as she had earlier today?

"Otto, how will I ever survive that day? I shall always think of the tenth of August as the day that all my children left, August leaving to fight a war and Hannah and Elsa fleeing to America to escape that very same war," Hedwig's voice was soft but full of sorrow. "I do not know that I shall be able to bear the pain of that day. I feel it already in my heart and soul. I know what we are doing is right, yet I am not sure that I can bear the ache that will live within me until we are all together again."

"What is there to say, my love? I understand. This war is only two days old and already its eagle's talons are tearing this family apart."

Hannah closed her eyes again, wiping the tears away one more time. The love in this family enveloped them all and yet that very love fostered the secrets she was sure they all held locked in their hearts, and cultivated the sacrifices that no one else must ever know were there. Love, secrets, and sacrifice, the incongruous ingredients for a bond that would carry them through, no matter what happened.

"There, that's the last of my things" Hannah straightened up from putting a few more things in the huge trunk sitting in the hallway. "I still have some room left, Elsa, if you need some."

Elsa stepped to the door of her room and looked at the trunk. "You can't possibly have that much space left." Elsa was astonished. "Surely there are more things that you want to bring with you."

Hannah laughed, looked around her room, it was almost empty. "The only other thing I could possibly do is fold up my room itself. This may be a very big trunk but I do not think my room will fit."

"Georg and I will make sure that you have a room once we get to America, you can leave this one here." Elsa came into Hannah's room laughing.

"Thank you Elsa, I know that you will make sure I have everything I could ever need."

"Just leave the trunk open. I must keep some things out for the baby. You can be sure, though, I will be able to use the rest of the space. Every time I travel, I seem to have more things to pack than I have places to put them."

Back in her own room, Elsa folded another dress as Momma walked into the room. "Where have you been Momma, I haven't seen you for a while?"

"I have been up in the loft. I have many things stored there. Look what I found."

"Momma those are the cutest little lederhosen I ever saw. I didn't know they were made so small."

Momma held them up, "They are cute. These little leather shorts belonged to your brother when he was just about little Gus's age."

"They're perfect. Just like the men wear with the little leather ties on the side of the leg and embroidered suspenders. They even have the little button flap in the front," Elsa squealed with delight. "Are you sure you want to give those to me? Louisa is expecting and she could be having a boy. Shouldn't August's son have them?"

"I have other things saved for them. I want you to have these."

"Thank you, we will have fun showing off Gus in his German fare."

Hannah interrupted, "Momma, I've finished my packing. May I go to Greta's house for a while, she and Ingrid want to say good bye."

"Of course you may. Please be back by suppertime. August, Louisa, and Genevieve will be here tonight. You know that I have been planning one last special family dinner."

"Momma, don't say such things." Elsa chastised. You sound like we are all going to die or something."

"I do not mean it like that. It is just that I am going to miss you all so much." Momma's voice began to waiver. "No, I swore to myself that I would not think of that now. Tonight is to be a celebration. That is all. A Celebration!"

"Thank you, Momma for letting me visit my friends. I'll be home by four o'clock, I promise." Hannah left as quickly as she could so neither her mother or sister could see her face, knowing it would betray her true feelings.

"Look at her run down the stairs like any carefree sixteen year old." Elsa said, "I do believe that she has accepted the decision to go to America and may even be looking forward to the adventure."

"I do not know, Elsa. She has gotten very good at hiding her feeling. I believe she understands it is the best for her," Momma said. "However, I am not sure that she is happy about the decision. You will need to be very thoughtful of her and pay close attention to how she is acting."

"She'll be okay. I may not be able to do things just the way you do but I can guarantee you that I will always be there for her."

"I know that. Just try to be aware of her moods too. That is all I am asking." Momma looked at her daughter, eyes brimming with tears. "I am very proud of you for taking on this responsibility. Thank you, for being you."

"You may cry. I know how sad you are. You don't have to hide from me." Elsa enveloped her mother in her arms. "Your secret is safe with me. I love you, Momma."

Hedwig pulled away from her daughter and looked at her beautiful face, now so serious. "I woke up this morning telling myself that I would not cry today, no matter what happened, but I just cannot help it, the tears come no matter how hard I try to will them away.

Elsa thought, it is only going to get worse, Momma. The men may say that this will all be over soon, however, deep inside I fear they are wrong this time.

* * *

Elsa watched her mother moving about the kitchen so efficiently, as she joined her, baby in arms. "Everything smells wonderful. Look at all of this decadent food. I believe you could make a feast out of bread and water if you had too," Elsa said.

"You will learn. I could not do all this so easily when I was your age."

"Momma, may I have your recipe for lebkuchen. I can't resist that delicious confection of dried fruits and nuts nestled in those wonderful spicy cookies." Elsa sat down and bounced Gus on her knee. "Every year I try to make them but they never turn out as good as yours. Mine are always too hard. They never seem to get soft like the ones you make."

"Of course, you may have my recipe, though I truly wonder if it will make a difference," Momma sighed as she continued to peel apples for a tart she was making. "You need to let them sit in an air tight tin, my dear. I know you. You want to eat them before they are ready. They will get soft, if you are patient."

"But Momma they are so good, Georg and I both want to eat them right away."

"Well, patience never was one of your virtues. Remember what Grandmamma Brauer always used to say? She had to start the cookies at Easter so they would be ready for Christmas." Hedwig arranged the apples in the pastry lined pan.

"I do remember, I always thought she was just teasing."

"She was. But there was certainly some truth in her statement too."

"Hand me that sugar please." A noise interrupted the conversation. "I think someone is knocking at the door," Momma said. " Will you check while I finish up this tart?"

"It's most likely just the post, but I'll check." Elsa put Gus on his blanket on the floor and opened the front door. A young man in uniform stood on the stoop.

"May I help you?" Elsa asked.

"Frau Muller, I am Paul Ulhman, Ingrid Schneider's cousin."

"I remember you. Please come in."

"I am wondering if Hannah might be home?" Paul asked.

"Actually she is at her friend Greta's house. She should be back in a few hours."

"May I leave a message for her?"

"Of course you can. Please come in and have a cool drink and some of my mother's wonderful cookies."

"I don't want to bother you."

"You are not bothering us. Momma, look who is here." Elsa called leading Paul into the kitchen.

"What a pleasant surprise. Please sit down while I get you something to drink. It is such a warm day," Momma fussed. "I am sure you must be uncomfortable in that heavy uniform."

"I would appreciate that, thank you. Ingrid told me that Hannah would be leaving soon and I had hoped to see her before she left. I have been very busy these last few days but the General gave me hour or so off to come and say good bye."

Elsa came back into the room after picking up Gus. "I know she'll be very sorry she missed you. Would you like to leave a message for her?"

"I have written her a little note, just in case I could not talk with her. Will you see she gets it?"

Momma laid her hand on the young soldier's shoulder. "Of course we will see she gets your note. Thank you for coming. I want you to remember that you will always be welcome in our house when you are in Dusseldorf."

"Thank you, for your kindness. I must be on my way." Paul stood and executed the perfect court bow for the women as he left.

"What a delightful young man," Elsa said. "Did you seem nervous to you?"

"I do not know about being nervous. He certainly is polite. Hannah could do much worse than that one," Momma said.

* * *

"Look at that child go. I cannot believe that he is just five months old. He has grown so much in just the few weeks that he has been here." Momma stepped out of the child's determined path across the floor. "Who would believe that a child his size could crawl the way he does. He is amazing."

"I believe that he is the most beautiful baby that I have ever seen," Louisa grinned at the baby who had stopped to play with his stuffed bear. "I am very envious of you Elsa. I only hope that my baby will be half as cute as Gus."

Genevieve, sitting in one of the big overstuffed chairs in Hedwig's comfortable living room, looked at her daughter, "Do not be silly, child. Of course, your baby will be cute. All babies are cute. You are just nervous because this is your first child. Everything is going to be fine,"

Elsa scooped Gus up before he reached the stairs and set him back on his blanket. "Louisa you are too kind, Gus is certainly a cute baby, however he can be a handful. It has been wonderful to be home and have Momma's help." She nodded at her mother. "I am looking forward to returning to America and am so glad that Hannah will be coming too. I am sure that she will be a big help taking care of Gus."

The back door slammed and Hannah announced, "Momma, I am home,"

"We are in the parlor, dear. Come and join us. The men are all out in the barn, most likely taking about the war."

"Did you have a good visit with your friends?" Louisa asked.

"Yes, we made a solemn pact that we would be friends forever. We even put it in writing."

Elsa interrupted, "Hannah, you had a visitor while you were gone."

"What do you mean a visitor?" She pulled out a chair from the dining room table and sat down. "I can't think of anyone who would come to see me."

"Well, this person specifically asked for you and when you were not here, left quite crestfallen." Elsa teased her sister.

"Elsa, who are you talking about and why are you laughing so?"

"What do you mean laughing? I would not laugh at my sister."

"Elsa, please, who are you talking about?"

"Here," Elsa handed the note to Hannah with great fanfare. "This strange person left you a note."

All eyes were on Hannah as she opened the folded piece of paper. Her face became more flushed with each line she read.

"Hannah, are you blushing?" Elsa asked..

Not sure how to react to all of this, Hannah ran up the stairs to her room slamming the door behind her.

"Elsa, I believe you were a little hard on her." Momma chided, "You seem to have forgotten how emotional you were at age sixteen."

"You're right, as always, I'm going to have to be very mindful of those things. Perhaps I just don't want to relive all the travail I put myself through at that age."

"I am sure we all went through those things as teenagers, and then tried our best to forget," Genevieve said.

"There goes that baby again straight for the door this time. Elsa you had better pick him up before he gets into something that will hurt him," Momma said.

Elsa got up to get Gus and she saw a man come to the door. With the baby in her arms, she opened the door and found herself face to face with a man in uniform for the second time that day.

"May I help you?" Elsa asked.

"Does Herr Georg Mueller live here?"

"Georg is visiting here. I am his wife"

"Is Herr Mueller here now?"

"Yes," Elsa replied, a feeling of foreboding crept through her.

"May I speak with him?"

"I am his wife," she repeated.

"I understand. I have my orders. I must speak only with Herr Mueller."

"Georg! Georg! Georrrrg!" cried Elsa running out the backdoor. "Georg, please come now. Georg! Georg!"

"What is it? What is wrong?"

"At the door. A man. In uniform. Wants to see you!" She barely got the words out.

"Calm down now, Elsa. What are you talking about? What man?"

"At the door. In a uniform."

"Alright. Everything will be fine." Georg stepped onto the porch from the garden path. "Come with me and we will see what this is all about." He put his arm around his wife, still holding the now crying baby, and led her back into the house.

"My name is Georg Mueller. My wife said that you wanted to see me." Elsa stood just behind her husband. "How can I help you?"

"Herr Mueller, I have a letter for you. May I see some proof of your identification?

Georg got out his passport.

The man looked at Georg's picture and then asked, "Will you please sign here?"

Georg did as he was asked.

"Thank you." The man handed an envelope to Georg and left.

Georg stood staring at the envelope. The seal of the Imperial Army stared back at him. He opened it and took out the single sheet of paper dated with today's date, Saturday, August 8, 1914.

What is it Georg?" Momma asked. "What does it say?"

Georg read the letter, "Herr Georg Mueller, you have been called to active duty in the Imperial Army of Germany. Please report to duty on Friday, August 14, 1914 to the First Army Headquarters in Düsseldorf. General Weisenger signed it."

"NO! NO!" Elsa screamed. "NO! This cannot be true. We do not live in Germany. We are Americans!"

Gus started to cry and Louisa jumped up. Going to Elsa she gently took the baby from her arms. Whispering in his ear, "Hush baby, it is alright. Hush, sweet baby, do not cry. Your Momma will be fine. Settle down sweet baby." She kept her voice very soft and soothing, as she rocked the crying baby. "Let us go and look at Grandmomma's pretty flowers. Hush, now little Gus. Everything will be fine. That is a good boy," she crooned as Gus began to calm down.

"NO! How can they do this? Georg, how can they do this? Tell them that we are Americans."

"Elsa, calm down! Let me think."

"I cannot calm down. We have to do something now. I know our ship leaves on Wednesday the twelfth. We'll just get on the boat and leave. They'll never know we're gone."

"Elsa, you know that's not true. They'll know as soon as they check my passport who I am. I will not be allowed to board the ship. We cannot try to sneak away.

"No, No, No," Elsa keened.

Dropping the letter on the table Georg tried to calm Elsa leading her to a chair.

"What is all the commotion?" inquired Papa as he and August entered the house. "What has happened?"

Momma stood in the dining room staring at the letter then looked at her husband, "Otto, This is the same letter that we saw just days ago with August's name on it. Dear God, how can this be happening? Not both of them!"

"I too, am wondering what this world is coming to," Papa replied.

"No, no, no. Please, God, do not let this happen to us. No, no, no," Elsa continued crying. "Noooo."

"Hush now, Sweetheart. Let me think. You, little Gus, and Hannah will go back to America. I will stay here and fight. Then I will join you as soon as the war is over."

Suddenly, no longer crying Elsa shouted, "Absolutely not! I will not leave without you. I could never leave without you."

She jumped to her feet and began beating on his chest. "If you have to stay then we will stay as well. This war is not going to separate us."

"I think that Georg is right, Elsa," Papa said. "You and Hannah should take Gus and go back to America. It will be much safer for all of you."

"I said No!" Looking at her father with fear and anger, "I will not leave without my husband." Crying again, "Oh, Papa how could this happen?" She fell into her father's welcoming arms. "Why did we ever come here?"

As if from far away, Elsa heard her family talking. Her father had his big arms around her and seemed to be saying something about war being cruel and being strong. She could hear Momma too, talking about family and Georg, telling her not to cry. They did not understand. In one short minute, her whole world had changed. Before that man knocked on the door she was secure and now….now….

Georg leaned against the rail of the front steps, cigarette in hand. I guess I should buy a pipe. My American cigarettes are nearly gone he thought. He stared at the window of the second floor room where he knew Elsa still slept. The letter delivered yesterday announcing his draft into the German army had upset her so that Otto had called Dr. Ostermann, who had come and given her a sedative.

Much to Georg's surprise, Louisa arrived early this morning and was now upstairs sitting with Elsa. He knew that tomorrow August would leave for the Army and yet here Louisa was with Elsa. What did she say, "She wanted to be with Elsa when she woke because Elsa would need someone who understood what she was going through." Louisa promised to stay as long as Elsa needed her.

Georg closed his eyes and tried to make sense of what had actually happened yesterday. Elsa became so upset that he had not had time to consider just what transpired. They would not be leaving for America tomorrow, of that much he was certain. Their whole life had changed in the blink of an eye.

How had the Imperial Army found him? Of course! His passport, it was on file in some government office alerting them to his visit in the country.

Going to war meant that all young German men must fight, even those who had been living in America for the last four years. He was still a German. In his heart, he knew that he would always be German.

He glanced at the newspaper that lay at his feet. He had read and reread the article and yet he picked it up again. Germany had invaded Luxembourg on August 2 and Belgium on August 4, even though Belgium was a neutral country. According to the article, the plan was to invade France by way of Belgium, not necessarily the shortest route, but with a bit of luck, they could catch France unprepared.

The city of Liege in Belgium had become an obstacle. That key city lay on the steep west bank of the Meuse River. Twelve ancient forts, six on each side of the river, had defended the city for a thousand years.

The city of Liege was the rail hub for eastern Belgium. That, coupled with the strategic importance of the river, made it critical that Germany gain control of this city. General Otto von Emmich was the commander in charge and had a force of 60,000 men.

The Germans had not expected much resistance, but a Belgian force of more than 25,000 men fought hard to defend the city. Both sides suffered heavy casualties. This morning's paper indicated that the city of Liege had finally fallen to Germany but all twelve forts were still defended by Belgians and continued to put up a stiff resistance. Those forts would have to fall before Germany could continue its dash for France.

Georg put down the paper, dragged on his cigarette, and considered the ramifications of the plan. Yes. Germany would need all the men that were available, to fight this war. The talk of this being a two front war grew steadily every day. The plan seemed to be to defeat France and then move on to Russia.

Letting go of the paper, Georg watched it float back onto the stoop. He knew that he was going to fight, just not where or on what front. He stubbed out the cigarette on the sole of his shoe. What did all this mean? Just a few days ago, he had been almost envious of August. Now that the reality of the situation was upon him, just how did he feel? He loved his country and wanted to defend the Fatherland against all enemies. Yet, there were other obligations, especially Elsa and Gus. What if something should happen to him? Who would take care of them? Otto and Hedwig would always be for there for them. Elsa though, needed a husband and Gus a father. Then there was his job in America and their house? He looked up at the window and wondered if Elsa was awake yet. He knew he must make arrangements to assure that his family and property were cared for. When that was done he would be prepared for whatever this war might bring him.

Glancing up at the window again, Georg blew a kiss to his wife, "Do not worry, Elsa, I will take care of you and our son." Leaving the stoop, he started toward town. He must find a telegraph.

***

Elsa struggled to open her eyes from the drug- induced sleep. Where was she? Something was wrong; this did not feel like her room with its beautiful view of the Maumee River. Where were Gus and Georg? Someone was sitting in the chair. Louisa! What was Louisa doing in her house in Toledo?

Elsa shook her head and realized it was a dream. She was actually in her childhood room in Germany. She remembered they were visiting Momma and Papa. Then the nightmare that was the day before hit her. The day had started out to be such a nice day. She helped Momma prepare for the family gathering that evening. She and Hannah laughed about packing the trunks. Gus crawling toward the door. She picked him up and there was a man in uniform at the door. He wanted to speak to Georg. In a rush it all came back, Georg, the letter, the shock, Everything!

She realized that someone else was in the room. "Louisa, what are you doing here?"

Careworn and fighting to keep her own emotions under control, Louisa got up from the chair by the window and sat on the side of the bed. "It is alright, Elsa. I'm here for you."

Still struggling to clear her head from the drugs, she remembered something else, "August, he leaves soon, you should be with him."

"You need me more than he does right now." She momentarily stared out the window, a tear slid down her cheek. Resolutely, she wiped it away and patted Elsa's hand, "I will be here for you whenever you need me. We must stick together, you and me."

"Louisa, I can't do this." Tears trailed down Elsa's cheeks. "Why did this happen to me? I'm supposed to be going back to America. Why me?"

"Elsa, I cannot tell you why this is happening to any of us. I want you to know that no matter what you are feeling or thinking you can talk to me. I will not judge you or your feelings."

"I....Georg, what if something....what if something happens to him?" Now the tears were flowing freely. "I don't want to be alone. What will I do?"

"I don't have the answer to that question. I'm afraid too, so very afraid. I keep trying to remember what Hedwig told me just days ago." Louisa got up, walked to the window, looked down at the street and saw Georg, a determined set to his shoulders walk toward town. "She said we must be strong for the men. We must never let them know how we really feel." She turned back to Elsa. "Most people don't think of me as a very strong person, but I am."

"Louisa, I just don't know if I can be strong, not with Georg in danger."

"Yes, you can. It will be alright, Elsa. I'm here for you." Louisa walked back to the bed and sat down, embracing her sister-in-law. "Together we will get through this, no matter what happens." Her voice grew firmer, "From this day forward we are sisters of the closest kind. Not sister in blood, we are sisters in war

Chapter 14
The Farm outside of Dusseldorf
August 12, 1914

Hannah looked at Papa, his face so serious. Normally he was full of fun on their weekly drive out of the city to visit Franz and Hans, the retired coach horses. They both loved Onkle Adolph and Tanta Margried Beckenbauer's farm where the horses lived their life of leisure, grazing on grass and nibbling oats.

The Beckenbauers had been part of her family for many years before she was born, even though there was no blood relation. Onkle Adolph and Grandpapa Kruger were soldiers together when Prussia fought with Austria more than 50 years ago. They had fought like brothers and kept that relationship alive long after the fighting ended.

"What is wrong, Papa? You look so solemn today."

"Ah, Leipchen, so much has happened so fast. I was not surprised about August's conscription but I never expected Georg's. The pace of change is almost more than this old man can take in."

"You are not old and you must not talk that way. I'm going to be here, Papa. You can count on me."

"I know that. Do not let your mother hear me say this, but I am glad that you are not leaving." A smile began to form on Papa's face.

Their comfortable Mercedes glided around a curve. Hannah got her first glimpse of the farmhouse built into a hill. Papa said that earth from the hill helped to keep the house warm in the winter and cool in the summer. The huge linden trees that shaded the whole front of the house looked even bigger than usual today. She thought that the house always seemed dark, windows on only one side, but she had to admit that it was cool in the summer and toasty warm in the winter.

They drove up the lane and the rest of the building came into view. In the middle next to the house was a second house. It was actually the barn. This part of the building shared a fireplace wall with the kitchen. The animals fortunate enough to reside on this farm were warm all winter long. Equipment, food and hay for the animals kept in the open end of the building were accessible all year around. This layout was especially efficient on cold winter days. Onkle Adolph could take care of his animals and other farm chores and never leave the warmth of the building.

"Papa, how come Onkle Adolph and Tanta Margried never come to town?"

"There is no need. They grow rye to make flour for bread, the oats for the animals and you know how large their vegetable garden is. The two cows provide milk and butter. They use the goat's milk for cheese."

"And pigs, don't forget the pigs." Hannah laughed. "We wouldn't have all the wonderful sausage without Onkle Adolph's fat lazy pigs."

"I think your mother appreciates the chickens most. What would she do without those fresh eggs each week?"

"I appreciate the eggs too and all the wonderful breakfasts that Momma makes with them." Hannah licked her lips at the thought of this morning's mouth-watering fare.

"They have everything they need here, and we are lucky to have such great friends. However they are getting older."

"I think they must be at least in their seventies."

"I would say closer to eighty."

"Is that why you always try to help Onkle Adolph fix something when we are here?"

"That is part of the reason. I just enjoy spending time with the man. He is like a father to me. You know that he and your grandpapa, my wonderful papa, were best friends in the war with Austria. Onkle Adolph saved my papa's life and they were like brothers ever after. Now, I only have Onkle Adolph and I really look forward to these few hours each week with him."

The auto came to a stop in front of the house. Hannah jumped out. "I wonder what delicious treats Tanta Margried has this week?"

"Hurry on in. I am sure she is waiting for you. I see Adolph is working on his plows. I will go see if he needs my help."

***

"Tanta Margried, the bread looks wonderful and is that your special apple kuchen that I smell?"

"Yes, it is. What a surprise to see you." Tanta Margried grinned, bent over from years of hard work on the farm. "I did not expect to see you today. I thought you would be on your splendid voyage to America."

"I am not going to America."

"What are you talking about, child?

"So much has happened." Hannah sat at the big kitchen table while Margried cut a piece the scrumptious apple cake.

"Well, do not keep an ancient farmer's wife in suspense. Tell me what transpired to change all the carefully laid plans."

Hannah took a bite of the cake. "Mmm, this is so good."

"You are teasing me. I could be dead before you get around to telling me your story."

"Well, if you insist." Hannah laughed, shook her head, letting those beautiful locks of hair fly free, and then got very serious. "Georg has been told to report to the Imperial Army on Friday and Elsa refused to leave Germany without Georg. She was very upset, but I don't think she'll change her mind."

"How do you feel about that? You seemed to be looking forward to going to America." The older woman poured a glass of fresh milk and set it down in front of Hannah.

"Tanta Margried, can you keep a secret? I haven't told anyone else."

"You know you can tell your Tanta anything and it will stay a secret just between you and me."

"I really didn't want to go to America. I felt like I was running away. This is my country too. I am a girl so I can't defend Germany on the battlefield, but at least I can work at home to help make sure there is a place for the men to return." Hannah stopped for a drink of milk.

"I understand you feel an obligation to be a good citizen, to do your part." Margried poured a cup of coffee for herself.

"Momma and Papa thought they were doing the best thing for me, but I'm glad I'm not going to America."

"I hope that you will choose your causes wisely. I know that you will do your duty, whatever that may be." Margried patted Hannah's shoulder.

"Thank you, Tanta Margried. It helps to know you appreciate my decisions.

"I pray that you do not have to experience the ravages of war. It is far more than any young person should be forced to endure." Margried had a faraway look in her eyes that Hannah did not understand.

***

Otto took Adolph's place at the grinding wheel. "Here, Adolph let me help you sharpen those plow blades."

"I appreciate it. My back seems to tire quickly these days." Adolph sat on a bale of hay and lit his pipe. "Tell me, Otto, how is the war going? We hear nothing out here on the farm. I look forward to your weekly visits so I can catch up on the news."

"Germany has invaded Belgium, in an attempt to catch France with their pants down. However, Belgium decided to fight back rather than give Germany safe passage."

"That should not have been a surprise."

"I do not think that the Generals expected that. It always seems to be a surprise for our Generals when other nations do not just fall down in fright before the mighty German army."

Adolph laughed, "What you say about our generals is so true. You know that your father and I fought together in the Austrian war of '66. We were sure that nothing could defeat us. We believed in Bismarck and everything that he was doing for the new German Federation. If it were not for Bismarck there would not be a Unified Germany."

"I remember my father telling me about his time with you fighting that war. It seems that every generation of Germans has a war to remember."

"Otto, keep your eye on that grinder or you will be sharpening your fingers and not the plow blade." The old man puffed on his pipe. "The Germans have always been warlike people. We have a long history of domination going all the way back two thousand years. There was a bloody series of wars throughout all those years. When we were not at war we were bouncing between princes and kings and churches."

Otto held up the blade and sighted the edge, admiring his work. "Our borders have changed so many times that no one knows where the real Germany lies,"

You are so right," Adolph got up to get another blade for Otto. "We have been invaded by everyone from the Romans and Huns to the Vandals and Franks to the Saxons, Bohemians and Prussians. No matter who we faced, we always fought with valor and pride,"

Otto took the next blade, fitted it into the grinder and began working. "You should come into the city more often and see how the young people today dress as officers in the army with their epilates and spats and fake medals on their breast pocket, just to show their patriotic feelings. I wonder if they think this is just a grand adventure."

"It has only been in the last fifty years that Germany has been a unified country." Adolph walked to the open end of the building and knocked out his pipe of a post. "You cannot expect the German mentality to change just because we now have a single emperor and a line drawn on a map that says Germany. We have been destroyed and rebuilt more times than man can count." He turned back to his younger friend a tired look on his face. "It may happen again. Who is to say that the Germany of today will be the Germany of tomorrow?

"I just doubt the Generals are ready for a modern war?"

"Do not criticize the German military leadership. They have a long past to call upon. The German people have always triumphed and we should expect no less this time. I have faith and history to tell me that we Germans will prevail one more time."

"Adolph, as usual you cleared up my thinking. You are wise and know our people well. I sometimes forget that you are so much more than an old German farmer. You are a historian and philosopher who understands the German mind better than anyone I know. Thank you, your insight always helps to clarify my thinking."

Chapter 15
Dusseldorf, Germany
October 1914

Hannah could see the twinkling of the lanterns in trees as they walked toward Hagen Brau. They reminded her of fireflies on warm summer evenings. She thought of so many festivals she had enjoyed here with her family. Tonight, however, her anticipation was not just for the festival. She was looking forward to seeing Paul. Ingrid said that he would be here if he could. She hadn't seen him for the past two weeks and was hoping that he would be here tonight. Her friends waved a greeting as soon as she entered the garden gates.

"Papa, may I sit with Ingrid and Greta, please?"

"Of course you may."

Hannah moved from behind Gus' carriage and Elsa stepped into her place. Leaning over, Elsa whispered in her ear, "Is your friend Paul with them tonight?"

"I don't know, but I hope so." She started toward the group, then called over her shoulder, "Thank you Papa, I'll see you later."

Hedwig grinned at her husband and chuckled, "Otto, I believe our little girl is growing up."

"I think you may be right, although I am not at all sure I like the idea." Otto glanced at his daughter almost dancing across the lawn to join her friends.

"I remember the first time Louisa told me about August," Genevieve commented. "She was smitten right away. August was such a nice, well-mannered young man that I could find no reason to object. Look at them now, expecting a baby."

"Mama, you are embarrassing me," Louisa chided. "Why do you say such things?"

"It is true and you know it. There is nothing about which to be embarrassed. August is a good man and you fell in love with him, that's all."

"Your mother is right, Louisa. You have nothing to be embarrassed about because you love your husband," Hedwig chimed in. She smiled at her friend, "Thank you for your kind words about our son. I only wish he and Georg were with us tonight, instead of off fighting a war." Hedwig had a catch in her voice, "I miss them both so very much."

"Come now, Momma," Elsa's voice gentle, "we promised that we would not let anything destroy our evening. We're going to be happy and celebrate Oktoberfest with our friends. We will not think of unhappy things this evening. Remember, Momma, we women must be strong. You keep telling us that."

"Listen to your daughter, Hedwig," Otto admonished. "Tonight is for family, laughter and good fun. Enjoy! No worrying tonight,"

"You are right, as always, Otto. Thank you for reminding me. Look there is a table, we had better grab it quickly, or we may be standing all night."

***

Ingrid jumped up as Hannah approached, "Hannah, you look beautiful tonight. Is that a new dress?"

"Yes, it is one of Elsa's. She said that I needed something different." Hannah twirled around. "Do you really like it?"

"Oh, Yes. It's perfect for you."

"Do you think that Paul will like it?"

"If he doesn't like it, I do," Erik, a friend from school, said. "I don't understand what you see in this Paul. What makes him so special?"

Greta frowned at her schoolmate, "Erik, you could never understand. All you think about is how girls look and not what we think or how we feel. You need to grow up."

"What has gotten it to you tonight, Greta? I was only joking with Hannah. You know you are more my type anyway."

"That is just what I'm talking about," Greta argued, "I'm only your type because of the way I look. You know you don't have a chance with me."

"What's going on here?" Paul asked as he approached the table. "It sounds like the war is here at Hagen Brau instead of in France. Greta, are you alright?"

"Of course I am, but how nice of you to ask." Greta looked at Erik, "You see that is how a man should speak to a woman." She looked back at Paul and patted the bench. "There's a seat here by me."

"Thank you, but I think I'll take this one next to Hannah." He smiled.

Ingrid joined the fray, "Doesn't Hannah look beautiful tonight?"

"She certainly does." Paul took his seat by the vision in blue. "I hope you dressed up just for me"

"Why would I do something just for you?" Hannah said with defiance. "I am dressed this way because I wanted to try a different style. These are American clothes. My trip to America was cancelled, so I will just have to try out my new style here in Germany,"

"Ah, the girl with spirit is back." Paul grinned. "You know, that is what I like about you. You are different from the other girls."

Hannah felt her face begin to flush.

"You seem to enjoy putting me in my proper place, although I must admit that Greta was definitely giving Erik a run for his money earlier."

"I only stated the obvious." Greta raised her chin in a mock superior pose.

"Erik, what do you say we buy these girls a stein of beer? I think we need to do something to get in their good graces again, don't you agree?"

"Yes, I do, Paul. Yes I do. What will it be ladies, Hagen's October Amber?"

Greta began to sway as the band took up their instruments and played the first strands of a waltz.

"Greta do you suppose that I could interest you in a dance?" Eric asked.

"Well, there doesn't appear to be a better choice since Paul only seems interested in Hanna. Do you promise to behave?"

"For you, I would do anything."

Greta heaved a huge sigh and headed for the dance floor.

Ingrid laughed. I think Greta really enjoys every minute of the attention that Erik gives her.

Paul nodded his head, "I think you may be right."

With couples on the dance floor, the band now began the waltz in earnest. "Hannah, I believe they are playing our song. Will you dance with me?" Paul asked.

"How can that be our song? I didn't know we had a song," Hannah replied as she shook her head and looked the other way.

"Woman, if are you are trying to make my life miserable tonight you are certainly doing a good job of it."

"Well, it is fun to watch you squirm," she giggled.

"Please, take pity on a poor lonely soldier boy," Paul pleaded dropping to his knees.

"Alright, when you put it that way, I guess I have no choice. I must do my patriotic duty and dance with you." Hannah got up and gave Paul her hand.

Once they were out on the wooden boards that served as a dance floor, she relished the feel of his arms around her. He was so strong, yet held her with such tenderness she felt she might melt. His golden blond hair reflected the moonbeams and his eyes, soft as velvet, were the richest shade of brown that she had even seen. She wondered if she was actually dancing. How could she be, she was sure her feet were not even touching the floor. When she was with Paul, she felt as if the entire world were right, even in this time of war. She hoped that this moment would go on forever. Perhaps if she closed her eyes and wished on a star, she would never have to wake up from this dream.

Paul could hardly believe that this wonderful creature was dancing with him. She was so beautiful tonight. It was not just her clothes. She had a look about her that he had not seen before. When he looked into her brilliant blue eyes, he felt as though he might drown in their depths. Her gorgeous auburn hair was the color of smoldering coals in a fire and felt like silk on his cheek. The sweet aroma that emanated from her was almost more than a man could bear. If he were smart, he would leave this dance floor, this garden, and run as fast as he could from this angel with whom he was dancing. Yet he knew that he would never be able to do that. Each time that he was with her, he found it harder to leave."

"Hannah, I've missed you these last two weeks. I think about you all the time. Sometimes when I'm driving and I'm so tired that I can't see straight, I think of you and you give me the strength to complete my mission."

"Paul, I don't know what to say…."

"I know I should not speak this way. We have known each other for such a short time. I knew the first time I saw you, that you were different." He looked Hannah in the eyes. "We live in such a strange time. It is not right for me to be talking this way."

He pulled back just a little. "You are so young. I do not want you to take what I am saying the wrong way."

"I think I understand your meaning." Hannah couldn't look at him. Her voice got very quiet. "I think of you all the time as well." She knew the blush was on her cheeks again.

"Each day I read the paper that Papa brings home and I wonder where you are and if you are safe." She finally got the courage to look him in the eye. "I know I may be younger than you, but that doesn't keep me from having feelings for you."

Paul whispered in her ear. "Let's go for a walk. There are so many people here."

They left the dance floor and wandered off toward the back of the garden where there was a grove of trees. As they sat on the ground in the shade of the trees, Paul put his arm around Hannah. "You are so beautiful. I get lost when I look into your eyes."

"Paul, I…."

Softly he put his finger on her lips to shush her. "Do not say anything." Tilting her chin up, he very gently kissed her. Her lips felt as though they were made of satin and she tasted of sweet honey. He had been longing to do this since the moment he met her. "I don't want to frighten you. Tell me if you want me to stop."

"Yes, I mean no. I have never kissed anyone before." She didn't know what she was saying. She had dreamed of kissing him many times but her fantasies were nothing to compare to this. She was not sure what she should do next, so she did nothing. He looked at her with eyes that seemed to mirror everything that she was feeling. She knew this was right. In the depths of her being, she understood that this man was her soul mate.

He drew her into his arms and kissed her again more deeply this time with a longing that surprised even him. This time she responded and put her arms around his neck. He knew, in that moment, that he would do anything to be with this woman. He had a duty to his country, an obligation that he could not ignore. This night, though, had given meaning to his life. He would stay safe and come back for her. He was sure that he was falling in love with her.

Chapter 16
Düsseldorf, Germany
November 1914

"Hello, is anyone home," Hanna shouted as she entered the house.

Genevieve straightened her back from bending over the kitchen table. "The girls are not back from market yet, Hannah, and your mother is in the garden," Genevieve sighed. "I am in the kitchen getting these vegetables ready for dinner."

Hannah noticed there was a pot bubbling on the old wood stove as she entered the kitchen. "What is that wonderful smell?"

"It could be the potatoes on the stove but I suspect what you smell are the pfeffernuesse. They are your brother's favorite cookie and Louisa makes them for him every year at Christmas. She finished them just before she and Elsa left for market. Would you like one?" Genevieve offered.

"Oh, yes I would, please," Hannah, replied eagerly reaching for the cookie. She took a bite of the delightful little anise confection. "Umm this is wonderful. Thank you"

"How was school today?"

"The same as always. I really don't like school and now there are so few people.

"What do you mean? Have people actually left?

"Yes they have! There used to be 20 people in my mathematics class and now there are only 10 and most of them are girls. I see no reason to continue in school, now that we are fighting this war.

"How can you say that? You should feel privileged that you can still be in school," The older woman scolded.

"I want to do my part to help the war effort. Everything is more important than school now. All the men off fighting the war and the factories need women to do the work. Many of my friends are going to work." Hannah looked up from pouring a glass of milk and met her mother's glare as she entered the backdoor, arms full of turnips from the garden.

"What are you talking about, Hannah. Nothing is more important than school."

"Momma, you know I don't like school. I would be much more useful if I were working at the munitions factory."

"Never! You will finish your schooling. I will not have you speak of this again." Hedwig stamped her foot. "Do you hear me?"

"But Momma. Bu…"

"No buts. You will finish school; your father would never allow you to leave your education to go to work." Her voice was rising. "War or no war you will complete your education."

"That is not true, Papa would understand. I just know he would. August, Georg and Paul are all fighting for the Fatherland. What good did school do for them?" Hannah turned and started from the room.

"Turn around, Child!" Hedwig was angry now. "What are you talking about, education useless? Of course education was important to all three of them."

"Education does nothing to help the cause. I need to be useful. I feel very strongly about this, Momma."

"I do not care how strongly you feel. We will not discuss this further. Do you hear me?"

"Why will you not listen to me….?"

"I have spoken and that is that. There is already enough upheaval in our lives." Hedwig slumped into the closest chair, her voice sounded tired now, "You must continue to go to school. It helps to provide a sense of normalcy for us. Do try to understand how important it is for you to do this. We all NEED for you to go to school."

Hannah slowly recognized what looked like despair on Momma's face. "Yes, Momma, I will not speak of it again," Hannah answered. *But we will speak of it again, Hannah thought to herself. Am I the only one in this family who understands what this war is doing to our lives? You are wrong, Momma, if you truly believe that my staying in school will keep our lives normal.*

Elsa and Louisa's return from the market at just that moment gave Hannah a good excuse to change the subject. "How was the market today?" Hannah asked.

"Quite good," Elsa answered, "we found some very nice fresh sea bass. It should make a good fish stew."

"That is wonderful, give it to me and I will prepare it," Genevieve said.

"Was there any mail today?" Louisa asked.
Louisa sounded more tired than usual today, Hanna thought. "There were a few things but nothing for you."

"Still no letter from August, I just do not understand," Louisa whispered, tears welling in her eyes.

"I am sure he has written, but we have no way of knowing how long it takes to get mail from the front," Elsa said.

"That is easy for you to say. You got a letter from Georg just two days ago and you have had other letters from him as well. Why is it only me that gets no letters?"

"Georg is very busy. I am sure it is hard for him to find time to write," Elsa's voice sounded surly.

"Georg is not even fighting. He is off in some nice safe factory somewhere designing newfangled toys for the army he cannot even tell you about. He may be busy, but he certainly is not in danger," Louisa's voice was rising with each word.

"I have not heard from Paul since I saw him at the Oktoberfest more than a month ago," Hannah added hoping to make Louisa feel better.

"He is not your husband! August should have written!"

"Louisa, you need to calm down," Hedwig put a hand on her daughter-in-law's shoulder. "Here, sit down."

"Take your hands off me. I do not want to sit down."

"Louisa, please, darling you do need to calm down as Hedwig said," Genevieve put her arm around her daughter.

"I agree with Elsa," Hedwig said, "I am sure that he has written to you. August is a man that loves words nearly as much as he loves his wife. I always called him my poet. Surely you will get a letter soon."

Louisa leaned on her mother, deflating like a balloon with a hole, till she looked as if she could barely stand. "I don't know Hedwig, perhaps you are right," she said, the tears finally spilling from her eyes. "I think I will go to my room and rest awhile. The marketing seems to have taken its toll on me today. I need to lie down."

Hannah watched Louisa closely as she climbed the stairs. There was something about her that did not seem right. She was sure there was more than not hearing from her husband. Nevertheless, what did she know about pregnant women. The others did not seem worried.

* * *

"August, I swear you write more than any man I have ever known. You always have that journal in your hands."

"It is my way of finding peace in this hell hole we live in. If I did not write, I would go crazy, just like half the men out here. It is the only thing that keeps me sane."

"Your wife must have a stack of letters a meter high by now."

"Mind your own business. You write your letters and I'll write mine."

"Hey, man, what did I say? I was just commenting on how lucky your wife is to have a husband like you."

"Just leave me alone."

"Okay, Okay."

August's thoughts traveled inward I am sorry my darling Louisa, I miss you more than life itself. My entire body aches for your touch. I would give the world just to see your smile or hear your beautiful voice. I am so afraid that I will die out here and never see you again. This never ending cesspool of quicksand attacks my mind dragging me under, only to let me up just enough to get my bearings before it begins sucking me back in. Therefore, I write in the journal you gave me that day just before I got on the troop train. When I write, I lose myself in the words. For just a short time, I am that man you learned to love so long ago, a whole man in body, mind and spirit using beautiful words to weave a tale. Perhaps when this is all over I will be able to share it with you, but for now I must keep it to myself. I hope you can somehow forgive me. I know you must wonder why you receive no mail from me. Soon, my love, soon. He picked up the pen and began another letter like so many others that he had written in the journal.

November 11, 1914

All is quiet just now. There is the occasional stray bullet that flies overhead, but I am safe for this moment, lying in a trench that serves as home. We have been moving north for days. The land of Flanders is beautiful and green with fields of grain ripe for the harvest. The brilliant shades of red, orange and gold in the trees are breathtaking. All around us there is an aura of peace and serenity. To these gentle people, war seemed only a gloomy forecast to be dismissed as unreliable until we marched into their land. With pick and shovel we have dug trenches through this portrait worthy of a master and rendered it forever changed.

We have brought the war to these peace loving people who want nothing more than to harvest their grain, gather their roots and truffles, and salvage enough food to stem their hunger through the coming winter. I am reminded of Onkle Adolph and Tanta Margried with their beautiful and bountiful farm. How would they survive were thousands of strangers to come across their farm and indiscriminately dig up their land? With these thoughts in mind, I believe that we all try to leave some of each farm untouched for the innocent civilians.

The soft clay of the soil makes it exceptionally good for earthworks. We Germans were the first to begin digging these trenches and have chosen the high points wherever they are advantageous.

The French have also built a system of trenches in response to what we Germans have engineered. I would guess that the distance between these two rows of earthworks is about two hundred meters. Of course, that varies depending on the lay of the land. The land between the two lines is fondly known as no-man's-land. It belongs to no man and no man is safe there.

At night, you can see the fires on the opposing side. And often you can hear voices and sometimes singing. It is so strange to hear a French ballad being sung from the enemy camp and soon men all around you picking up the strain and singing the same ditty in German. This sometimes goes on for hours.

Life in these trenches is a living hell. It is extremely muddy, very cramped and filthy beyond your imagination. Everything is caked with multiple layers of this insufferable mud, a combination of clay, water, urine, and blood. We cannot bathe, as clean water has to be brought from at least a mile away from the trench. What clean water there is must be reserved only for drinking or cooking.

There is no room to stretch out for sleeping. We try to stay off the bottom so that our feet do not rot from constantly being in the water. At night, we often huddle together, to provide each other warmth as there is little dry clothing and blankets and the weather gets colder each night. In many areas, we must walk bent over; the trenches have not been dug deep enough to protect our heads.

The worst part, though, is that the guns are never silent. The shells and bullets are banging and whistling overhead in a constant barrage that leaves me always wondering where the next shell will hit. After dark, the machine guns and rifle-grenades pick up the chorus. The French seem to fire six rounds to our one. Quiet usually reigns from midnight until dawn. That is the time when I can hear the screams and moans from those sick and wounded all around me. Often I hear men begging to be put out of their misery. They just want to escape this hell, and, for many, death seems the only possibility.

"Kruger, get up here. We need your help with the gun."

"Yes, Sir, I am on my way, Sir." Stuffing the journal into his breast pocket, August headed for the machine gun nest.

"Corporal Ulhman, the post has just arrived and there's a package for you."

"Thank you, Lieutenant." Paul was sitting at a desk in the front room of the converted farmhouse that served as headquarters for the German First Army in France. This once elegant room with its rich gold brocade draperies, plush Aubusson carpet and graceful Louis XIV furniture, now replaced with utilitarian military desks, chairs, and file cabinets was quiet this late December afternoon. The draperies that still hung at the windows were open to let in the bright winter sun, the carpet covered with mud from hundreds of dirty boots.

Paul glanced at the desk where the mail sat. There was a package with the familiar scrawl he knew as Hannah's handwriting. His heart leapt and sank all at the same time. He picked up the package and took it to his bunk in the room he shared with three other men, also couriers. He sat holding the package, debating whether to open it or not, his emotions in a turmoil.

"Corporal Ulhman, the Captain needs you."

"Yes, Sir. Thank you, Sir." Paul left the package on his bed and reported to his superior.

Several hours later Paul returned to his bunk and stared at the package, still unopened. Filled with reluctance, he slowly sat down and very carefully opened the box. Inside a knitted hat and scarf and a tin of homemade Christmas cookies awaited him, along with a letter. He put on the hat and wrapped the scarf around his neck, he could feel the warmth of Hannah envelope him. How he missed that girl! In his thoughts constantly, no matter how hard he tried to erase the feelings, she would not leave. The kiss never should have happened for it had sealed his doom. Doom, a strange word to describe a kiss, but surely that was what he felt. He knew with no trace of doubt that Hannah was the right one for him. Nevertheless, he also knew he must never see her again.

There was a war and he was actively involved. No more than an hour ago, he had been at the front slogging through the mud of the trenches. Today relative calm prevailed with only the occasional rifle shot across no-man's-land. No one on either side was much interested in firing on this Christmas Eve. Men wanted rest and quiet. Reluctantly officers indulged men their wishes. They wanted confrontation no more than their men did.

An almost serene tranquility exuded from the trenches. The weather had turned cold and only a few billowy white clouds moved lazily across the sky, the wind having ceased to blow. Sunlight warmed the men as it reflected off the new fallen snow creating ice diamonds that sparkled with brilliance. They were opening packages, reading and writing letters, and sharing gifts of baked goods with their fellow comrades, the dead and wounded already taken from the trenches to the hospital or morgue tents. Only the dead in no-man's-land still remained untended awaiting their rescue.

The illusion of quiet Paul experienced at the front today was a false impression. When this night was over the war would begin again with a fury that would take the lives of many. All that was rational within him dictated that he must not become involved with anyone, especially Hannah, who seemed so young and vulnerable. Each of her letters expressed her apprehension for his safety and well-being. Was it fair to allow her anxiety for him to continue?

Pulling the scarf closer around his neck, he inhaled her perfume as it drifted up from her handwork, and remembered her feel in his arms when they danced. He had never been in love before, was not even sure what it meant to be in love. Yet, somehow, Hannah had become the most important person in his life. As a result, he was convinced that he must find a way to end this madness and torment for them both.

The unopened letter stared up at him from the bed. Ignoring it, he went to his desk. The quiet in the room seemed so strange. Closing his eyes he escaped to the refuge of happier days in the palace gardens of Vienna, his hands idly sketched one of the gardens from memory. This particular rose garden had never been his favorite but as he sketched, on this cold December day, he imagined the vibrant colors, velvety textures, and delicate scent of roses, Hannah's sent.

Working with unusual diligence, soon several varieties that had not actually been in the garden, found their way onto the paper. He must write Obergardener with these new ideas. If only this war had not happened. He would be working his own way up to obergardener at some fine estate or palace and be free to pursue his ever increasing interest in Hannah.

Hannah, sweet Hannah, her letter seemed to call out to him. Try as he would to resist the call, he could not. Returning to the bunk, he slowly opened the envelope. Hannah herself seemed to flow from the envelope and enfold him in her sweetness.

Dear Paul,

I hope this letter finds you well. You have been in my thoughts nearly constantly these last few days. As I knitted this hat and scarf, I felt your presence. I would close my eyes and could feel your arms around me as we danced that last time at the Oktoberfest. That was such a happy night.

Even though there was war, it seemed so far away and unreal. We were together and nothing else mattered, at least to me. When you kissed me so gently, I thought that my world had ended and begun all at the same time.

Paul closed his eyes and once again felt her lips on his. His hand touched the scarf, fingers closing in its softness.

I hope that you have gotten my previous letters. I have written to the address that Ingrid gave me, but I have not heard from you. I know you must be very busy and have little time to consider the likes of me.

You have no idea how wrong you are. You seldom leave my thoughts.

You probably think that the feelings I have for you are only those of a smitten schoolgirl. However, they are very real to me.

I do not think you foolish. My feelings are so real as well.

I had, perhaps mistakenly, felt that you had feelings for me also.

It was no mistake.

Your kiss given so lovingly and the look that you gave seemed to speak volumes to my naive eye. If you could find it in your heart to answer my letter, just to let me know that you are alright, it would mean so much to me. I will not bother you any more, nor will I write to you again, if that is what you want. If you are not comfortable writing to me, please write to Ingrid and tell her. She will tell me what you say.

Oh, Hannah, what am I doing to you? I must end this madness.

I pray that you share my feelings, however, I will understand if you do not. I beg you, please do not keep me wondering and worrying that you are dead or wounded. I know that you would not intentionally be cruel to me but this worrying and your silence is unbearable. I could stand the worry about your wellbeing if I knew you cared. I am sorry if I have upset you with my ramblings.

Paul let the letter drop to the floor and closed his eyes. He saw Hannah standing there in her American clothes with her hair done up so sophisticated, the unruly tendrils escaping and dancing to their own music. Her laughing eyes so bright with mischief as she quipped her responses to his comments. When they danced, she fairly floated across the floor in his arms. Then, when he had held her as they sat under the tree, her eyes were no longer full of mischief, only wonder and adoration. The sweet rapture of that single kiss would carry him through all that this war had to give him, if only he would let it. She would be there for him, waiting when this madness was over. Waiting, with her arms and heart open for him. He knew this with a certainty that burned into his soul.

Eyes open again, he looked around the cold room. This was war and in the harsh reality of daylight, his sense of all that was right and good could never allow him to subject Hannah to the heartache that war inevitably produced. After all, she already had a brother, brother-in-law, and an uncle fighting and he could not let her be concerned for his safety also.

Somehow, he had to find the courage to tell her that he did not care for her and she need not write to him again. She must get on with her life, forget about him. Should he survive this war, then perhaps, he would see her again.

The situation was entirely his fault; he should never have shown interest in her in the first place. He pursued her, meeting her family and trying to make a favorable impression on her father. How wrong he had been. This conflict had been looming then and he had known it.

Why had he allowed this to progress so far? The beauties at the palace had never tempted him. How then had this little minx gotten so far under his skin?

I am not a coward, yet somehow writing to Hannah and telling her that we must not see each other again is almost too unbearable to face.

He had not answered any of her letters because he could not bring himself to end it. Her letters were in a leather pouch inside the breast pocket of his uniform close to his heart. Each day he read and reread every one of them. How could he face the days ahead knowing that he would receive no more letters from her?

Yet he must. He must stop this. He was hurting her by his very silence. She had expressed that in her letter today. She was beginning to believe that he did not care for her.

He would take advantage of that and write her now, tell her that he had never cared. It was just a fling for him. He would love to see her again but she was to have no feelings for him as he would never have feelings for her.

Yes, that is what I need to do. I need to be crass and uncaring, nonchalant, the typical soldier just looking for a good time. Hannah would never like someone like that.

He rose and went to his desk. Pen poised over the paper, his mind made up that he would somehow gather the courage to end this once and for all.

Christmas Eve 1914
My Dearest Hannah,

The hat, scarf, and cookies are very much appreciated. I am well.

I spend the greatest part of everyday traveling between the headquarters and the front delivering messages. Usually it is only minimally dangerous. There is not much fighting behind the lines. I am lucky to have a dry bed most nights. I carry a side arm, but to date, I have not had to use it. The biggest problem I encounter comes from bad roads. I have had one or two spills from my motorcycle because the roads are so full of ruts, holes, and mud.

Today however is a beautiful day. The bright sun reminds me of your smile and the sky is a blue that only your eyes could rival for brilliance. The white clouds are drifting past in a way that reminds me of the way you seem to float on air when we are dancing. The snow has kissed the ground with gentleness that only you could understand.

What am I doing? This is not the letter I wanted to write. This is not a letter saying that I do not care and yet these words are pouring from my pen, almost as if by their own will.

Paul's conscious mind seemed to have no control over what he was putting on the paper. Tears seeped from his eyes, traversed his cheeks, and found their way to the paper on which he wrote. They were tears of loneliness and longing for the decision that he must make. He should be blunt, cruel if necessary, because that was what was best. His mind, a very good mind to be sure, told him that he must end it.

His heart however, a heart never before tried, was breaking, telling him that he must never leave Hannah. She was to be the source of his strength and comfort in the long hard days to come. Head or heart, to which should he listen. Never had he felt so conflicted.

He had always followed his head. When his father told him he had arranged for him to receive training with the local nursery owner and he was to leave home and go there to live, Paul understood and went willingly. Years later, when Herr Hessel told him that he must leave Leipzig for Vienna and the apprenticeship at the palace, he had gone, knowing that it was the best for his education.

When his apprenticeship was finished, he volunteered for the German army. Again, he followed what his head had told him. He could have stayed at the Palace. Obergardener had begged him to stay and become a gardener of full employ. But his head told him that he owed the responsibility of service to his Germany for advantages afforded him in his young life. He must repay the fatherland before he could continue his life.

Why then, was it so very hard for him to listen to his head this time? Those other decisions had been difficult, yet he had never agonized over them, as he was this one. This was tearing him apart. He wanted only to be with Hannah, no matter the consequences.

I am thinking only of myself. I need to think of Hannah and what is best for her. Wait! What did she say in her letter? Paul dropped his pen, ran to the bunk, picked up Hannah's letter from the floor, where it had fallen.

There it is 'We were together and nothing else mattered, at least to me. When you kissed me so gently, I thought that my world had ended and begun all at the same time.' I feel the same way.

Suddenly, he knew he could not give her up. In a few short months she had become a part of the very fabric of his being, sure that his soul would depart and life would not be worth living were he to give her up.

Somehow, his heart seemed to be winning the battle that raged within him. Perhaps it takes more courage to face my feelings for Hannah and walk the unknown road with her, than to end our relationship with a lie.

Where the road would take them he knew not, but he was now confident that they must walk the road of life together.

He picked up his pen and continued to write:

My wonderful Hannah, I am so very sorry that I have not answered any of your letters. I can only say that it is the coward in me that has kept me from writing. I have made every excuse, telling myself that if I did not write that you would stop and I would not have to face my feelings. Then I told myself that it would be best if we did not see each other again so you would not worry about me. There is a war, after all.

Can you ever forgive me for treating you so poorly in my attempt to sooth my own inability to face the reality of my feelings for you?

When I read your letter today and you said that you felt that your world had ended and begun all at the same time, I knew just what you meant. I too, feel that way and know that I can no longer deny my feelings for you. I have tried. Oh! How I have tried. All the time knowing that loving you was all that I wanted in this world.

Yes, Hannah, I must tell you that I love you. Thoughts of you are all that keep me doing my job. Your letters are close to my heart always and all I need do is touch them and I can feel your presence with me. I cannot predict what will happen in this horrible war but if you will wait for me, I will do everything within my power to come home to you. No man could have a better Christmas gift then I have received this day. The knowledge and acceptance that I love you and the hope that you will return that love is a blessing that I shall treasure all of my days.

Yours forever with love,
Paul

Hannah tore the paper from the pad, wadded it up, and threw it on the floor to join the growing pile, with such force that had it been anything heavier it would have made a dent. Her grunt of exasperation did not even begin to express her frustration. Try as she would, she just could not get the words right. She had read and reread Paul's letter and with each reading, her feelings grew stronger.

She closed her eyes and tried to think of something else. Upstairs on the third floor, Hannah knew that Momma and Genevieve sat with Louisa. Dr. Ostermann had given strict orders that she was not to get up. Her contractions were frequent and it was much too early for the baby. She was to stay quiet in hopes of prolonging her pregnancy a few more days. He had made it clear that he doubted Louisa would go full term, but every day could make a difference for her baby's life.

Bright sun filled Hannah's room with an illusion of warmth that did not reflect the actual temperature outside, or Hannah's mood inside. It was a cold and crisp, but altogether a beautiful day for January. Perhaps she should get dressed and go for a walk. She was still wearing her pajamas and had not even thought of combing her hair. Anything would be better than trying to write this letter. It was just too difficult.

In the parlor downstairs, Elsa enjoyed solitude while Gus took a well-deserved nap. He never stopped moving these days. Beginning to walk, all he wanted to do was explore every nook and cranny of Grandmomma's house. Today he had decided he was big enough to take a try at the stairs. He did not fall, thank goodness, but only because she caught him just as he started his climb.

Elsa picked up the needlework that lay in her lap and admired her handiwork on the gown she had made for Louisa's baby. The fabric was from a blanket that had been Gus's. She had sewn the little gown with her own hands and just now finished embroidering a row of roses around the bottom.

Of course, it is not what she would have done for the baby were she at home in Toledo. She closed her eyes and pictured the scene. Emma Klein, her neighbor, and she would had taken the streetcar downtown and gone to Lyons Department Store. There in the children's department she would have found the most beautiful gown of the softest material and made sure that there were matching hat, booties, and blanket, and she would have had it wrapped in the special paper you can only get at the Lyons Store. While she was there, she would have picked out the cutest little boy's navy blue and white sailor suit for Gus. Then Emma and she would have taken Gus in his carriage up to Ladies Fine Dresses and Elsa would have picked out something just a little daring to intrigue Georg.

After that, the three of them would have gone to the very top floor to the Tea Room. Her mouth watered as she thought of ordering her favorite Chicken-a-la-king. That creamy mixture of delicate vegetables and little pieces of tender chicken served over the flakiest pastry she loved so much. It was so very different from the heavy German food. She liked German food, of course, especially all the good things Momma made. Still, the delicate mixture seemed like heaven this afternoon. All of the waitresses would have stopped by their table to tell her what a beautiful baby she had and how pleased everyone was that they were all having lunch with them today.

She missed being in her home in America with her friends and her own life. She missed Georg so much sometimes it was a physical hurt. Why had they ever come back to Germany? It still seemed so unfair. They were Americans; after all, Gus was even a citizen. He should not have to be stuck here in Germany, especially during this awful war. Elsa, lost in her own thoughts of America and how wonderful her life used to be, was startled by a noise. It took her a moment to realize that was someone at the door. As she got up to answer it, she saw a man patiently standing there in a German uniform.

Her head swam with terrible thoughts. Someone was dead or at the very least badly hurt. Which one? Oh, please Dear God; don't let it be Georg. She did not want August or Ernst to be hurt either, but please do not let it be Georg. With her heart in her throat, she went to the door. She really wanted to run in the other direction, up the stairs and hide behind the skirts of her mother. Yet, she knew she was a grown woman and she must act so. Very gingerly, as if it might explode in her hands, she opened the door and stared at the man who stood there.

"Frau Mueller, Elsa, good afternoon. Do you remember me? I am Paul Ulhman."

"Why, yes, of course. How nice to see you," she said, dumfounded with relief. "What are you doing here? Oh, please excuse me, where are my manners, Do come in."

"Thank you. I had to come to Dusseldorf and was able to arrange to get a little time off. I was hoping that I might be able to see Hannah."

"Yes, of course, please come in and have a chair. I will get Hannah for you. I know that she will be very excited to see you."

Elsa walked to the stairs with a grin on her face. "Hannah, please come down stairs, you have a visitor." She called. When there was no answer, she called again. "HANNAH, you have a visitor."

"Tell whoever it is that I don't want visitors right now." Hannah sounded rather distracted.

"Hannah, you need to come downstairs now."

"Did you not hear me? I do not want to see anyone."

"Hannah, do come down. NOW"

"Who could possibly be so important?" She grumbled. "What gives you the right to order me around?" Hannah opened the door and stepped out. "I am your sister, not your child. You have no right to tell me what to do."

"I know you are my sister, but you need to come downstairs!"

"Oh, alright. Here I am downstairs. Does that make you happy?"

"It does make me happy. Look who has come to see you." The words were barely out of her mouth when she saw the look of stark horror on Hannah's face. It was only then that she noticed her sister's disheveled appearance.

Hannah turned and ran back up the stairs, screaming, "How could you do this to me? I hate you."

"Hannah, please…."

"Why are you so mean?"

"Hannah, let me ex…." the slamming of the bedroom door shook the whole house.

The look on Paul's face clearly showed his stunned reaction to Hannah's behavior. "I thought she would be glad to see me."

"She is glad to see you, or at least will be soon. This is entirely my fault. I should have realized something was wrong when she did not want to come downstairs. She has been up in her room for several hours and I don't think she has combed her hair or even gotten dressed. Please make yourself comfortable while I will go up and try to talk some sense into her.

By the time Elsa got upstairs, Momma had come down from Louisa's room. "What is all of this commotion?"

"I seem to have made a terrible mistake," Elsa's voice apologetic, "at least terrible in Hannah's mind. Paul Ulhman has come for a visit. She is upset because I did not warn her. I am going to attempt help her get ready to see him, if she will let me in her room." She looked toward the closed door with trepidation. "Would you mind going down and talking with Paul?"

"That would be my pleasure." Momma said a smile on her face. "When Hannah is presentable, I am quite sure that you will find us in the kitchen. I wager that I can tempt Corporal Ulhman with something to eat," Momma laughed as she started down the steps.

Elsa knocked on the bedroom door. "Hannah, please open the door."

"No! Go away!"

"I'm sorry, darling; I should have told you who was here. Please, let me in."

"How could you be so mean?" Hannah asked as she opened the door a crack.

"I said I was sorry. Let me in and I will help you fix your hair and find a pretty dress to wear."

"Where is he now?"

"Momma is with him. She is going to feed him, so we have a little time. Please, I know you want to see him."

"I don't know if I want to see him. What should I say? I look so awful. How could you let him see me this way?"

"Everything will be fine. Let's get you fixed up," Elsa said as she gently pushed the door open.

Flinging herself on the bed, Hannah sobbed, "I think you should just go away and tell him to go away, too."

"You don't really feel that way. Do you?"

"I'm so confused. Nothing makes sense anymore."

"Perhaps I can help you." Elsa ventured another step into the room.

"How can I trust you after what you did?"

"I'm your sister and I love you." Elsa gently closed the door.

"Oh, alright, but I still am not sure I want to go back downstairs." Hannah lay with her face to the wall.

"Let's try that pretty light blue dress we bought to take to America. I'm sure I have stockings that would match and I have a blue satin ribbon that would be perfect for your hair. When I'm finished you will be the most beautiful girl that Herr Ulhman has ever seen."

"He has already seen the ugliest girl ever."

"Don't say such things." Elsa looked around the unkempt room. "What have you been doing up here all day and what is all this paper on the floor?" Then Elsa saw the letter lying face-up on the bed. Without picking it up, she read just a few lines and realized why Hannah was acting so out of character.

"Hannah, my little sister, I think understand what is happening, you truly care for this young man and he for you. It changes a relationship so much when those feelings are out in the open. The first time a man tells you he loves you can be terrifying. I know that this must be hard for you and if you are not ready for this kind of a relationship, you must tell him."

"It is not like that at all." Hannah slowly rolled over. "I think, no, I know that I love him too, but I have never loved anyone before and I'm not sure how to act. What do I do, Elsa? You know about these things. You have been in love so many times."

"Well, I don't know about many times."

"You and Georg are so perfect together. I just do not know what to do."

"My advice to you is to be yourself. You are the person he fell in love with. He doesn't want you to change. Just be yourself and everything else will fall in place."

"What do you mean?"

"You're trying too hard. Here, sit up and let me help you get ready. I'm so sorry, Hannah, I played a mean trick on you. Can you forgive me?"

"I guess so." Hanna got up from the bed and walked to the mirror. "One of the things that he says he likes about me is that I don't agree with him on every little thing and that I have my own ideas about things." She turned to look again at her sister. "Is that what you mean about being myself?"

"Yes, exactly, you need to be the person he fell in love with."

"Thank you, Elsa." She put her arms around her sister and a tear slid down her cheek. "I love you and am so glad you are my big sister."

A little later Hannah came down the stairs looking very different than she had just an hour before. She was dressed in a pale blue wool dress that reached to just above her ankles, the bodice was pleated with vertical tucks. The white collar matched the delicate white cuffs, tiny pearl buttons on both collar, and cuffs echoed the row down her back. The whole affair tied at the waist with a darker blue satin sash that accentuated Hannah's emerging hourglass figure. Elsa had brushed Hannah's hair until it shone and tied it at the nap of her neck with a matching blue satin ribbon. The overall picture was one of a lovely young woman who most certainly had the radiating glow of new love.

Paul jumped to his feet when Hannah entered the kitchen. "You are so beautiful!" he exclaimed. "You take my breath away."

Hannah blushed and turned her head away. Catching sight of Elsa, her head nodding almost imperceptibly, she turned back to face Paul. Elsa said be yourself so she would. "Thank you for those very kind words, but what are you doing here? Should you not be off fighting a war somewhere?" She saw Paul begin to smile. "I am sure you have much more important things to do than spend an afternoon with me."

Now it was Paul's turn to be caught off guard. He seemed to stumble around for the right words. "Perhaps you are right, but for today, believe me when I say nothing is more important than spending an afternoon with you." He could not believe how beautiful she was. Her eyes matched the deep blue of the ribbon in her hair. And that hair, that gorgeous hair, how could one person have such beautiful hair?

"Frau Kruger, may I have your permission to take Hannah for a walk in the warm afternoon sun?"

"Certainly you may. Enjoy yourselves on this beautiful day," Momma smiled as the couple put on their coats and departed through the front door. "My little girl is growing up and becoming a lovely young woman. Elsa I am not sure that I am ready for this."

"Momma, you have no choice. I believe that those two may have a future together."

"You may be right. Paul is certainly a very nice young man. Hannah has made a good choice."

"How is Louisa feeling?"

Elsa recognized the worry in her voice when Momma spoke, "I am very concerned for both she and the baby. I fear that she is going to have that baby very soon, no matter what Dr. Osterman says. A woman knows about these things. Louisa is not strong physically and this is going to be very hard emotionally, as well."

"I agree. If there are problems with the baby, I'm not sure that Louisa can survive it. I think that I'll go up and check on Little Gus. Lord knows how he slept through all of this fuss. I'll stop in Louisa's room and see how she is feeling."

Hand in hand, Paul and Hannah walked toward the river. Neither spoke. Words were not necessary. Talk would come later. At this moment the touch of a hand and the knowledge that the other was there was enough to make each of them content. Life had changed for them in very subtle ways in the last few weeks. Just beginning to understand that they were somehow meant to be together, they also knew that many more pressing things in their lives were to be confronted first. So for now, just being close was enough.

As they approached the river, the sounds of water gently lapping the quay reflected their mood. The river was quiet today. A tug pushing a barge full of coal floated past barely creating a ripple. A lonely bird sang a sweet song as it perched on the naked branch of a tree and chipmunks scurried about hunting for nuts and any other treats that humans may have left. What little wind there was blew the smoke from the factories' tall chimneys in the opposite direction of Paul and Hannah.

They found a bench and sat gazing at the city across the river. In the afternoon sunshine, it was a beautiful vision. The sun reflected in windows made the city seem bright and clean. They could see vehicles moving but could not hear the raucous sound of traffic. At that moment, there were no military vehicles in sight. People seemed to be going about their daily lives with no sign of war. It was just a beautiful winter's day, created for this special pair to savor.

Paul was the first to break the silence, "I saw August about a week ago. I had to go north with a dispatch and just happened to pass where his unit was resting. He was in good spirits and seemed to be quite healthy."

"What good news!" exclaimed Hannah. "Louisa will be so glad to know. Perhaps that will help lift her spirits. She's having a very difficult time with the baby."

"Have you heard from Georg and your uncle?"

"Yes, we got letters from both of them just after Christmas and they were both well. Georg isn't at the front. He's working in a factory, designing something that is very secret. He seems more excited about what he's doing in every letter. Ernst is in a submarine helping to guard the northern coast. He has been involved in one or two skirmishes but nothing too serious thus far."

Paul smiled at Hannah. "I'm glad to hear that."

"What about your family?" Hannah asked. "Ingrid told me that you come from a very large family. Yet I cannot remember ever hearing you speak of them. Surely some of your brothers must be involved in the war."

"You're right; I do have a large family. There are thirteen children all together. I'm the youngest boy but have two younger sisters."

Hannah's voice filled with awe, "It must be wonderful to have so many brothers and sisters."

"Well, perhaps sometimes." Paul had a strange look on his face. "To answer your question about the war, I have written home, of course, but hear very little back. I can only hope that everyone is safe. Come; let's speak of happier things. I know that we must live with this war, but just now I want only to enjoy being with you."

Hannah smiled, her cheeks the color of new roses, whether from the gentle wind or the blush of love it was hard to tell. No matter, she looked beautiful to Paul.

Later in the afternoon as they walked back toward the house, Paul immediately recognized Hannah's alarm when she saw not only her father's auto but that of Dr. Osterman as well.

"Oh, dear! The doctor was here this morning and had not planned to return until tomorrow. Something must have happened with Louisa," Hannah dropped Paul's hand and ran toward the house.

Hannah burst through the front door and found Papa pacing across the room. "Papa, what has happened?"

"Louisa is in labor and the doctor says that he cannot stop it. There appears to be some other complications as well."

Hannah couldn't remember when she had seen such a look a worry on her father's face.

"He mentioned something about the baby being breach." Otto looked toward the stairs as if waiting for something or someone. "The women are all upstairs trying to help and I am down here wondering what is happening. I wish that August were here. He needs to be with his wife."

"I'm going up to see if there is anything I can do to help." Hannah called as she ran up the stairs.

Paul walked through the door just in time to hear Otto speaking. A plan began to form is his mind. "Herr Kruger, perhaps I can help."

"Corporal Ulhman, how good to see you. Hedwig said that you were visiting Hannah. I am glad to see that you are well."

"Thank you, Sir. I couldn't help but hear what you said about August. I was telling Hannah earlier, that I saw August about a week ago."

Otto looked surprised. "Is that so?"

Not sure how to respond to that, Paul continued, "You may know that I'm assigned to General Weisinger and as a part of my duties have contact with many other generals and persons of command. I could speak with the General and inquire about the possibility of obtaining an emergency furlough for August. I know it would be unusual but I would like to try."

"I am sure that Louisa would be eternally grateful. However, I would not want you to do anything that would put your position in jeopardy." Otto looked back at the stairs again.

"I'll go right away. I don't know if the General will agree to this, but he is a good man who cares about his men. If I'm successful, I'll go to the front and bring August here as soon as possible." Paul started for the door then turned back. "Please consider what to tell Hannah. I don't want her to be terribly disappointed if I'm not successful. Assure her that I will return before I resume my duties at the front."

"Good luck and God sp...." The sound of Louisa's scream drowned out Otto's farewell.

Paul strapped on his leather helmet and jumped the pedal to get the engine of the motorcycle started. The smooth purr told him he was ready to go. What in the world would he say to the General? He must have been crazy to even suggest such a thing as trying to convince the General to give August a furlough. Then he heard Louisa's scream in his head again. Her cry had erupted as he was leaving the house. She sounded so helpless and scared. If Hannah were in her situation, he knew he would want to be there and he was certain that August would want to be with Louisa.

General Weisinger's office was looming and Paul had still not decided what he was going to say. He made up his mind as he entered the building. "Corporal Ulhman, here to see General Weisinger." He saluted to the officer on duty.

"The General is in his office; however, I do not see your name on his list."

"This is a personal matter please ask the General if he will see me."

"I'll make him aware that you're here. Have a seat, Corporal."

Paul sat on the familiar hard bench and went over in his mind just what he would say. He knew that it was a long shot. Still he kept hearing Louisa's cry and seeing the look on Otto's face. He would do what he could.

Finally, after what felt like hours, the officer on duty roused him from his thoughts. "General Weisinger will see you now, Corporal Ulhman."

Paul was resolute as he followed the officer down the hall; he would do everything he could to get August home, if only for a few hours.

"Corporal Ulhman, this is a surprise. To what do I deserve the honor of having my dinner interrupted by you?" quipped the General.

Paul swallowed the lump in his throat, "Thank you General for taking the time to see me. I have a personal request, sir. The sister of a very dear friend is having a baby and there are serious complications. I came to respectfully ask if you could possibly see your way clear to give her husband a short furlough to come home and see her. The doctor has said that it is very possible that neither she nor the baby may survive."

Without looking up from his plate the General asked, "The sister of a dear friend? Just who is this friend?"

"My friend is Hannah Kruger, sir. She is my girlfriend, and it is actually her sister-in-law, Louisa Kruger, that is having the baby. August Kruger is with the First Army in Flanders, Sir. I saw him just a week ago, when I was delivering a dispatch to his commanding officer."

The general still had not looked up, "How do I know that this is not just a ploy to get some man home to see his poor lonely wife for a few hours?"

"Dr. Osterman is the doctor, Sir. He can vouch for the seriousness of the situation."

"I know Dr. Osterman; he delivered my son, a good man. Still this is a very unusual request. Why have you come and not someone from the family?"

"You gave me a two-day leave when I delivered my dispatch this morning, Sir. After I had cleaned up, I went to see Hannah. That was when I learned of Louisa's condition. I volunteered to speak to you. I don't believe anyone in the family would have even considered coming to you.

The general stopped mid bite. "Humm."

Encouraged, Paul went on, "Herr Kruger was nearly overwrought with concern, something that is extraordinarily unusual for that man. He is not a man of easy emotion."

Putting down his fork, the commanding officer finally looked at Paul, "I can see that you are enormously concerned. I hear it in your voice. Yet, I must be especially careful not to set a precedent here."

Paul shifted from one leg to the other, "Sir, you did not hear Louisa's scream nor did you see the look of concern on Herr Kruger's face."

The General turned and stared out the window. "I believe that you have always been honest and certainly you are an extremely trustworthy messenger."

Paul shifted again wishing he could sit down.

The older man tented his fingers as he continued to stare out the window. "I will grant this man a furlough, providing his commanding officer can spare him. I am counting on you to get him here and back to his unit as required."

Paul breathed an almost audible sigh.

General Weisinger swung his chair back around. "Get me that pen and paper there to write the orders."

"Thank you, Sir. I will be forever grateful, as will the Kruger family."

"Here are the orders for Corporal Kruger. Be careful, son. I trust you to keep this little transaction in complete secrecy."

"I will, Sir. Thank you!"

The general went back to eating his dinner as Paul left the office.

* * *

Several hours later, Paul rode in the dark of night through a thick fog, on what used to be a road but now was more a muddy track full of frozen ruts. It took all of his concentration to keep the motorcycle upright and going forward. The landmarks began to look familiar where he had last seen August's unit. He remembered a large farmhouse that served as headquarters and in the front were some holly trees. He had to find those holly trees.

There, just up ahead was a stand of trees in front of a large house. Yes, they were holly trees. That must be the house. Barely able to stand, he dropped his cycle on the frozen drive and climbed the steps. The officer on duty stumbled and then stood at attention when Paul opened the door. He has probably been dozing, Paul thought. Now he is trying to cover his weakness with gruffness.

"What do you want, coming in here in the middle of the night?"

"I have a dispatch from General Weisinger for Captain Engels."

"The Captain is asleep. Can it wait?"

"I do not believe so, Sir. The General's instructions were to deliver it immediately upon arrival."

The duty officer did not look happy. "Very well, wait here. I will arouse the Captain."

Paul had not read what General Weisinger had written. He wondered how Captain Engels would take the request. He did not have long to wait. The Captain was coming now.

"Corporal, you have a dispatch from General Weisinger for me?" The Captain barked.

"Yes, Sir. Right here Sir," Paul answered, coming to attention and saluting the captain.

The look on the Engels' face was unreadable as he considered the contents of the dispatch. He looked at Paul but said nothing. Paul stood silently at attention.

When the captain spoke, it was not to Paul. "Lieutenant, will you please find Corporal August Kruger and have him report to me promptly."

Turning back to Paul. "At ease Corporal, there should be some food and coffee in the kitchen." The Captain's voice was accommodating. "You look pretty beat. I should think that you have been riding all night and are now going to take Kruger back to the General's office. A little coffee will do you good."

Paul relaxed just a little, "Yes, Sir. Thank you, Sir. The food and coffee are welcome. I am fine, though. I have gotten very used to long hours."

"I suspect you have. Nevertheless, rest a little while you can."

"The General is expecting Kruger shortly after daylight and the ride back will be longer than coming here. With two on the cycle, I cannot travel quite as fast. We will leave as soon as Kruger is ready."

***

Awakened from a sound sleep, August was not sure what was happening. Lieutenant Hoch was standing over him, quietly speaking to him. The words seemed to make no sense. What was he saying, the Captain wanted to see him at once. The cold damp air was beginning to take its toll on his joints; he got up slowly and followed the Lieutenant to headquarters.

"Corporal Kruger reporting for duty, Sir." August saluted.

"Kruger, I have just received a dispatch from General Weisinger requesting that you report to his office as soon as possible," Captain Engels stated flatly. "What do you know of this?"

"Why? I do not understand."

"No need to understand. The dispatch is very specific, ordering you by name to report to the General's Headquarters immediately to attend to a very important matter. You will leave within the hour. Please report back here as soon as you are ready. You are dismissed."

"Yes, Sir." August saluted, turned and left to collect his pack. Questions filled his mind; what could the General possibly want with him, why would he request him specifically, how did the General even know who he was? This was all very strange.

***

Within the hour, Paul had refreshed himself and was back at his motorcycle waiting for August. The stars still bright in the sky and the air almost eerily quiet were deceiving. Paul knew the sun would be rising all too soon and the cacophony that accompanied the brutality of the hostilities would begin again. Pacing, he was anxious to get on his way before it all began.

Just then, the door of Headquarters opened and August came out with the Lieutenant. Paul had hoped that August would come out by himself. As they walked toward him, he could see a question and perhaps recognition on August's face. Paul bent down as if he were checking the tires, making sure that his face was not visible when the pair stopped in front of him.

Lieutenant Hoch spoke, "Corporal Kruger, you are to travel with the courier back to the General's office."

"Thank you, Sir," August sounded puzzled.

Paul kept his head down as he climbed onto the motorcycle. "Corporal Kruger, I hope you are prepared for a long cold ride." Paul tried to muffle the sound of his voice in his scarf. "My orders are to have you in the General's office as soon as possible. Have you ridden a motorcycle before?"

"Yes sir, I am quite familiar with this particular model vehicle. I have a friend who is also a courier."

"Good, climb on and we will be on our way." Without looking at his passenger, Paul stood astride the vehicle and waited for August to mount behind him. When they were safely several miles down the road, he would stop and tell August the reason for the secrecy and the purpose of the trip.

The ride was exhilarating. The cold air felt good on his face, as August pondered the strange orders. So many questions were dancing in his head and no answers were forthcoming. No matter what the reasons, it was good to be away from the front, if even for a short time. The General's office was in Dusseldorf, perhaps he would be allowed time to see his family. Louisa's baby was due soon and it would be very good to see her.

August touched the journal he kept in his shirt pocket. Suddenly filled with guilt, he thought of all the letters he had not sent. How would he ever be able to explain to Louisa? Was she angry with him? She had every right to be. There was no explanation for his conduct, only cowardice. All the excuses he had made these many months now seemed so hollow. Other men anxiously awaited mail call, read their letters with eagerness and answered them. Not he, the mere thought of burdening Louisa with his dark thoughts was beyond his imagination. Therefore, he stayed silent and wrote in his journal. Now the thought he might see her made his guilt overpowering.

The sun was visible in the southeast sky when Paul decided that it was time to take a break. He found a wide grassy area bordered by trees, no houses or other buildings in sight. that he felt was a good resting place. Gently, he slowed the cycle and pulled over to the edge of the rutted dirt road. Paul put his feet down to steady the bike and August followed suit.

Paul carefully climbed off and waited for August. When August's foot touched the ground, his knee buckled and he went down. Reaching down to help him, Paul smiled. "August, you will learn that you have to give your body time to adjust after a long ride before it is willing to hold you upright. Here let me give you a hand."

"Paul, is that you?" August asked. "What do you know of this? Have you conspired somehow to take me home, perhaps?"

"It is good to see you, August. Conspired? Well, perhaps. However, I promise that I have done nothing wrong. The orders from the General are genuine. Although, I did have a little something to do with their issue."

"What is going on? This is all very confusing?"

"I am sure it is. Let me start at the beginning. First, I need to tell you that this little trip has to do with Louisa and your baby...."

"The baby is not due for several weeks yet."

"I will tell you what I know. I had a short leave and went to visit your very lovely sister. I am sure that you realize I am quite smitten with her. Hannah told me that Louisa was having some difficulty and that the doctor had confined her to bed rest. When we saw the doctor's auto in front of the house..."

"Is she alright?" August's voice filled with anguish. "Tell me, what do you know?"

"I know very little. I left immediately and went to General Weisinger's office. I have done a lot of work for him and felt that if you were to get a furlough, he was our best chance.

"Paul, I do not know what to say to you. Why would you do this for me?"

"I would do this for anyone. However, I care for your sister very much and, as a result, her family is exceedingly important to me. I think that we had better get started again. We still have about two to three hours to travel before we reach Düsseldorf. Are you up to the ride?"

"You bet I am. I cannot believe that I'm going to see my family soon. I can only hope that they will all be alive and well when we get there. Thank you, Paul, for all that you are doing for my family and me. I don't have the words to express my gratitude."

Chapter 21
Later that Morning
Düsseldorf, Germany

It was nearly noon by the time they reached General Weisinger's office. "Corporal Kruger reporting per General Weisinger's orders." August saluted the officer on duty.

"The General is expecting you, please report to his office. You are expected as well, Corporal Ulhman."

General Weisinger stood as the two men walked into his office. "Good afternoon, men. You made good time."

"I did my best, Sir." Paul saluted.

"Corporal Kruger, you are to report to your home immediately. I spoke with Dr. Osterman and I understand that your new daughter is doing well, Kruger. However your wife is having some problems."

"Ulhman, please see that Kruger gets home as soon as possible. I will expect to see both of you here in my office at noon the day after tomorrow. You are dismissed"

"Thank you, Sir," August answered, his voice barely audible.

"You are both good men. Take care of what you need and then we must get on with this war." Weisinger shook both men's hands. "Congratulations, Kruger, on your new baby. My best wishes for your wife. Now go."

August did not know what to think as the two men left the office. He was a father. He had a daughter. What was happening with Louisa? She had to be alright. "Paul, how quickly can you get us across that river? "

"We will be there before you know it. Let's go. By the way, congratulations!"

The ride across the river seemed much longer than usual for August. It was like a dream. The river was flowing quietly, the edges frozen in jagged shards. Small white patches of snow covered the banks. Traffic seemed to crawl; even on the motorcycle that could weave in and out it felt like it took hours to get from one side to the other. Down the Bruckestrasse, seemed another hour just to drive four blocks. The turn onto Dorfstrasse, now the house was in sight. There was Papa's auto. Next to it was another auto, probably that of Dr. Osterman. Off the motorcycle and up the steps. The door opened and he was in his mother's arms.

He had not realized just how much he missed his mother. There were Papa and Hannah, Elsa and Little Gus. Where are Louisa and the new baby? Catch your breath; come now breathe, everything is going to be fine. Settle down, August, you are home – YOU ARE HOME!

His mother's voice startled him out of his reverie, "August, my August, you are alright, home, standing here in my living room."

"I'm fine, Momma." He hugged her with more strength than he knew. Reluctantly, he let go. "Where are Louisa and the baby? I want to see them."

Otto clasped his son's hand. "They are upstairs, Son. The baby is very small, only about one kilogram but she seems strong and is breathing well." Tears shown in Otto's eyes. "We are taking turns holding her to our flesh to keep her warm. Even I have taken my turns." He looked away, lest someone see his emotions.

August, was too worried about his wife to hear everything Papa said, looked to his mother. "Louisa! How is Louisa?"

"Dr. Osterman is with her now," Momma voice was solemn. "She has lost a lot of blood and has not regained consciousness since the baby was born."

August had a look of question on his face.

"It was very difficult for her, son, very difficult." Hedwig's face was a mask. "I can only pray that you being here will help. She is in the loft room on the third floor. Genevieve is with her.

August took the steps three at a time. The door to the new room was open and he could see Genevieve sitting in the corner in a rocking chair, wrapped in a blanket with a very small head resting on her shoulder. His daughter, how small she looked. Dr. Osterman was sitting at the end of the bed monitoring Louisa where she lay so still and silent. Her skin looked like wax and had that gray color that he had seen much too often since the start of this war. It was the look that men had when they were close to death.

He fell to his knees beside the bed, gently picked up her hand and held it to his lips her skin cold to the touch. She has already left me, he thought.

"Dear God, please do not take my Louisa, she is the sweetest, kindest, most loving of women. She is so young and has just become a mother. This new baby will need her for her very life." His voice caught and he stifled a sob. "Please, dear God, I will never ask for another thing if only you will spare my Louisa. I know that I have asked for so much during this time of war but now, Lord, I need you more than I ever have before."

He laid his head on her arm. "Louisa is my heart; she is the reason that I fight this war to keep her and our new child from ever having to face such horror again." He raised his head and looked up, "God, if you ever only answer one prayer for the rest of my life, please answer this one. Louisa is the keeper of my soul. She is my only love. God, she is my very life." He put his head back down on her hand as the tears fell from his cheeks and flowed across her delicate fingers.

From somewhere far away, Louisa could hear voices. No, just one voice. She could hear August, the love of her life. Surely, she must be hallucinating; August was far away fighting the war. Something had happened. All she could remember was the terrible pain, screaming, could that have been her. Someone said something about a baby, her baby, but she could not remember if the voices said that the baby was dead or alive. It was all so vague.

The pain had gone on forever and then finally the sweet release from pain. She felt like she was floating. If she looked down, she could see the room. There was Mother in the corner wrapped in a blanket. Dr. Osterman was sitting in a chair near the end of the bed on which someone was lying quite peacefully. Wait, someone was on the floor. It was a man she did not recognize, he had long hair and a beard and he was talking. Listen Louisa, listen what is he saying? The voice sounds so like August.

August lifted his head again with one more imploring look to the heavens, "Lord, please let her live. Please let my precious Louisa live!"

That face, that voice, it is August. He is in the room. Louisa knew that she must be either dreaming or perhaps dead. No, August really was in the room she could feel his tears on her hand. Now he was gently caressing her fingers. With all of her will, she tried to move them.

August felt the slightest movement in his hand. He looked and yes, her fingers were moving. "Louisa, wake up. It's me, August. I am here. Open your eyes, Louisa."

Louisa could hear his plea and she tried to comply. She wanted to see him but she was afraid. If she woke up would terrible pain return? She did not know if she could stand the pain. What if this was all a dream? Yes, that must be it. This was a dream. August was not really here in her room.

"Louisa, I love you more than life. Please wake up. You cannot leave me. I need you. Please, Louisa, wake up."

Perhaps it was not a dream, possibly by some miracle; he was really kneeling beside her bed holding her hand. She must try, he sounded so sad. She would endure any pain to take the sadness from August. Fighting her way through the fog, she finally opened her eyes. "August is that really you?" She tried to speak but could only manage the merest of whispers.

"Louisa, you are awake! My darling, I love you, I love you," August exclaimed, tears streaming down his face.

"I love you too," she managed this time with more voice.

August looked from Louisa to the Doctor. "Will she be alright?"

"It is too early to tell, but I believe she now has a chance. You have given her the will to come back to us. She will still need a lot of rest. She has lost a large amount of blood but waking up is crucial and she is here with us now," the doctor replied.

"Louisa, you have to try to stay with us. I need you. Our baby needs you. I know that you can do this. August gently caressed her face and then kissed her forehead.

"I will try," she said with what seemed every reserve of her strength.

"Let her rest now. She needs all of her strength to recover," instructed Dr. Osterman.

"Yes, Doctor. I will go now and let her sleep." He watched as she closed her eyes again, a smile on her pale face.

"August, come and see your daughter," Genevieve said quietly from the corner where she had been unobtrusively observing the scene unfold in front of her. It was with great relief that she too began to feel perhaps Louisa had a chance.

"She is beautiful and so tiny," August beamed at his new daughter.

"Would you like to hold her?" Genevieve asked.

"Yes, more than anything I want to feel this child in my arms, but I cannot yet. I have been in the trenches with war and filth and death. I must bathe before I can allow myself to hold this wonder child. She must never know the filth and stench of war. I will be back soon to meet my child."

Turning to leave the room August saw his father standing in the doorway. "How long have you been there?"

"Long enough to be reminded just what a loving and noble man you are. It would be an honor to prepare the bath for you, Son. I will do so right away. Welcome home." Otto turned his back and hurried down the stairs as tears spilled from his eyes.

August sat in the large galvanized tub as his father continued to fill it with hot water. He had scrubbed and rinsed and scrubbed some more in an effort to wash away the horror of war. "Papa you cannot even begin to understand how wonderful it is to have this opportunity to be with you and the rest of the family. I am, indeed, a very privileged man."

"May I cut your hair for you and help shave your beard?" Papa asked.

"Thank you, but no, Papa, even though I am sure I look very strange to you, I need the warmth of the long hair and beard in the frigid trenches."

"I understand Momma has found some clothes for you while she is washing and mending the clothing that you had on. Son...." Papa stopped.

"Papa, it is not necessary for you to say anything more. So many things have happened in such short time. It is more than even you, the stoic king, can bear. Sometimes I think that you are not as unemotional as you would like us all to believe."

"I was raised to be strong," Papa said. "Men must not let others see their emotions."

August understood what his father was feeling, "What is happening to us is extraordinary. I can't believe that anyone would think less of you for acknowledging your emotions. Now, would you please hand me that towel so I can reluctantly get out of this heaven of a bath and go meet my daughter."

***

Half an hour later, August sat on the floor by Louisa's bed holding their daughter; both were smiling as they examined her from head to toe. "She is so tiny and yet so perfect," boasted August. His heart felt like it would burst from his chest, he was so proud.

Louisa smiled at her husband, "I did not believe I would ever see this, my husband and my daughter sitting here with me. Right this moment I am sure I am the luckiest woman in all of Germany."

Laughing, August said, "We must give this liebchen a name. What do you think?"

"I would like to name her Elsbeth Frederica."

"That is a lot of name for such a little girl."

"It is a name full of family honor," Louisa chided.

"I like it, a name of which she can be proud, Elsbeth Frederica Kruger it is!" August announced with pride. "Welcome to the world, Elsbeth. May you live a very long and happy life." With that, he kissed the child's forehead and laid her gently in her Louisa's arms.

They sat staring at the beautiful infant they had created. No words spoken, their hearts full of love and peace, just becoming aware of the responsibility that bringing a new life into the world portends. This feeling perhaps intensified by circumstances in which they found themselves. Elsbeth intruded on the moment by making herself known with what began as a whimper and grew into a full-fledged cry, demanding recognition.

At just that moment, Elsa stepped into the room, "Is that my new little niece making all that noise? Louisa, it is wonderful to see you awake. We all feared for your recovery."

"Thank you, Elsa, I am feeling better."

"I believe this new little one is telling us that she is hungry. Louisa, are you feeling strong enough to feed her?"

"I am not at all sure I am able yet," Louisa answered.

"Luckily, this baby's cousin has just finished his dinner and very generously left a little for his new friend." Elsa smiled.

"What I am saying is that I would be delighted to feed her," Elsa offered. "I have plenty of milk, if you would allow me that honor, just until you are able to do it yourself, to be sure."

"Elsa, I would be eternally grateful if you would do that. She certainly is letting us know that she is hungry. I envy you the privilege of giving her the first meal."

August could hear the remorse in Louisa's voice as Elsa gently took the infant from her and turned to her brother, "August, do go downstairs and spend some time with our parents. They have missed you sorely. Louisa needs her rest and I will take care of this little sweetheart."

"Yes, sister dear, you always were the bossy one," August laughed. "Seriously, thank you for taking care of our precious child. I don't have the words to express my feelings of gratitude."

"Go, before you make me cry." Elsa kissed her brother's cheek and then busied herself with the baby.

Downstairs, the aroma of fresh bread just taken from the oven was nearly overwhelming for August. "Momma, I believe the one thing I have missed the most is your fresh bread. When I received your package at Christmas, I was more than willing to share all of the delicious cookies that you sent but I hoarded all of the bread for myself. I just could not bring myself to share even one morsel of that sublime perfection."

Hedwig blushed. "You always know just what to say."

"It is true, Momma, no one makes bread as good as yours."

"You certainly need to eat more bread. You are so thin, but you look healthy and for that I am very grateful."

"Well, give me a piece of that bread and I will begin work on this thinness," August answered as he cut a slice of the bread cooling on the counter.

"I will make an exception this one time, but you know that you are supposed to wait until we are at the table," scolded Momma, a grin on her face. "Do not let that happen again, for I would have to smack your fingers as I did when you were just a tyke."

Hanna looked up from where she was peeling potatoes, "That's not fair, Momma. You never let me take a piece early."

"You, my dear little sister, have not been away for months fighting the big bad English enemy."

"Only because I am a girl. I would go if I could."

"Now, children, no fighting today...."

A knock at the front door interrupted them. "I'll get it. That might be Paul," Hannah spoke, running for the door.

"He is a good man, Momma, a very good man," August praised. "I know of no other person who would have made the effort and taken the chance that he did so that I could come home. Hannah could not make a better choice than Paul."

"I know what you are saying, August. I agree with you," Papa added as he walked into the kitchen. "I have been worried about my little girl getting too involved with someone at her age. Paul and his actions have changed my mind."

Hannah opened the door to, indeed, find Paul. The two stood smiling at each other. Paul stepped into the house and took Hannah's hand. "Paul, I am so glad to see you. Did you get some sleep? You look much more rested then you did a few hours ago."

"Yes, I feel much better," Paul, answered as he leaned forward and kissed Hannah on the forehead.

Taken aback, Hannah did not know how to react. They were standing in the foyer of her house. Her whole family was there. Yet suddenly it did not seem to matter. These last few hours had been almost incomprehensible. The awkward discomfort she had felt just one day ago was gone. Now there no longer seemed to be a need to hide her feelings for Paul from her family. Paul, by his actions, had made himself a part of her life and this family.

Momma came from the kitchen. "Welcome Paul. We are so glad you have joined us for this simple meal. Dinner is nearly ready and I think that we should all gather around the table."

Elsa walked down the stairs carrying the contentedly cooing baby, snuggled in her arms, to join the rest. "August, perhaps you would like to introduce your beautiful little daughter to the family, before we begin."

"It would be a delight to do so." August hurried to the stairs. Taking the child from Elsa and holding her up so everyone could see, he said with halting voice, "It is with the greatest pride and love that...that...that I introduce to you the newest member of this family." He began, the tears were now streaming down his cheeks, as he held the tiny baby just a little higher, "Elsbeth Frederica Kruger."

"That is a very big name for such a little girl," laughed Papa.

August smiled. "I said the very same thing. Louisa scolded me and assured me that she will grow into this name of honor," August answered.

Momma walked toward August and the baby, arms held out. "I agree with Louisa it is a perfect name. Elsbeth, for your wonderful mother, Otto. How very nice to honor her memory."

Genevieve stepped next to Hedwig, with tears in her own eyes. "And Frederica for my dear Friedrich, if only he could be here to share this moment with us."

"I think that it is a beautiful name for a beautiful child. I am proud to be her Tanta Hannah."

August turned to Elsa. "Thank you for feeding and caring for this bundle of joy. I know that Louisa is looking forward to taking on the duties of mother as soon as she is well enough to do so."

"She is feeling much better and has asked me to instruct all of you to enjoy this meal together. She said she is going to sleep some and does not need to have anyone with her just now. Little Gus will be waking up soon and will want to join us. I will check on Louisa when I go to get him," Elsa said.

"Well then sit down and enjoy this fine dinner that your momma has made for us before it gets cold," Papa urged pulling out his chair at the head of the table.

"Momma, the sight and smell of this food is almost more than I can stand," August sighed. "I have been living on so little for so long."

"I know what you mean," Paul said. "When there is enough, it tastes bad."

Papa surveyed the table. "The sausages are from last year's pig."

"I helped make the sauerkraut this year," Hannah bragged. "It may be even better than what you and Papa make, August."

August looked at his little sister with a grin. "Do you really think you can make better sauerkraut than me? Never!"

"I bet I could make it better than you too, brother," Elsa chimed in.

August turned toward Hedwig. "Help, Momma, the girls are ganging up on me."

Momma laughed so hard the tears rolled down her cheeks. "Now, now children you must not fight."

"Would someone please pass the hot potato salad?" August asked. "I will waive judgment on the sauerkraut. I am absolutely sure no one can make potato salad better than Momma. Do not even try to fight me on that one." He asserted, looking at each of his sisters.

Hannah and Elsa glanced at each other. "You are right this time," Elsa agreed.

"Save some room. I made cherry kuchen for dessert. I wanted to make chocolate but I have not been able to buy chocolate at the market for several months now."

The family enjoyed the meal and talk touched on all manner of subjects, all of them carefully skirting the topic of war. Hannah marveled that they seemed to be able to talk around the subject that surely was in the front of everyone's minds.

Finally, August introduced the subject by asking, "Paul, did you have the same unusual and almost surreal experience that I did on Christmas Eve? It was something I shall never forget."

"I don't know what you experienced." Paul answered. "But I too felt that there was something in the air leading men to behave in a way that certainly did not reflect the tenets of war."

"I know what you mean," August replied. "It was such a beautiful evening where I was in Flanders. The sky was clear and the moon bright. Stars sparkled like diamonds, reminding us what eve it was. One of our men put some candles on a tree and set it up on the parapet of the trench, knowing that light might draw enemy fire. Then we all began to sing Stille Nacht, Heil'ge Nacht."

"Were you afraid that the enemy would hear you?" Elsa asked.

"There were a few stray shots and then nothing, just silence as we sang. Someone took out his harmonica and someone else had a violin. The music continued and, before long, the Belgians were singing too."

Hannah could not believe it. "The other side was really singing?"

"Yes, one by one we put our heads up above the edge of the trench and found ourselves staring at those we had been firing upon just hours earlier. They too, were carefully looking our way. Soon a few brave men from each side were climbing out of the trenches and making their way into no-man's-land."

"Surely, not," Momma said. "Tell me that you did not do that, Son?"

"Momma, you worry too much. On our side, my friend Sergeant Koch led the way with the lighted tree held high and planted it in the middle of the field. Soon there were men from both sides standing around the tree talking, laughing and singing. We shared our gifts of food from home and exchanged souvenirs such as buttons and emblems of our units."

"That must have been very strange," Genevieve mused.

"It certainly was. We spent the entire night out there together like old friends. When dawn began to break, we returned to our respective trenches and napped the rest of the day. There were no shots fired on Christmas day."

"Had the officers called a truce?" Papa wondered.

"No one had called a truce. We simply did not fight. It was not until the next day that shots again began to fly. A most extraordinary experience," August concluded with emotion.

"I too spent that night in a manner very similar to yours, August," Paul replied." On Christmas day, one of the British troops produced a football and soon the British, French and Germans were all out in no-man's-land playing a game."

"Did you play too?" Hannah asked.

"I did. It went on for hours with lots of laughter and shouting. Sometimes it was very hard to understand what was going on because of all the languages being spoken. In the end, we all had fun and no one mentioned the war."

"This all seems extraordinary. I wonder if it was like that elsewhere on the front?" Papa asked.

"I think it was all along the front. As I traveled delivering messages for the next several days, everyone seemed to be talking about the 'Christmas truce.' None was officially called, of course, the men just seemed to have decided that was the right thing to do," Paul answered.

"It is enough to make you believe that there is a higher power than man governing our actions," August said.

"I cannot agree with you more, August," Genevieve interjected. "I have always believed that God is ultimately in charge of our actions. Men may get us into wars, but only God can get us out of the situations created by man. On Christmas Eve, through him, the hearts of men were stirred to celebrate the birthday of his son and no war created by man could interfere. I know that you believe, August. I heard your prayer for Louisa and so did God for he answered you and my Louisa is getting better."

"I think that we all agree with you, Genevieve. We cannot blame this war on anyone but the men in power who led us down the slippery slope of poor diplomacy. I believe that God is always there watching out for all of us but he, in his infinite wisdom, has allowed man to make his own mistakes. This war is one of those horrendous mistakes." Otto said with sadness in his voice.

The words sounded strange coming from Papa, who wanted everyone to believe him a man of stone. Hannah looked at him, it was obvious how sincere he was, the look on his face and the tone of his voice belayed his feelings.

Listening to her father, even Elsa had tears in her eyes. "Perhaps we should take advantage of this special moment to all join hands and say a silent prayer of thanksgiving for this day and a prayer of safety for you August and Paul, my Georg, and of course Onkle Ernst, and hope for better days to come."

"May I join you?" A voice came from the stairs. "I am feeling much stronger and wanted to be with you all together," Louisa said as she sat down on the step.

"Louisa, how did you get down here?" August jumped up.

"In truth I have spent much of time you have been eating, coming down the stairs. I would maneuver one or two steps, then sit down, and listen to the pleasant words of conversation drifting up from below. Then pull myself up and manage a few more steps only to sit again and listen." Genevieve got up too. "Louisa, you should not have tried to come down, you are too weak. You could have fallen."

"I was determined to make my way down. I wanted to be a part of this family gathering too."

By the time she had finished speaking August had scooped her up in his arms. He carried her to the table where he gently set her down in the chair that Paul had hastily pushed to the table's end.

The mood at the table had changed with the sudden appearance of Louisa, though now there was even more reason for thanksgiving. They all joined hands and were silent for several minutes, each lost in his own thoughts and prayers. Finally Elsbeth, cradled in her grandmother Genevieve's arms, began to fuss and one by one the others, each in their own time, looked up.

Hannah felt as though an invisible veil of serenity, hope and strength now surrounded this family, and bound them inexorably together. Looking from one face to another, she understood that they would each need to draw on this moment many times to help carry them through the difficult months that she secretly feared were yet to come.

Hedwig gently removed Otto's arm from around her waist and edged out of the bed. He looked so peaceful now that he was finally sleeping soundly. Something was bothering him, more than just the turn of the war. For days now, he had been quiet and somber, even more than usual.

Putting on her robe, Hedwig once again heard Elsbeth crying from the room above. Not wanting to wake anyone else in the household, she felt her way up the stairs in the dark, stopped just outside the door to Louisa's room, and listened.

Louisa's voice was quiet, "Hush, my Liepchen, Momma is here. You must not cry. I know you're hungry but I have nothing more for you."

Hedwig could see through the crack in the door that moonlight shown on Louisa as she sat in the rocking chair, babe on her shoulder, the fatigue showing in her every movement.

Hedwig heard her whisper to Elsbeth, as if talking to her would help. "It seems like I have been living in this house forever. How I long to be back in my own house with you, and your father beside me. Oh, August, I miss you so very much. I love your family for all that they have done for my mother, Elsbeth, and me, but I want only to go home and be with you."

The baby whimpered again. Hedwig felt more than a little guilty, hearing her daughter-in-law's lament. Louisa's voice was so full of worry, it was no wonder the baby would not sleep.

Louisa continued, "How much longer can this go on? We are hungry and worried all the time. Mother and Hedwig put on their grandmother faces and do everything they can to make life comfortable. Yet I know they are worried too."

Hedwig made up her mind to go in, but stopped when she heard Louisa's next words. "Poor Otto, the only man in this house, seems to get older each passing day. The pressure of trying to support all of these people is taking its toll. He always walked as a man so confident and proud and now his head is often down and he seldom laughs. He hardly ever disagrees with anyone. It is almost as if the fire that makes him a man is slowly going out. Your grandfather is a good man, Liepchen, a very good man."

Tears rolled down Hedwig's cheeks as Louisa whispered about this man that she loved so much. Now Elsbeth made herself known again with more force this time.

"Hush, my sweet baby, how I love you. You are my little miracle. I do not know how you have survived. It seems that we have less food to eat every day and I make so little milk for you. If it were not for your dear Tanta Elsa, I know you would not have been able to survive. Do not cry, baby. Things have to get better soon."

Hedwig could take no more. She pulled her robe tightly around her thin body and opened the door of the room.

Louisa looked up, surprise and dismay on her face. "I'm so sorry if Elsbeth has wakened you. She's had a very hard night. Please forgive her, she is so small and cannot help her crying. I'm trying to keep her quiet."

Hedwig smiled at Louisa. "I am not upset with you, or her. No one else is awake; grandmothers are just tuned in to these things. You have been up most of the night with her and I thought perhaps I could help."

"Hedwig, she is not your responsibility. It's so early please go back to bed. I'll do my best to keep her quiet."

"Do not be silly. Let me take this darling child while you go back to bed. I will try to work my grandmother magic on her. You must be very tired and lonely, it shows in your eyes, though you try to hide it from me. Sleep will help."

Hedwig gently took her granddaughter in her arms and carried her down the stairs just as the light of dawn began to break. In the kitchen, she took a small clean cloth from the drawer and a jar from the middle of the big kitchen table. Back in the parlor, she settled in the big overstuffed chair. Elsbeth snuggled into her grandmother's ample lap while Hedwig twisted the cloth around her finger then dipped the cloth covered finger in the jar of honey. Finally, she lovingly put her finger to the baby's mouth.

Elsbeth at first pulled away from this new taste and feel. Hedwig was patient, playing with the baby's mouth, just touching it and then pulling away. Eventually the child became used to the sweet taste and began to suck eagerly on her grandmother's finger. Before long, she closed her eyes and was fast asleep as Hedwig gently rocked back and forth in her chair and thanked God for all the blessings that she had, even during this time of war and depravation.

It turned out to be a beautiful day. The sun was shining, finally, no rain. It seemed as if the rain would never stop this spring. Best of all, Hedwig had the house to herself. Otto gone to work, Hannah was at Ingrid's house, Elsa and Louisa had taken the children to the park and Genevieve had gone to visit a friend. The quiet was liberating.

Hedwig sat in the kitchen; pen in hand, contemplating the paper with her garden plans spread across the table. She must take advantage of every available inch of space for the precious vegetables. They were far behind schedule because of all the rain, and she wanted to get started today if possible. She even planned to plant vegetables where her prized flowers usually grew, for she knew they would need every morsel of food they could glean for next winter.

There were mere crumbs left in the cellar from last summer. All of the potatoes were gone. There was still some kraut and a few other vegetables along with a little sausage but even that was nearly gone. To make matters worse, there was so little available at the market. Most distressing was lack of flour for making bread. What was available was so expensive she could not afford to purchase any. The sound of the back door opening distracted Hedwig from her planning. Who could that be? No one should be home for several hours. Hedwig looked up to see Otto stumble into the kitchen.

"Otto, you are home so early today. What is the matter?" There was no reply as Otto sat in a chair.

"What is it? Has something happened?" Still no response.

The dark threads of fear began to weave their way through every fiber of Hedwig's body. "Otto, Darling please. Tell me what is wrong!"

"I was not able to purchase benzin again today. How can I drive my taxi without fuel? Yesterday they told me to come back today. Now they are telling me, perhaps next week." Otto's shoulders sagged as if the weight of the world were his alone to bear.

The look of defeat on his face cracked Hedwig's heart like a china cup hitting the tile floor.

"Without my taxi I cannot provide for my family. I understand that the government needs fuel to keep the war effort alive, but I need it to keep my family alive," Otto said as he laid a newspaper on the table. "Then I read this."

Hedwig picked up the paper. It was not a German paper but rather one from the Netherlands. She scanned the headlines

Ship detained and cargo confiscated as contraband within Dutch territorial waters.

Hedwig looked at her husband, his head on his arms on the table. Now she understood his mood of these last few days. Her eyes strayed to the end of the story:

What does all this mean for the future of shipping to any ports of the North Sea? Are all ports to be blockaded no matter the country and is all cargo to be considered "absolute contraband" whether bound for Germany or other countries? Is all of Northern Europe to starve as a result of Germany's actions? These are questions that loom large in the mind of this humble reporter.

Hedwig put the paper down. She did not care to read any more. She already understood the effects the war was having on her own family and in her heart knew that life was going to get much harder before it got better, if it ever got better. Looking at her husband of more than thirty years, she could see the terrible toll it was taking on him. His inability to maintain his livelihood and therefore provide for his family was killing him as surely as if he had been shot by a French bullet.

Finally, Otto raised his head and looked at his wife. "What am I to do, Hedwig? What am I to do?"

Hedwig just shook her head.

"I cannot continue to work without fuel and there seems to be very little left after the Kaiser takes his."

Hedwig had no answer. The silence in the kitchen lasted for what felt an eternity. Finally, out of desperation she offered an absurd idea, "You could go to the farm and get Hans and Franz. The coach is sitting in the barn just as beautiful as the day you retired it for the auto. Those dear old horses do not need benzin. Surely we could find enough to feed them." Hedwig said this, knowing in her heart that perhaps there would not be enough for the horses.

Elsbeth flashed into her mind, just this morning crying from hunger. The look of despair in Louisa's eyes. She would keep those secrets to herself. No sacrifice was too much to keep her family together.

"NEIN! That is a most ridiculous idea."

Hedwig blanched at Otto's vehement answer. She had not expected such a response.

"Woman, sometimes I wonder where you come up with such ideas. Do you really think that I would go back to driving a coach pulled by horses?"

"Otto, I just thou…."

"Well, do not think. It is not helping me."

Hedwig sat, silent. She knew from years with this man that it made no difference what she said or did. So let him rant. Soon he would calm down and be more reasonable.

"I would be the laughing stock of the drivers. I can just see it now. Look, here comes Otto and his two horses. He must think he is back in the last decade."

Hedwig could not help herself, "Surely, they would not make fun of you like that."

"You do not work with these men as I do."

"But you have been driving longer than most and have more experience. They look up to you."

"Well, that would stop, if I showed with old Hans and Franz, feed bags strapped to their muzzles. They would put a muzzle on me."

"I think you are exaggerating. You would just be showing good sense."

"GOOD SENSE, NOTHING! I will not do it!" Otto slammed his fist on the table, got up and stomped out of the kitchen. In the parlor, he opened the special box that contained his tobacco. Choosing his favorite, he filled his pipe, tamped it down, and lit a match.

Hedwig watched from the kitchen. She did not like his pipe smoke in the house but this day she said nothing. She just sat and watched. The feeling of trepidation was growing stronger by the minute. She saw the match hover over the bowl of the pipe for much longer than was necessary to light the pipe. Experience told her that when Otto was this angry, she must let him be. Eventually, Otto shook it out and left by front door, allowing it to slam with vigor, pipe in hand.

Dear God, what have I done? She thought. I knew I offered an absurd idea, but I did not expect this reaction. She got up from the big old table, rolled up the drawing of the garden she had been working on so diligently before Otto interrupted her. "I might as well put this away for today. I will get no more work done." She mumbled to herself. "Still this needs to be done. We need food for next fall and I will not let Otto and his attitude disrupt my work." Determination in her every move, she spread the drawings back on the table and began making notes.

Lost in her work, an hour passed and then another when Hedwig heard the back door open again. Otto came in, a thoughtful look on his face. "If I give the leather seats a good rub with oil and grease the joints, that old coach just might be useable again. The tin on the wheels look good and the spokes are still strong. I found an old can of wax and rubbed a little on one of the doors. You would be surprised at the shine I got."

Hedwig just sat and stared. Would she ever get used to his outbursts? She knew this was as close as she would ever get to an apology so she accepted it gracefully. "Do you need some help? I am sure Hannah would be glad to work with you when she gets home from Ingrid's house."

"Send her out to the barn; I will be happy for her help. We will need to go to the farm and get the horses. I think I have just about enough benzin for that trip."

"I will tell her."

"Come to the barn if you need me." He went back outside, whistling, his unlit pipe in his hand.

* * * *

Later that day Otto and Hannah came to a stop in front of the old farmhouse. Things were too quiet for a warm spring day. As the two climbed from the auto, Adolph came out of the house, concern written on his ancient face.

Otto immediately thought the worst. "What is it, Adolph? What is wrong?"

"Ah, it is Margried. She has slowly become more and more ill. Now she has no strength, and I fear no will, to get out of bed. Her coughing and wheezing are so strong that she can barely breathe. She is failing and I do not know how to help her. I worry that she will not be with me much longer."

Hannah rushed into the house followed by the men. Margried lying in her bed, her eyes closed, looked very old and frail, indeed. Hannah picked up her limp hand. "Tanta Margried you must wake up, it's me, Hannah. I've come to see you."

Slowly the old woman opened her eyes, her voice barely a whisper. Hannah put her ear close to Margried's lips to make out the words. "I didn't make a kuchen."

Hannah offered a strained laugh, "You are silly Tanta. I don't come to see you only for your wonderful kuchen. I come to see you because I love you. How can I help you?"

Margried struggled to sit up, racked by a sudden bout of coughing. After a few moments, she spoke with a little more voice. "I fear there is very little you can do. I believe that my days in this world are numbered."

"You must not talk that way. I'll take care of you." Looking at her father, who had come into the room, Hannah said, "Papa, I must stay here with Tanta Margried until she gets better. Can you find a way to get the horses back to town without me?"

"Certainly. Adolph and Margried need your help now."

Adolph looked at Otto. "What is this about taking the horses to town? You have no place for them."

"I am no longer able to purchase benzin for my taxi. I need the horses so I can use the old coach."

Adolph seemed skeptical. "I do not know if they are strong enough anymore. They are both very old. They may not fare well working in the city again."

"We are being forced to make changes in our life, Adolph. I need the horses to help me provide for my family. Even with the money I earn, there is very little to buy in the markets these days."

"There is still plenty here on the farm. Although, I must admit that I am very slow getting the crops in this year. The fields have been so wet that I have not been able to plow."

Otto listened to his beloved old friend and began to understand that wet fields were not the only problem; the will of this ancient man had faded as well. This magical place presided over by the sage who was Adolph, had been Otto's refuge from the city for most of his life. Today as he looked up at the brilliant green hill behind the house, he imagined an emerald sea dotted by the sails of early summer flowers and it astounded him. The picture, a peaceful pastoral scene, could have been painted by one of the masters.

Looking around this beautiful place, no one would know just a few hundred kilometers away men fought, men died and the war raged on. Otto made up his mind at that very moment what he would do.

"Adolph, Hannah will stay here and help with Margried, until she is better, and I will assist with the crops."

"What do you know of farming?" Adolph growled. "You are nothing but a city boy who never planted anything in his life."

"Ah, you are so right, but I have lived with Hedwig for so long that her natural talent for raising things has surely rubbed off on me. "

"That is about as likely as a snow storm tomorrow."

Otto laughed for the first time that day. "I said nothing of doing all the work. I said I would help you. I have always been a quick study and am sure that I can learn much from a master such as you."

The old man harrumphed.

"Together we will farm this land and keep our families alive."

"But what of your important work as a taxi driver? You have always told me how much they need you in the city"

"For now, this is much more important. The crops we plant will keep us all from starving next winter. I never wanted to be a farmer but suddenly the thought is very appealing."

Adolph stared at Otto, "Surely you do not mean this."

"Yes I do! Now, I need a list of supplies. Then help me hitch the horses to your old wagon and I will go back to town and tell Hedwig of my decision. I will see you tomorrow, my friend, and together we will farm this land."

Otto drove the horses back to town. A vitality he had not experienced in many months flowed through him. There seemed a purpose to his life again. This morning the news of war and the blockade, no fuel for his taxi, and his feeling of helplessness had nearly crushed him. Now the prospect of being able to provide food for his family had breathed a new life into him. He whistled a bright tune that matched his mood as he brought the horses to a halt in front of his house just as the sun was setting.

Chapter 25
September, 1915
The Farm Outside Düsseldorf, Germany

The rocking chair creaked a sweet song while Margried gently cradled the sleeping Elsbeth on her generous lap. How she enjoyed having the babies in her house. They helped her to feel alive and useful again. Only a short time ago she had accepted that surely she would die. The day Otto and Hannah arrived had been the worst yet. Then the angels themselves had swopped down to take care of both her and Adolph.

The next day Hedwig and Genevieve appeared, followed by Dr. Osterman. While Genevieve applied the horrible smelling, but wonderful feeling poultices to her chest, Hedwig made the glorious chicken soup that Hannah so lovingly spooned into her mouth.

Within days, she began to feel better and soon was able to sit up again. However, it was the babies who had truly given back her will to live. Little Gus, so full of life and such fun to watch as he toddled around the house laughing at everything he saw, and Elsbeth, such a good baby, with smiles that could brighten even the darkest heart.

Now all the women were busy in the big old farmhouse kitchen with its sturdy square block table by the window, surrounded by eight cane-bottom chairs with the ladder-backs, so straight and tall. The pump on the counter by the sink added its squeak to the endless din that comes in a busy kitchen. It was hot for this late in September and the air was stifling, Hannah stood at the big old wood fired stove, sweat dripping on her already damp blouse, "Momma, the water is boiling. Are the jars ready yet?"

Hedwig stopped peeling tomatoes and looked at Elsa, doubled over in laughter. "Elsa, stop laughing and finish putting the lids on those jars. You are wasting time and we need to finish those beans so we can get the tomatoes done today, as well."

"But Momma, Louisa is being so silly that I simply can't help myself, she is talking just like August would and it is so very funny."

Margried watched the girls from her chair. "It is good to hear all of you laughing and see you working together. What a wonderful summer this has turned out to be. The harvest is more than adequate. There should be food in our pantries for winter. Most important to me, is that I am feeling so much better,"

"We are all thankful, indeed," Hedwig, agreed. "However, if we do not finish this preserving the girls will not think it is so funny when their stomachs are complaining next spring."

"Yes, Momma, we'll get back to work," Elsa said with mock seriousness.

"I wonder how the boys are faring these days. Have you had word of them recently?" Margried asked.

"I have a letter from Georg that came just two days ago. He has some very exciting news. You know that he has been working in a factory that makes aeroplaness." Elsa began putting the lids on the jars. "He helped in designing some of the newest models. The latest one on which he has been working is called the Fokker monoplane, which means that it has only one wing and is very modern." Elsa got a faraway look on her face as her hand hovered over a jar. The lid seeming suspended in midair.

"I knew you would find another reason not to finish your job. I need those jars." Hannah complained, stomping her foot.

Elsa ignored her sister but resumed putting the lids on the jars. "Georg says that it is the best and fastest aeroplane ever made. Now he tells me that he has actually been flying in the air himself. One of the best pilots in Germany has been working with Georg. I cannot remember his name. Let me check the letter. It's here in my pocket."

"I do not care if your husband falls off a cliff or who his friends are. I need those jars." Hannah demanded.

"Just be patient. I'll get you your all important jars. But first I want to find that pilot's name. Yes, here it is. His name is Oswald Boelche and Georg says he is the best German pilot and is going to be the first to use this new plane."

Hannah's anger began to fill the room. "Elsa, put the stupid letter away and get me those jars. It is very hot over here."

"Okay, here are your precious jars. Are you happy now?" Elsa picked up two of the jars and made as if she were going to throw them.

Hedwig hurriedly wiped her wet hands on her apron, stepped between the two young women, and spread her arms, "Girls, no fighting. Elsa, carefully hand those jars to Hannah. And you Hannah, outbursts like that will not be tolerated."

"Yes, Momma!" was almost a chorus as both girls contritely did as they were told.

The kitchen became deathly quiet for a few minutes. Finally, Louisa spoke up. "Elsa will you finish telling us about Georg?"

Hannah looked from Louisa to Elsa, turned, and walked out of the kitchen into the parlor. Muttering under her breath.

The very thought of Georg again brightened Elsa's thoughts. A smile returned to her face when she said, "Certainly, it really is very exciting. Let me read you what his letter says:

I cannot even begin to describe the feeling of sitting in that vehicle, with goggles on my eyes the wind blowing around me. I began to move forward down the field and as the speed increased, the feeling of exhilaration was like nothing I ever experienced in my life except...

Oh, I can't read that part," Elsa laughed shyly.

"Read some more, Elsa. I want to hear about this aeroplane ride," Louisa said.

"Are you sure? I don't want to bore you."

Genevieve spoke up for the first time. "I think we all want to hear more."

"Alright where did I leave off? Oh, yes, here,"

I went faster and faster and finally pulled back on the rudder and the nose lifted off the ground and before I knew it, I was airborne.

I cannot imagine being off the ground," Louisa gasped. "Please keep reading.

I kept climbing and climbing until I was above the trees and finally I was as high as the clouds. Suddenly all the cares and worries of life just fell away and it felt like only the birds and I inhabited the skies on this beautiful summer's day. I looked down and could see for miles. Everything was green, warm, and so full of life. It is a feeling that is truly indescribable.

Hannah could not help but hear the discussion in the next room. Listening, enthralled by the story of Georg and the aeroplane she meekly reentered the kitchen. "I think flying would be exciting."

I don't know," Elsa said silently accepting her sister back into the circle. "Let me read the rest:

I felt at peace with God and the world. The worries and threat of war seemed to exist no longer; this time truly was for the birds and me alone. I wish that I could share this experience with you. I know you would love the feeling as well. I did not want to come back to earth and all its harsh realities, but of course, eventually I had to, there is only so much fuel. Even the landing was a new and exciting undertaking. I touched down with just a little bump and soon was sitting in front of Oswald, who was laughing and said I had a look of intoxication on my face. 'You will soon be a pilot, like me. I see it in your eyes. Once you have been in the skies there is no other thing on this earth that will satisfy you.' I fear he may be right for I have thought of nothing else, but when I can go up again, ever since my feet touched the ground.

"I can't read the rest to you because his words are just for me," Elsa said with a rosy blush on her face.

"It sounds to me like he has a new love in his life." taunted Louisa. "Are you not just a little jealous?"

Elsa was immediately defensive. "Of course not! Georg will never love anyone or anything more than me. I am not the least worried."

"We all know that Georg will never love anyone but you, Elsa." Genevieve commented emphatically. "Although, it does sound like he is very much enamored with this flying." The older woman shook her head. "I cannot even imagine what it must be like to be flying in the air. I am sure that I would not like it all. I want to keep both of my feet on the ground where God put them." She stomped her feet for emphasis. "Flying should be only for birds, surely not for people."

"I could not agree with you more," Margried chimed in. "If God had wanted us to fly he would have given us wings. I am sure that he did not mean for us to fly and people who attempt it are just tempting fate."

"Oh, I think that it would be wonderful to be up in the air and away from all this madness here on earth. I can understand just how Georg feels," Hannah exclaimed with a wistful look on her face. "I would love to try flying, to feel the wind in my hair and the sun on my skin. How wonderful to see the tops of trees and houses. It would be like being a part of a completely new world. I'm sure that I would love it."

The ever-pragmatic Hedwig gently brought the group back to reality. "All of this talk of flying and new worlds is not going to feed us this winter so we had better get back to work before your father comes in here and finds us all sitting and talking rather than doing our jobs."

When Elsa next spoke, there was just the slightest quiver in her voice, "Yes, Momma, of course you are right. We will get back to work. Nevertheless, I am very glad that my Georg had this new experience. I do worry though that he will want to stop being a designer of aeroplanes and want to become a flyer of them."

"Momma, Momma." The sweet sounds of a baby's voice from the other room indicated to all that little Gus had awakened from his nap. Very soon, the sound of little feet running preceded the crying child into the kitchen. He climbed up into Elsa's lap and laid his curly blond head on his mother's shoulder. A picture of Madonna and child could not have been sweeter.

"Here, my big boy, let's get you changed so you can go out in the barn and see Grandpapa," Elsa whispered in his ear. Suddenly Gus no longer wanted anything to do with cuddling but began wiggling, trying to get down, eager to get started on another adventure in the barn with his most wonderful Grandpapa. Running as fast as his little legs would carry him, he headed for the door that led to the barn. "No, no, first we must get you ready. Come with me and soon you can play in the barn." Dutifully, the little boy followed his mother.

"Elsa is such a good mother and she is so gentle with Gus. You should be very proud of her, Hedwig." A smile crossed Margried's face. "When she was growing up I was not so sure that she would turn out this well. Maturity has been very good to her."

"Yes, she has grown up and I agree that she is a wonderful mother. However, there are times when I still see the old Elsa. I worry, should this war go on too long, how she will manage. I am not sure that she is as strong emotionally as she wants us all to believe," Hedwig's voice was full of concern.

"I worry about us all, should this war continue much longer," added Genevieve. "We have been very lucky so far. Every night and every morning I pray that we will survive this terrible time and soon all be a family again. Surely this war cannot continue much longer."

****

Otto and Hannah were perched on the high driver's seat of the beautiful old carriage much later that evening as the family traveled home over the well-known roads. Otto's voice broke the silence, "What a perfect end to a perfect day. Hannah, do you remember our last ride out here in the taxi so many weeks ago?"

"Yes, it seemed like the whole world was crashing in on us, but everything turned out so well."

"I love to feel the wind gently blow when I am driving and see the sky full of stars, the clip clop of the horse's hooves the only sound. I did not realize how much I missed that when I was driving the taxi."

Hannah agreed smiling in the moonlight. "The children are both asleep, and I would not be surprised if Momma and Genevieve are too."

Otto drifted back into his own thoughts: It is so quiet; one would never guess that a war raged just a heartbeat away. When they reached the house, Otto gently lifted the sleeping Gus from Elsa's arms, "I will carry him up to his bed while you help the others into the house," he offered.

"I will see what the postman has brought us today," Hedwig said as she walked toward the front door.

The house was dark. Otto stopped briefly to light a lamp before taking the sleeping child up the stairs. He walked slowly through the parlor, lighted only by the moonlight streaming through the windows suddenly startled by a sound that could only have come from an animal in very great pain, a sound so bone chilling that he knew at once it was not an animal but his own beloved Hedwig in great distress. He quickly, but gently, laid the sleeping child on the sofa and ran into the dining room to find Hedwig sitting in a chair near the table, her whole body rocking as she clutched an envelope to her chest, the sound that escaped from her indescribable and filled with such pain.

Otto fell to his knees in front of her and looked at the woman he loved. The woman with whom he had spent the majority of his life, who had shared all of his joys and sorrows and he knew what was in that envelope. He knew what it would say. He just did not know who. Did not want to know.

He could not look, for he knew that his life would never be the same again. The contents of that envelope would forever change the very fabric of this family and his life. Gently Otto rose, put his arms around Hedwig, and cradled her as she rocked and cried. What could he do? How could he help her? No answers came for there were no answers.

Ever so carefully, he pried the envelope from Hedwig's hands. He turned the envelope over, his worst fears confirmed. There on the front of the envelope was a wide black border indicating to all who would see just what terrible news was contained within.

Otto looked at the envelope without seeing it. Someone from his family was gone forever. Fear kept him from looking at the embossed seal that would tell who. He laid the envelope on the table and turned again to hold his wife. How he loved her. He was such a fortunate man to have found this wonderful partner in life. Now they had lost someone dear to them and they would struggle through together. "I love you, my dearest Hedwig. You, and only you, make my life worth living. We will get through this together." He gently rocked with her as he held her head to his chest. This cherished woman who was in so much pain.

Finally, after what seemed an eternity, Otto eased away from Hedwig and again picked up the envelope, turned it over and looked at the seal.

Chapter 26
Early February 1916
Düsseldorf, Germany

Hannah put her hands over her ears trying to block out Momma's scream. That animal- like sound just would not go away. The letter with the black border lay on the table staring up at her. Onkle Ernest's name forever engraved in her memory.

Slowly she opened her eyes, shaking her head to clear it of the dream that had awakened her every morning, since that terrible day so many months ago. It had been such a beautiful day at the farm. She remembered how she and the other women had worked and played, joked and teased, while canning the wonderful fresh vegetables they had been eating all winter. She remembered the ride home that evening, she, sitting with Papa up on the bench while he so skillfully drove the horses. The stars shown in the sky creating a beautiful tableau of light, then they arrived home, Mama's scream, the letter. She lived it over and over again.

She rolled over in her bed and pulled the ancient down filled comforter up over her head, not quite ready to face the frigid air that filled her room. She knew Papa would soon quietly open her door and gently speak her name. As she waited for him, she allowed her mind wander over the last few months.

Everything had changed and nothing had changed since that beautiful September day when they came home to find the letter with the black border. She was often ashamed of herself, for she felt such relief that it was not Paul or August or even George. Certainly, she did not want Onkel Ernest to be gone but if someone in their family had to die, she was glad it was not one of the younger men. She thought this emotion was wrong and yet she could not shake the feeling.

Momma however, was devastated that her only brother was gone. They had been so close. Momma was ten years older than Ernst and after their mother died she had raised him like her own child. Hannah was sure she missed him as if part of her own self had died. He had never married or had a family, because he had dedicated his love and life to his beloved Germany. If there had ever been a true patriot, it was Onkle Ernest.

Momma seemed so much older these days. She moved more slowly, as though the weight of the world were hers alone to bear. She never complained, yet you knew that she had more aches and pains then before. There were days that Hannah thought she was older than Tanta Margried. Sometimes she would sit and stare out the window for hours and only the children, little Gus and Elsbeth, seemed to cut through the fog that was a like an invisible shroud around her.

Elsa and Louisa had taken over much of the responsibility of the day-to-day keeping of the house and family together. Papa finally had to give up driving the coach to town every day the horses were just too old. Hans had become lame and it was time to give them both a rest. Papa, after much loud discussion, had taken a position driving a trolley, but not before making it very clear to anyone who would listen that he thought this job was beneath him. He only did it because his family needed him.

Hannah thought how dramatically her life had changed as well. She no longer went to school but worked in the munitions factory on the other side of the river. She and her friend Ingrid spent their days making bullets. It was not difficult work but the hours were very long and she was always exhausted when she arrived home. She contributed all of her pay to help the family but it seemed to make no difference. The store shelves were empty and there was little to buy, especially food. The family survived because of last summer's bounty from the farm. Nevertheless, the larder got smaller each day and they all knew, although no one said anything, soon there would be nothing left.

"Hannah, it's time to get up," Papa whispered. "I am going down to start the fire."

"I will be down soon," she whispered back.

She continued to lie in the warm cozy cocoon of her bed, just a little longer, listening. It was quiet, very quiet outside. Last night when she went to bed the sound of rain turned to ice rattled against the windows, while the crash of ice breaking and falling from the limbs of every tree had kept her awake for what seemed hours.

Yesterday they had awakened to a cold winter rain that had quickly frozen and covered everything in a sheet of treacherous ice, making travel very difficult. Now there was just silence. The rain must have stopped she thought. She lowered the covers and peeked out the window. What greeted her was a veritable winter wonderland. A blanket of snow embraced the landscape so soft, white, and pristine that surely angels must have painted this new picture. She could not remember ever seeing a snow so beautiful. Yet, she realized this incredibly beautiful and serene scene must hide treacherous snares for anyone trying to move about outside.

Quickly, she got out of bed and dressed in the several layers of clothing that she had laid out the night before on the foot of her bed. The last things that she put on were her apron with the big pockets and the wonderful warm sweater that Momma had made for her.

She pictured Momma as she painstakingly unwound the yarn from an old sweater of Papa's and made it anew for her. The sweater was warm and made of love and she knew that she would always treasure it, no matter how worn it became.

Hannah picked up her shoes and quietly made her way down the stairs, moving precisely to avoid each place on the ancient boards that would groan their displeasure and possibly disturb the sleeping family. It was only four in the morning and much too early for the rest of the household.

The smell of the wood fire in the kitchen warmed her heart even before she could feel the warmth on her body. Papa was sitting at the big wooden table near the old stove reading. He was always reading anything that he could get his hands on with news of the war. Sometimes when there was no newspaper he would reread the one from the day before or even week before over and over again.

There on the table a steaming cup of bitter tasting chicory coffee beckoned her sit down. How anyone could call this coffee was beyond her. However, it was hot and she was grateful to see it ready for her. There was also a bowl containing some of the leftover stew from yesterday. Cereal was no longer available. The best they could do for breakfast was to add water to last night's dinner stew to make a sort of soup in the morning.

"Papa, have you looked outside yet this morning?" Hannah asked.

"I certainly have," he grumped, "this beautiful day is not fit for either man or beast to travel. There will be no trolley today and you will not be going to the factory. I should have let you sleep."

"You know I was awake when you spoke to me. We will all enjoy a day at home together. Perhaps when the sun comes up I will take little Gus outside and make a snowman. What fun that will be." Hannah smiled at the thought. "Maybe we can even make Momma smile."

She sat and slowly sipped her coffee, thinking of how cute Gus would be all bundled up trying to walk in the snow. A sudden overpowering chill, the intensity compelling beyond credence, overtook her. She felt frozen to her very soul. Death could not have been colder. Moreover, for just a moment she had a strange other worldly feeling. It was almost as if she were in another place. Never had she felt so alien and filled with trepidation in her own world before. She tried to shake off the feeling with a shudder and wondered what could have caused such a strange sensation.

* * *

Paul stood on the knoll under his favorite apple tree, the delicate pink and white petals infused the air with perfume of the gods. Endless lawns and gardens of the Schoenbrunn Palace stretched out before him, a vast quilt, precisely made, to cover the bare ground. Everything was perfect, just has Paul had imagined it. He loved the spring and early summer gardens. All of the bulbs from the Netherlands, planted with such meticulous care in the fall, formed the riotous patterns of color that he had so carefully envisioned, as he laid them out in the fresh earth. There was an immense feeling of gratification when the patterns began to materialize each spring. He never ceased to marvel that he, a poor boy from Leipzig, could have so much influence on such a beautiful place.

Look, there, off to one side, was the new rose garden that he had designed that Christmas Eve. How confused he had been, trying to sort out his feelings for Hannah. He designed this delicate garden just for her with all of the love in his heart. What a glory it was to see it now actually come to fruition.

The memory of that long frigid winter of indecision was making him tremble now. He felt so cold, and so wet. He experienced a sense that he would never again get warm. Why was he feeling so wet on this beautiful early summer day. So wet! Cold to the bone, especially his feet and legs. SO COLD!

He opened his eyes and tried to lift his head. The pain knocked him back. He struggled to no avail to move his arms; it was as if they were made of lead. Cautiously, he looked around and began to realize that he was lying on a bed of ice covered with a blanket of snow.

The rain had turned to snow. He remembered riding his motorcycle with an extremely important dispatch for headquarters in Bonn. The rain coming down steadily for hours before it turned to ice. The roads, so treacherous he had slowed down just to be able to stay upright.

When did the snow start? He could not remember. Why was he lying on the ground? Where was his motorcycle? Surely, he did not stop to sleep, not on a bed of ice. He must get up. This was, perhaps, the most important dispatch he had ever carried. When he tried to move again the blinding light and magnificent pain overtook him.

"Hannah, will you dance with me? The music is so sweet tonight. They must be playing just for us."

The look on Hannah's face was one of laughter and love. They were sitting on the ground under 'their special tree,' away from the rest of the crowd, where they could be alone. The evening was grand; moonlight shimmered through the branches above its silver beams caressing Hannah's lovely face. There was no place on earth that he would rather be then here with his arm around Hannah, holding her close to him, looking into her eyes and gently kissing her perfect lips. They stood to dance and he pulled her close. The feel of her next him so exquisite he was not sure he could bear it. Their bodies molded together as if they were one, dancing to the music in their hearts. Surely, he would take this feeling with him into eternity.

***

"Well, it is about time that you woke up. We were beginning to think that you preferred your own private world to the real one."

The voice was deep and rich with just a note of gruffness in it. Paul slowly opened his eyes and quickly closed them as the blinding light assaulted him.

"Come on, try again. I know that you can do it. It is time to wake up now," the disembodied voice chided him.

Once more, Paul opened his eyes, very slowly this time giving them time to adjust to the bright light. He tried to turn his head and found that he could not, nor could he move his arms or legs. He could move only his eyes. Cautiously he attempted to look around and find the source of the strange voice. There, next to him an apparition in white.

When he tried to speak, he found that his mouth was parched and only a squeak would come out. "Where ...."

"Do not try to talk. You are in a hospital in Bonn. You had a rather nasty spill with your motorcycle that left you lying in a ditch covered with snow."

His eyes were beginning to focus and now he saw the speaker was a very large woman dressed in white standing near the foot of a bed.

"You are a very lucky young man. A company of soldiers marching on the road above spotted your motorcycle. They began searching for the rider and found you at the bottom of a steep ravine almost completely covered in snow. We are still not sure how long you were there, but it must have been at least several hours because your blanket of snow had nearly obscured you from view. You have a number of serious injuries, the most dangerous of which is that you were nearly frozen."

"How long...have...have...I... been here?" he asked.

"Oh, I would say that you have been playing sleeping beauty for about five days now. I am the wicked witch, here to scare you into waking you up. You have been lounging around here long enough and it is time for you to wake up and get busy trying to heal those wounds."

Ever so slowly, Paul tried to turn his head again, more successfully this time. He had a much more inauspicious outcome when he tried to sit up.

"Not so fast. You are not ready to get up and run races quite yet. You have a dislocated shoulder and a broken leg. Here let me help you get a little more comfortable."

The lady in white very gently helped him ease up to a different position on his pillows so he could see his surrounding a little better. There were other men in beds all around him. As he slowly regained his senses, he remembered his reason for coming to Bonn.

"My motorcycle? The satchel – dispatch?"

"I will try to get a message to the men who found you. They have checked in several times to see how you are doing. I am sure they can answer some of your questions about what happened."

With that, the woman patted his arm, turned, and left to talk to another man in another bed. Paul closed his eyes and sank back into the pillows. What had happened to the dispatch? He knew it was important and he had let his superiors down, something that he had never done before. Closing his eyes, he once more succumbed to sleep. There were no dreams of Hannah this time, just troubled images of his motorcycle, snow and a never-ending road that led to the General's office.

Chapter 27
Three days later
Bonn, Germany

Paul stretched his leg without thinking; the pain jolted him back to reality. He opened his eyes and took in the scene that played out around him. A room filled with beds, each occupied by a man in some stage of recuperation. Blood-soaked bandages were everywhere on heads and chests. Many men seemed to be missing an arm or a leg or both. Though very much encumbered by his own injuries, he was sure he would heal and leave this place. He was not so confident about some of his roommates.

"Hey, beautiful, where have you been? I've missed you."

In a room filled with noise the sudden cat call caught Paul's attention.

"I thought you had left me for another guy," this from a different bed.

"Sweet cheeks, where's my kiss?" yet another bed.

By now all eyes, including Paul's, focused on a beautiful young nurse making her way down the aisle between the seemingly endless row of beds. She was tall and blond and carried herself with an air of confidence. Several times, she stopped and spoke to someone but always in a very professional, never personal way. She was friendly, but aloof. Paul was sure that she must spend her days warding off these sad and lonely men.

Finally, she reached Paul's bed and much to his disappointment gave him only a passing glance. He spent the rest of the day watching the door through which she had entered, hoping she would walk through the room again. She was strikingly beautiful, yet there was also something else, something almost familiar about her.

***

A few days later Paul was lying on his bed when a young man approached him..

"Corporal Ulhman?" A man in a ragged captain's uniform asked.

"Yes," Paul's voice was tentative. "How can I help you?"

"I think that it is I who can help you. I am Captain Köhler. My company and I found you on the road about three weeks ago."

"How wonderful to meet you!" Paul was genuinely surprised to see this man. "I am so grateful. I surely would have died if not for you and your men."

"You gave us quite a scare. We found your motorcycle lying on its side at a curve in the road but there was no sign of a rider."

"How did you find me?"

"My men began searching and finally found you at the bottom of a small ravine near a little stream. If you had rolled ten more feet you would have been in that water and most likely drowned."

"I don't know how to thank you enough."

"I'm just glad you made it. When we finally got you up the hill it took another two hours to get you to a field hospital."

"I did not know I was at a field hospital."

"The medic said that you were in pretty bad shape and did not give us much hope that you would make it. When I checked back a few days later and you were gone, I assumed the worst. No one knew anything about you. I had picked up the satchel from your motorcycle and wanted to give it to you.

"You have my satchel?"

"Yes, I checked back at the field hospital again when I was visiting one of my men and the medic I originally talked to was there and he told me they brought you here."

"If you have my satchel, do you know what has happened to dispatch I was trying to deliver?"

"When we found you I checked your satchel I found the dispatch, figured it must be extremely important, why else would you be out in weather that bad. I took it back to camp and had another courier deliver it to General von Stoltenberg."

"I don't know how to thank you. Not only have you saved my life but my job as well. There just are not enough words."

"I wanted to make sure you were going to be okay and bring this back to you. You have some personal things here I am certain you do not want to lose."

"Hannah's letters!" Paul had been so worried about the dispatch that he had forgotten about them.

"I assure you I have read none of them. Every man deserves some privacy, especially in times like these. When you get better, maybe I will see you on the road again sometime." With a salute, he was gone.

Paul, still reeling from this welcome visit, at first ignored the catcalls. Every nurse who came through the room got them but when the mysterious blonde came through, they were different. He became aware when one man, Rupert, who occupied a bed on the other side of the room, was particularly obnoxious. The woman smiled and patted the end of his bed, acknowledging him as she walked past. She continued through the room and when she got to Paul's bed, she stopped and picked up the chart from its hook for the first time. She quickly scanned it as was her usual manner with other charts and started to put it back on the hook. Then she stopped and looked at it more carefully looking at Paul and then back at the chart and at Paul again. The chart clattered on the floor when it fell from her hand.

"Paul, Paul Ulhman is it really you? I can't believe it."

He just looked at her, "Do I know you?"

"It's me Greta Metzger, Hannah's friend."

The next thing Paul knew she wrapped her arms around his neck.

It took Paul a moment to recover. Now he understood why she had looked so familiar. This was Greta, of course. Why had he not seen that. He remembered Hannah had written something last spring about Greta moving to Bonn with her parents. "Greta, how wonderful it is to see you. Hannah didn't tell me you were a nurse."

"I'm not really a nurse, just a volunteer. They need so much help here I try to come as often as I can. I'd hoped to go to the university but the war changed my plans, as it has for so many of us."

"Tell me what to you hear from Hannah?" Any connection to Hannah warmed Paul's heart.

"Oh, Paul, I really want to sit and talk with you, but I can't just now. I don't work tomorrow but I will be here the next day. I would love to spend some time with you after my shift if that is alright with you."

"That would be wonderful. It's so good to see you. It's like seeing someone from home."

"For me too. I miss Düsseldorf and Hannah and Ingrid so much. I just hate it here in Bonn. Nevertheless, Papa will not let me go back. He says it is too dangerous there and it is safer for me to be here in Bonn with him. I really must go now but I will see you day after tomorrow."

With that, she walked out of the room leaving Paul in a daze. He only became aware of his surroundings when he heard the other men in the room teasing him, especially Rupert. "I bet you think that you're really something special now. What do you have that rest of us don't? For the life of me I can't see what makes you so special."

The other men began to laugh which only spurred Rupert on. "I know! She must really feel sorry for you. She actually gave you a hug and you just lay there? What kind of man are you?"

The room seemed to rock with a chorus of "What kind of man are you?"

Rupert was on a roll now. "Not my kind of man. If she had gotten that close to me, she would never have gotten away. I sure don't understand what she sees in such a poor substitute of a man."

"Poor substitute of a man!" the chorus of voices echoed.

Before Paul could think and come up with an appropriate, witty comment, the words fell out of his mouth, "Greta is my girlfriend's friend. We haven't seen each other for years. We are just friends that's all."

"Yeah, Yeah, just friends. I've heard that one before. Sure, just friends. I know she feels safe with you because you're such a coward...."

The jeering went on and on. Paul turned his head away and tried not to listen to the comments.

"Pauly Boy, where's your girlfriend today?" Rupert called. "Has she forgotten you? What did you do, scare her away?" He chided. "I still don't know what she sees in you. Such a little boy!"

Paul was so tired of these endless comments. He had become the whipping boy of the ward with Rupert stirring up the crowds from morning until night. Thankfully, he was now able to get up and move around on crutches and he tried to spend as little time as possible in the ward. This afternoon he planned to meet Greta out on the wide front porch of the building and take in some of the beautiful early spring sun. It was still cool but the flowers were beginning to bloom and the smell of spring was in the air. The lawn in the front of the building had begun to turn green while the tips of the limbs of the giant old trees were no longer brown, but not yet green. They were that in-between color, almost yellow, that told you the limbs were softening and would soon be full of life again. Paul, too, was beginning to feel full of life again. His injuries were healing well. Soon he would be able to leave this place. The first thing he planned to do was visit Hannah.

The day was so beautiful. He did not want to just sit. He began wandering along the walk that surrounded the large building when Greta caught up with him. "Where are you going?" she asked. "I thought we were going to sit on the porch."

"I want to take a walk. I don't even know what is in the back of this beautiful old building."

"I'm not sure you want to know," Greta sighed. "But you seem determined so we'll walk together. This was once a school, you know, filled with the voices of laughing children running, playing and learning all day long. Now instead of children laughing, men are moaning, crying and dying."

And making life miserable for others, Paul thought. He did not want Greta to know how awful life had become for him on the ward.

"You truly are one of the lucky ones, Paul. You will be going home and all in one piece. So many of these men who do survive are not whole men either physically or emotionally any more. This is a terrible war that seems to be going on forever."

They rounded the corner of the building and there stretched out in front of them almost as far as they could see down a gentle hill were small white crosses, row after row after row of them. "I didn't know there was a cemetery here too." Paul said.

"A very make-shift one. This started out as only a hospital, but the men kept dying and there was no place to put them. Someone came up with the idea of burying them here on the hill, just to have somewhere to put the bodies until family members could come and claim them. The problem is that so many have died and so few families have claimed the bodies."

Paul hobbled over to a row of crosses. On each cross, there were initials and a date.

"These crosses don't even have a name on them and the ink on some is so faint that you can hardly read the numbers." He bent down to look more closely. "How are people going to identify these bodies when the war is over? This is terrible. This is no way to run a cemetery. No way at all."

Reluctantly, Paul straightened up, the pull of the faded crosses almost physical. They continued on their walk and eventually came to the front of the building again.

"It is time for me to leave. Can you make it to your bed on your own?" Greta asked.

"Of course I can. I'll be leaving soon, remember. Before I go back to work, I hope I will get some time to go and visit Hannah. I miss her so very much."

"I'm sure they will give you some leave time. Will you will go back to being a courier?"

"I should hope so, as soon as I am able to handle the motorcycle again. I think I was quite good at it."

"I'll see you tomorrow." Greta smiled and gave him a kiss on the cheek. "It's so wonderful to have someone to talk to. Hannah is a very lucky girl to have found a man like you, Paul. Not many men are as kind and understanding as you." With that, she turned and walked away, leaving Paul with a strange feeling of sadness for her.

He sat on the porch a while, putting off the return to his ward as long as possible. He dreaded facing Rupert's tirade one more time. The sun faded, turning the spring sky a brilliant orange. He finally garnered the courage and started back into the building. He could hear the men laughing and talking as he approached the room.

Suddenly all the jocularity ended as if a switch had been turned off. The sound of his crutches echoed in the silence. Paul felt the burning stare of each man's eyes as he walked down the aisle between the beds. No one said a word.

Finally, he reached the space at the end of Rupert's bed. King Rupert, as Paul had started to think of him, lay in his bed, the Supreme Antagonizer surrounded by his loyal toadies. Silence had now reached the deafening level. The slap, slap, slap of his crutches the only sound.

"Hey, Pauly Boy, do you really think you can ignore me? You are not going to get off that easy."

Paul refused to acknowledge him.

"You were gone for a long time. Did you and the pretty little nursie have some fun off in an unused corner of the building?"

The toadies snickered.

"What was it like, huh? I will bet she was good. Anyone who looks like her is sure to have lots of practice with men, know just how to make them happy."

The room got quite again. This was going too far even for Rupert.

"Was it good, Pauly Boy – real good?"

Paul stopped.

"But then, how would you know what is good. You are just a little boy."

The rage was building.

"What was your job? Let me see if I can remember. Oh yes, motorcycle courier. What kind of job is that? Certainly not a job for a real man."

Paul's wrath, now a volcano, threatened to explode.

"I bet they gave you a motorcycle because you were too soft for a gun, too much of a baby."

Slowly Paul turned to face Rupert, the volcano of furor erupted with the force of Mt. Vesuvius. Throwing his crutches to the floor, he lunged for Rupert's head, began hitting him with all the raw force, and pent up frustration, that weeks of listening to this abuse had created. "You bastard, how dare you talk about me!" He punched and punched, not caring how much it hurt his own hands. "And Greta, you will never talk about her again. I swear I will beat you to a pulp."

Paul became aware of other people around him but he did not care. He could feel the bones in Rupert's face crack, and still he did not stop. He wanted to hurt Rupert for everything he had said, and even more for the things he had said about Greta.

It finally took several men to pull him from Rupert. He continued to swing, his anger a beast, over which he had no control. Nothing mattered but the tremendous desire to rid the world of Rupert, never to listen to his abuse again.

Chapter 29
A few days later
Bonn, Germany

The guards that pulled Paul from Rupert led him to a different room on the opposite end of the hospital. Doctors decided that it would be far better for him to sleep in another ward, at least for one night. Someone got his meager assortment of personal belongings and brought them to his new bed. Admonished, he was not to go to the other area for any reason what-so-ever. He had no trouble agreeing to that restriction. The last thing he wanted was to ever see Rupert or hear his deprecating words again.

The next day, Paul allowed himself to reflect on what had happened. He knew he was wrong and yet there was little remorse. Rupert was a cruel man and Paul could not forgive him for his comments about Greta. Still, he knew his own behavior was unconscionable.

As the days passed, guilt for his actions began to eat away at him. Finally, one morning he awoke and could no longer live with what he had done. He had never felt so ashamed in all his life. How could he have let his anger get the better of him? He was an educated man, chosen for his job as a military courier because of his ability to follow directions and his trustworthiness. His position was one of which to be proud, not ashamed. He could no longer lead himself on and say that he had been defending Greta's honor. Truth was he had simply been mad, mad beyond belief. He needed to go and apologize to Rupert, no matter how much pride he had to swallow.

He made his way down the long hallways until he found his old ward. Almost sheepishly, he opened the door and looked in. Everything was quite. This seemed as good a time as any. Stoically, walking down the aisle between the rows of beds, Paul sensed that somehow things were different. He reached Rupert's bed. It was empty. He turned to the man in the bed next to Rupert's, what was his name? He could not remember. "Did Rupert finally get up and go for a walk? All he ever does is lay in that bed."

"Rupert is gone."

"Where did he go? I want to tell him I'm sorry for what happened. How I behaved was way out of line."

"No, you do not understand. Rupert is gone! You never understood did you. Your own little world was all that mattered. You never bothered to get to know the rest of us. Rupert died last night. He knew his time was coming. That is most likely why he was so obnoxious. He knew his time was almost up."

Paul could not believe what he was hearing. Slowly he sank down onto the bed that Rupert had occupied for so many weeks. "Why did he die?"

"Rupert was a brave and true soldier. No enemy bullet killed him though. The trenches killed him. He was the ultimate hero, but few will ever comprehend what he went through. The doctors still do not know how he lasted as long as he did. He got a burning fever but that did not keep him down. The smell of rotting flesh got so strong his trench-mates could not stand it. They took him to the field hospital and from there he was brought here."

"What are you talking about, rotting flesh?"

"The doctors could not get his boots off because the blood and rotting flesh of his feet had melded into the leather of his boots and become a solid mass the likes of which the doctors had never seen before. They finally cut the boots off and found that the flesh of both feet was completely gone. Even the bone had begun to rot away. The gangrene had progressed well up his legs."

"Surely he knew this was happening."

"Of course he knew something was wrong, but he just kept doing his job, being a good soldier."

"What happened when he got here?"

"The doctors amputated both legs above the knees hoping that would be enough. Of course, it was not and they went back and took both legs off as far up as they dared. Even then, they could not stop the gangrene. It was in the trunk of his body and there was nothing they or he could do."

Paul was puzzled "I never heard him complain of pain."

"He was continuously in excruciating pain but he never let on. That was how he got in the mess he was in to begin with. Had he complained when his feet first began to have problems from all the water in the trenches, perhaps he would still be alive with two legs on which to walk."

"Did he have a family?"

"He had a wife and two small children. He talked about his kids all the time. You were too busy in your own little world to care about any of the rest of us. Do you really know anything about any of us?"

Paul's guilt grew stronger, not only did he not know anything about these men; he could not even remember their names. What kind of an animal was he? "Please, tell me more about Rupert."

"I think he was probably a really good father. He was a butcher before the war. He had his own shop in some small town, I cannot remember where. To hear him tell it he was also involved in running the town and was the first to volunteer for the army when the war started."

"Where will they bury him? Will they send his body home to his family?"

"I expect they will bury him out back to be forgotten like all the others. It's a shame; Rupert really was a good man."

Paul just sat on the bed not knowing what to think. He had expended so much time and energy hating this man that he had not even realized that he had a life, a story. He certainly had not thought of him as one who might die a hero and leave a loving family behind.

Paul's thoughts moved to August and Louisa and the sweet new baby who was a year old by now. What about Georg, Elsa, and little Gus. This man was no different from them. His wife and children would be just as grief stricken as either Louisa or Elsa would be. It was then he knew he must do something to keep Rupert's memory alive. What he had not done in life he would do for him in death.

Paul left the ward, he headed toward what he thought must be the office area. He wandered around the huge old building, opening and closing doors until he found what appeared to be administrative people. A woman sat at a desk. "Excuse me." Paul looked at the sign on her desk, "Frau Shubert, I need to speak to someone about the cemetery."

"I do not know what you are talking about. We have no cemetery here. Now if you will excuse me, I am very busy."

"What do you mean there is no cemetery? Behind this building there are hundreds of graves with white crosses."

"Oh, that. It is not a cemetery, just a holding area, a place to put bodies until families come to claim them. You are keeping me from my work." Frau Shubert said with some vehemence.

"Well then, who can I speak to about the holding area for bodies?" Paul asked, his belligerence boiling from his mouth.

"No one is really in charge of that area. We just put the bodies out there and then when a family comes to claim them we send someone out to dig them up again."

"I am sure that you must have a listing of whose body is buried in each grave. May I please see that list?" It was more a command than a question.

The look on Frau Shubert's face was one of extreme distaste. "Who are you, young man? Why are you asking me all of these questions?"

"I, I...." Paul stammered, realizing that he had gone too far with his demands, began to modify his demeanor.

"I do not have to give you any lists."

"I am sorry. It is just that I have a friend who died sometime during the last two days and I wanted to know where his grave is," Paul answered more respectful this time.

"Well, why did you not say so? Coming in here making demands will do little to help your cause."

"I truly am sorry. I'm just so upset about my friend."

"Who is your friend?" Frau Shubert grudgingly asked.

"His name is Rupert..." Paul suddenly realized that he had no idea what Rupert's last name was. "He died last night. Surely you can help me."

"I will do what I can." She picked up several sheets of paper from a corner of her desk and began running her finger down the page. "Ah, here it is Rupert Barnhart, died March 28, 1916."

"Where is his grave?"

"I do not know if they have him in the ground yet but I suspect his grave will be somewhere near the bottom of the hill, unless they find an empty spot closer to the top."

"What do you mean you do not know where his grave is? Surly there must be a plot showing the empty spaces." Paul's disgust was beginning to show again.

"Look, only three men died last night so just look for yesterday's date and the initials R.B." She threw the papers back on her desk. "Now, go away and leave me alone or I will call the guards."

Paul could not believe what he was hearing. He left the office and found his way out to the cemetery. Bewildered he tried to find Rupert's grave by wandering up and down the rows of randomly placed crosses. Some of the cross's markings were so faded he could barely read the date or initials. Finally, after much searching he found what must the right one. It was a fresh grave and the initials and dates were right. Using the crutches for support, he lowered himself to his knees, ignoring the pain he carefully ran his hand over the roughly painted cross. "Rupert, I am going to do everything in my power to see that you get home to your family and have a proper burial. One fit for the hero that you are. Every man in this field deserves a proper burial. If it is the last thing I ever do I am going to see that it happens for you."

He was just struggling to get up when Greta came around the corner of the building. "Paul what are you doing down there? Frau Shubert tells me you have been causing trouble."

"Greta, you are just the person I need to see. You must help me get the list of men buried here. There needs to be a plot or map showing which soldier is in each grave. If bodies are claimed that needs to be noted."

"I think I can get you the lists, but you will owe me. Frau Shubert is not my favorite person. She can be very difficult."

Paul kept talking, his excitement growing. "And I need some grass seed, lots of grass seed. Without grass, these bodies are all going to wash down the hill in the next big rain. Will you help me, Greta? Please, I need to do this."

"There is a war going on, remember? There is not enough food and you want grass seed."

"Please, Greta. These men deserve something better than this. Do you know that witch in the office told me there was no cemetery here, just a holding area. For many of these brave men this will be their final resting place. They deserve to have their names on their crosses and grass to cover their heads. I was afraid that asking for flowers was going too far."

"I will see what I can do."

"One more thing, Greta. I know your father has influence with lots of officers. Do you think that he could get me an assignment to do this cemetery thing for a while?"

"Paul, sometimes you really ask too much. I said I would do what I can. It seems obvious that you are serious about this and if I know anything about you, it is that when you make up your mind to do something, nothing is going to change it. I will talk to my father.

"Grass seed, where am I going to get grass seed?" She mumbled as she turned and walked back toward the building.

Chapter 30
June 1916
Braun and Bloem's Munitions Factory
Düsseldorf, Germany

Hannah's eyes searched the room. The shrill cry still echoing off the walls. Sweat from her face pooled on the table in front of her; caused by heat or tension, she was not sure. Herr Yeager was looking in the direction of the turmoil across the immense open space filled with long worktables.

Surreptitiously she slipped the cold piece of metal into the pocket of the big white apron that covered her drab brown dress from neck to hem. Her fingers momentarily touched the other three slender projectiles it joined there. Still morning and already four pieces lay nestled together, safe from view. Herr Yeager's vigilant eyes shifted her way. Quickly she withdrew the handkerchief that protected the secret cache; clutching the cloth she swiped it across her forehead.

Who had screamed? She straightened up, hand pressed to her aching back.

Only an hour until her lunch break, she could make it. Another scream cut through the din of the constant clang of the stamping machines echoing around the room like a giant steel ball bouncing against tin walls. She watched Herr Yeager moving away from her, across the room. There, near the door, someone was on the floor?

Hannah glanced toward Ingrid at the next table. Their eyes met for just an instant. Immediately both girls looked back down at their work, Hannah filling and capping the 9mm cartridge shell casings, Ingrid stamping them with the B&B brand of Braun and Bloem's munitions factory.

At last, the bell rang precisely at twelve o'clock signifying the beginning of their lunch break. Women poured out of the steaming factory, gulping fresh air like drowning men, trying desperately to clear their lungs of the fumes and suffocating heat of the factory floor.

"Ingrid, did you see who fainted this morning?" Hannah asked her friend pushing stray hair from her damp forehead.

"No, I was afraid to look."

"Me, too. Quick, over there is a table. Let's get it so we can sit down a while. My back is killing me."

"There's Petra. Let's ask her to join us. Petra works on that side of the room, maybe she can tell us what happened." Ingrid pushed through the crowd of women. "Petra, over here."

"Hannah, how do you always manage to get the best table in the yard?" Petra practically fell onto the bench. The shadow from the huge linden tree fell across her, temporarily shading her from the blazing sun.

"Just luck I guess," Hannah rubbed her back. "Or maybe I am so tired of this miserable factory that I do whatever I can to get out first."

"Well, I like this table because it is the farthest from the factory door." Ingrid chose a seat with her back to the building. "Why do we have to be watched like children even on lunch break? I swear Herr Braun's personal police never get tired of trying to catch one of us breaking a rule."

"Do you know what happened this morning, Petra?" Hannah bit into her apple.

"Frau Wiesenberger fainted"

"Isn't she expecting a baby?" Ingrid asked.

"Yes, they just carried her out, and put a new girl in her place."

"Is she alright?" Hannah massaged her back again.

"I don't know," Petra looked worried. "What will she do if they don't let her back on the floor. Since her husband came home from France, he's not himself and never leaves the house."

"I talked to her last week," Ingrid said. "She told me that she no longer gets his military stipend so she has to work."

Hannah glanced up and whispered, "Quiet everyone, here comes Herr Yeager."

"Well, well, if it is not my favorite group. Are we having a good day girlies? I certainly hope so, especially you Fraülein Kruger. Watching you makes my long hours standing on the floor worth the effort."

"Go away and let us eat our lunch in peace, you big bully," Hannah growled.

"Why, Fraülein Kruger, why would you say such things? Surely you know that I am your best friend at this wonderful place."

Hannah felt her anger grow. She clenched her fist, under the table, until her nails bit into her palm, "You are no friend of mine. Now, please let us eat our lunch."

"Since you ask so nicely, I will do just that. I look forward to seeing you back inside." He lumbered off, a bear with a limp.

Hannah slipped her hand in her pocket and fingered the four shells that lay there. "I hate that man."

"I can't stand him either." Ingrid screwed up her face. "He thinks he's so important because he's a floor guard. I wonder why he isn't on the battlefield like all the other men his age."

"Someone told me that he was old man Braun's nephew," Petra said.

"He must be something to somebody because he's too dumb and too ugly for anything else," Hannah said.

"Hannah, be careful what you say to him. I think he could be really dangerous." Petra picked up her lunch things and put them back in her apron pocket.

"I agree with Petra," Ingrid said. "You need to be careful."

"He doesn't scare me. He's all talk. What could he possibly do to hurt me?"

"There goes the horn. Time to go back to work already?" Petra's voice sounded weary.

"I'm afraid it is. Four more hours of drudgery." Hannah pushed herself up from the bench and started back toward the building.

"Hannah, is your father driving the trolley tonight?" Petra asked as she walked through the factory door.

"Just like always. We'll meet at the bench after work."

Back at her workstation, Hannah picked up an empty case and inserted the explosive and cap in the end. Then she carefully measured out the correct amount of propellant, poured it into the case and gently tamped it down. Next, she inserted the bullet and crimped the edges of the case to hold the bullet in place. Finally, she rolled it around in her hand, satisfied that it was correct she put it in the box beside her, picked up another, and began the process again.

Her mind drifted to the letter from Paul that came in yesterday's mail. He was still working on the cemetery behind the hospital in Bonn. His leg was healing nicely and he would soon be able to ride his motorcycle again. She dreaded his going back to the front. He mentioned making a trip to Düsseldorf and she dreamed of how she would feel when she saw him again.

Her hands moved automatically: filling, tamping and crimping, while her mind conjured up scenes in the garden at Hagen Brau. They sat under their favorite tree and looked into each other eyes. Paul's hand slipped around her waist and pulled her closer while his other hand gently traced the outline of her cheek, then her chin and finally her lips. Soon his lips replaced his fingers and she felt herself melt as their lips met. Her own fingers trailing over his face… she felt a rough place where metal met metal. Suddenly back to reality, she looked at the metal projectile. It did not feel right, the bullet was too short.

She charily laid it on the worktable next to the measured line. Yes, it was just a millimeter too short. She had not added enough propellant. She looked around for Herr Yeager, did not see him. She palmed the cartridge, slid her hand off the table and into her pocket...

"Fraülein Kruger, let me see your hands. Now." Herr Yeager's voice sounded over her shoulder, full of menace. Hannah felt the hair on the back of her neck prickle, he was so close. How had he gotten there without her noticing? She raised both hands and laid them palm up on the table. Herr Yeager stood over her. She could feel him just touch her back. "Empty your pockets."

She glanced up and caught Ingrid's eye, who nodded ever so slightly. Knowing that she had no other choice, she reached into her pocket and brought out the remains of her lunch, the handkerchief, a few other personal items including Paul's letter, and the coins for the trolley ride home. "This is all I have, sir."

I saw you put a cartridge in your pocket."

"You must be mistaken, sir. There is no cartridge here."

"I do not make mistakes. Come with me"

She started to pick up her things.

"Leave them." He grabbed her arm.

"Don't touch me. You're hurting me."

"I will do what I want." Gripping her left arm, he led her away.

Hannah looked back at Ingrid, but her eyes were down as she set the stamping machine for the next lot of cartridges.

"You women are all alike. You think you are too good to be caught. Maybe someday you will learn that nothing gets past Herr Yeager."

He led Hannah to a small room in the interior of the building. The room contained a table pushed against the wall and one chair. As soon as the door closed, he pushed her back against the table. "Take your apron off."

"I will not."

"That is how you are going to be, huh? You think you can talk back to Herr Yeager, Yah?"

"You don't scare me."

"I have no intention of scaring you. If you do as I tell you, we will have no problems. Now take off your apron."

"No!'

Herr Yeager reached out and grabbed both her shoulders, twisted her around until she faced the wall. He then began fumbling with the knot of the apron strings.

His breath stunk of the garlic from his wurst at lunch. She could feel hot air coming closer to her neck. His breathing became more rapid and nausea climbed in her throat as he continued to work on the knot. "Take your hands off me."

"What have you done to these strings, woman? Do you not know how to tie a proper bow?"

"Maybe I am trying to keep men like you from bothering me."

He finally got the apron strings undone and pulled it from her. "Now we shall see what you really have in there." He laughed as he turned the pockets up, out rolled five cartridges onto the table.

Hannah held her breath. What would he do now?

"So, I was right and look at this, not just one shell but five. My, my, this has not been a very good day for you, has it, Fraulein Kruger?"

"Everyone makes mistakes. What this company expects is unreasonable and they know it. That's why they have to employ thugs like you to keep a few harmless women in line." The sting from his hand on her face brought her up short.

"How dare you speak to me like that? I will show you how we make inconsequential women like you, respect men like me. He pushed her down on the chair, wrenched her arms around the back of the chair, and used her apron strings to tie her hands together. He began working on the buttons that lined the front of her dress from neck to waist.

Hannah struggled kicking him in shins. "Get your hands off of me," she shrieked.

He slapped her again, only this time he slapped her breast not her face. "See how you like that. Kick me again and next time it will be harder."

"You don't hurt me, you incompetent oaf." The vehemence of her words, like knives, slashed the air. She was certain no one could hear them but that did not stop her harangue of insults.

"I told you to shut up."

She spit in his face.

Wiping his face, he roared. "Now you have gone too far." Fiercely, he grabbed her hair, yanked her head back, took his filthy handkerchief, and stuffed it into her mouth. He then took off his belt and used it to strap her legs to the chair.

She tried to pull away but it was impossible.

He returned to the buttons of her dress. Finally getting them all undone, he pulled the sleeves off her shoulders further impairing her movement.

His hands began to explore her exposed breast, at first, almost tenderly.

Hannah tried to pull away.

"Don't pull away from me, woman. You will pay for that!" He slapped her breast again then began savagely twisting and pinching.

The pain was excruciating. Hannah tried screaming through the cloth but could not. She squeezed her eyes shut and tried to push the pain from her mind.

"You close your eyes, my dear. You like what I am doing, do you? Well, let me show you more."

Suddenly the pain stopped and she opened her eyes. He had taken his hand from her and was opening his trousers. They fell to his ankles as she watched. How ugly his hairy white legs were. She continued to watch in horror as he loosened his under garments and exposed himself. The monster that stood before her was revolting. She felt the bile climb in her throat. The gag in her mouth choked her.

He fondled himself with one hand as he lay hold of her breast with the other. Again he twisted, harder this time. His eyes glazed over.

She moved from side to side trying to dislodge him.

"You want to help do you?" He let go of her breast and began to rub himself against her face.

She turned her head away.

Suddenly he yanked the cloth from her mouth and frantically tried to replace it with himself. She bit down hard.

He roared.

She bit again before he could pull himself away. "I hope I bit it off!" she screamed as loud as she could.

At just that moment, the door flew open, "Klaus, what is going on in here?" Herr Braun demanded of his nephew.

"She was hiding mistakes in her apron." Klaus Yeager stood half-naked, blood dripping on the floor.

Hannah nearly laughed at the absurdity of the picture.

However, she wisely kept her thoughts to herself.

"For God's sake cover yourself! Then leave this factory. I do not want to ever see your face darken my door again."

"But, Onkle Leopold, she was stealing. I have only been teaching her a lesson."

"Shut up and get out of here. I will not have you make a mockery of me or my business."

"Onkle Leopold, please I need my job. What will my wife say when I tell her I have lost my job? I have children to feed. You cannot do this to me"

"Listen to you, blubbering like a baby."

"But...."

"Look what you have done to this girl. Get out of my sight, you make me sick."

Hannah watched Herr Yeager scramble across the room and out the door.

Herr Braun moved behind Hannah, untied her hands and carefully pulled the shoulders of her dress up never touching her skin. "Button up your dress and then I will undo your ankles."

Ankles free, she stood up rubbing her wrists and arms.

"Here is your apron."

Herr Braun sounded almost gentle as he handed her the white cloth. "Thank you sir.

"What is your name, Fraülein?"

"Hannah Kruger, sir."

"Fraülein Kruger, I hope that you will accept my apology for my nephew's behavior and I trust that you are not hurt too badly?"

Hannah said nothing.

"There will be no further discussion of this incident."

Hannah, head held high, walked from the room, never glancing at the cartridges that lay on the table.

Chapter 31
Immediately following
Düsseldorf, Germany

Hannah, hearing the door close behind her, trembled. She staggered into the shadow of a darkened corner. The cords of the rope, that had held her composure together, begin to snap one by one. Weak from the horror of the last hour, she slid down the wall and crumbled into the corner. Arms wrapped around her legs, she laid her head on her knees and sobbed, no sound escaping her lips.

How long was she there, perhaps minutes, possibly hours. Time had lost all meaning, desolation and anguish replacing every sense. Eventually the pain began to abate and consciousness gradually returned. What was she to do now? Could life possibly continue? She was physically alive but her soul was mortally injured. How could she face her family, her friends…Paul? Her body convulsed in misery. Time and space again lost all significance, only desolation remained.

Hannah's mind wandered in a barren desert of lonesomeness crying out for help. There was none. She was only beginning to discern that she must accept her fate and go on with her life. Life would be forever altered. Yet nothing was different. The world around her would never know what happened. What had Herr Braun said? "There will be no further discussion of this incident." Yes, he was right; there would be no further discussion of this incident.

Little by little, she began to uncurl, joints stiff from sitting on the cold hard floor. Awkwardly she finally managed to stand, glanced around to get her bearings, and saw a door at the end of the dim corridor, which led to the factory floor.

Hands smoothed her dress and apron as she moved towards the door. Once again back stiff and head high, she pushed the door open, ran her hand through her hair one last time, and began the trek across the factory floor to her worktable. She kept eyes focused straight ahead, deliberately avoiding any eye contact. The rope of her composure, now so tenuous, she knew that one look from a friend would render her incapable of continuing.

She finally reached her worktable to find everything as she had left it, all of her personal and private things strewn across the surface, where Herr Yeager had pawed through them. One by one, she picked them up and returned them to her pockets. All the while, she could feel Ingrid's eyes boring into her head as surely as if she was using a sharpened awl.

Silent questions bombarded her like a volley of grenades on the battlefield. She refused to acknowledge any of them. Keeping her eyes on her worktable Hannah picked up an empty case, put in the explosive and cap, measured the propellant, poured it into the case, tamped it down, inserted the bullet and crimped the edges. The routine brought back some sanity. As long as she did not make eye contact with anyone, she was certain she could finish her shift.

* * *

The blast of the air horn, signaling the end of the day, reverberated through Hannah's body, jolting her out of her self-induced stupor. Dear God, would she ever get used to that noise. Suddenly conscious of all the eyes on her again, she quickly put away the materials needed for her job and started out of the building.

"Hannah, wait for me," Ingrid called after her.

Hannah ignored the voice and kept moving.

"Hannah, wait."

She began pushing her way through the crowd of women anxious to get out of the building.

"What is the matter? Hannah!"

The sound of Ingrid's voice pounded in Hannah's brain. Now she could hear other women calling her name.

"Hannah."

She kept moving through the crowd.

"Are you alright?"

She pushed someone out of her way and finally got through the door.

"Fraülein Kruger, is there a problem?"

The sunlight blinded her, but she continued in the direction of the street.

"Hannah, wait."

The voices seemed to be coming from all directions. She had to reach the bench at the trolley stop. Then she could sit down and have time to think before she answered any questions. She knew that she must face the others. But how could she tell them what happened?

Finally, after what seemed an eternity she made her way through the swarming sea of humanity and saw the bench. No one was there yet. Running now, her breath coming in gasps, she stumbled to the bench and collapsed in a heap, like a punctured balloon. The exhaustion that overcame her was bewildering. She pulled herself into a corner, trying to make herself as small as possible.

"Hannah, what's wrong?" Ingrid's voice filled with concern as she plopped down next to her friend.

Hannah pulled away when Ingrid put a hand on her shoulder. "Nothing is wrong."

"How can you say that? Of course, something is wrong. You are acting very strangely."

"I have a slight headache. That's all."

"Hannah, you are my best friend in the whole world. I have known you since we were just small children. You cannot fool me. Something happened this afternoon. You can't hide it from me."

Hannah knew she was right. They were closer than most sisters. They often finished each other's sentences. Nevertheless, she could not tell Ingrid what happened. She just couldn't.

"You are right as always, Ingrid. Herr Yeager frightened me and I am very upset."

"What did he do?"

"Oh, nothing really. He was just all talk."

"Did he find your mistakes?"

"I finally showed them to him and left them on a table for him."

"Are you going to have your pay docked?"

"I don't know, perhaps."

"Why do I think you are not telling me everything? You have been acting very strangely since you returned to your worktable. Now there's a distinct quiver in your voice."

"I keep telling you. Nothing happened. Now, can we please stop talking about this? Look here come the trolleys." Hannah turned to look her friend in the eye for the first time. "Whatever you do, do not say anything to my father about this."

"But, he would want to know what happened."

"No."

"You know how he worries about you working here already."

"Yes, I know. He still thinks I am his little girl and he has to protect me."

"You know you love him for that."

"Please do not say anything to him. Please"

"If that is what you want"

"It is. Do you promise not to say anything?"

"I promise"

Hannah gladly took Ingrid's outstretched hand and pulled herself to her feet. The ache in her body from Herr Yeager's abuse seemed to be growing by the minute. Her knees ached, her wrists burned and there were no words for the pain in her breasts. She worried that bruises were showing on her face and arms. She just wanted to get home and hide in her room.

The third trolley in the line, number 21, was marked for the Reichsstrasse and the Rhein River. As women climbed aboard, many greeted their driver with a cheerful "Gutten tag, Herr Kruger." Hannah tried her best to sound cheerful as she changed the refrain to "Gutten tag, Herr Papa," as she always did. The women around her laughed, just as every other day and Otto grinned, exactly like every other day.

But, it was not every other day and Hannah held her breath as Ingrid climbed aboard behind her.

"Gutten tag, Herr Kruger."

Hannah waited, but Ingrid said nothing else and the girls made their way to a seat across the aisle and two rows behind the driver. Hannah sat by the window which was open to let the cool breezes into the stifling coach. Putting her hand on Ingrid's arm, she mouthed, "Thank you."

The twenty-minute ride to the river went smoothly. There were several trolleys in front of theirs. As they approached the river, the line of traffic slowed down. When it was their turn, the trolley made its way to the middle of the bridge. Herr Kruger called out, "Well, ladies, here we are again for no reason we must stop in the middle of this bridge."

Even before he finished speaking, several of the women, got up and made their way to the windows closest to the river. A soon as the trolley came to a full stop the women reached into their pockets and began throwing things out of the open windows. You could hear the splashing sounds as the well-aimed missiles reached the river far below. The daily ritual complete, the women sat down and the trolley began to move.

Hannah cringed when she heard the woman in the seat behind her speaking: "I wonder what would happen if someone from the factory happened to be crossing any bridge in this city just after shift change time and saw what was happening."

Another voice responded, "Let's hope that never happens. We would all lose our jobs."

Ingrid joined the banter, "I find it hard to believe that all those men at the factory are oblivious to what we do every day. I will bet that there are enough munitions at the bottom of that river to blow up half of this city."

"I know what you mean. I am a nervous wreck every day from the time we leave the factory until we have thrown the mistakes into the river," the first woman said. "But at least we will have a great story to tell our children when this horrible war is finally over and life gets back to normal."

Hannah wanted to scream for the women to stop talking. What did they know? Nothing. None of them knew what would really happen if they were caught with their mistakes. She alone knew and she wanted to stand up and shout at their ignorance. There was no story for their children here. There was nothing of this horrible experience that she would ever tell her children.

She felt the tears escape and begin to roll down her cheeks and turned her head toward the window. After today, how could she ever have children? Could she ever face a man again?

Her father's voice brought her out of her self-imposed isolation. "Hannah, no food for the hungry fish today? You must have had a very good day."

Chapter 32
Early August 1916
Düsseldorf, Germany

"There you go, Little Gus. You're ready. Go give Grandmomma a big hug." Elsa patted Gus on his newly changed bottom and put him down on the floor. "Momma will be back soon."

"Elsa, are you ready yet?" Louisa was standing with the front door open. "I was hoping we could get an early start this morning."

"I'm almost ready, Louisa. I had to change Gus and you know how he is these days, it is like changing the diaper on a tornado."

"Well, if you would plan your time better, we could leave sooner."

"You just wait; Elsbeth will not be that docile, well behaved, little girl forever. Soon she'll be just like Gus, running everywhere."

"When that happens, I'll know it takes more time and be ready for it. Will you please hurry up." Louisa cast Elsa a look full of scorn.

"I think I'm ready now. Let's get started."

"Finally, I thought if we got out early this morning maybe we could get near the front of at least some of the lines." Louisa was down the steps as Elsa came out the front door. "Do you have your ration card?" Louisa asked.

"You ask me that every day." Elsa slung her bag over her shoulder with a huff. "Have I ever forgotten it? No, I have not." She said with contempt. "Shall I get it out and show it to you?'

"Don't be silly. I just wanted to make sure we didn't forget anything." Louisa strutted on ahead.

Elsa stopped and looked at Louisa, a strained expression on her face. "By we, you actually mean me!" She reached a hand out to Louisa's shoulder. "Please stop and look at me. Why do you always treat me as though I know nothing?" Elsa was so angry that she felt the tears forming. "I'm just as smart as you and don't need you to make sure my life is run correctly,"

Louisa stopped and looked at her sister-in-law. "I wasn't implying that you weren't smart. It's just my way of making sure I have everything." She started walking toward the market again. "I hate to come back and lose our place in line." Louisa picked up her brusque pace. "It seems like all we ever do is stand in line and wait for our small share of food to be doled out by the government."

"Well, it always makes me feel as if you do not trust me. You have to take care of me or something," Elsa caught up to Louisa. "Look at me."

Louisa stopped one more time and looked at Elsa. "Well…."

"Maybe I'm a burden to you."

"Elsa, please, I didn't mean that." Louisa looked contrite "It's just…Oh, I don't know. This war has gone on for so long."

"Well, that's no reason for you to treat me the way you do."

"Sometimes I don't know what I'm thinking. I worry about August all the time and it makes me crazy."

"I worry about Georg too. I never stop thinking about him."

"On top of that there is so little food." Louisa began walking again, but more slowly this time. "Life is just so very hard right now."

"I understand. I keep thinking, if only we had gone back to America, everything would be different."

"Sometimes I forget that you're not really home either. I shouldn't complain." Louisa brushed at her face. "I don't think that Mother, Elsbeth, and I would have been able to survive on our own." Her eyes began to fill with tears. "It would have been too hard."

"We are really very lucky." Elsa began to feel a better. "At least we both have our separation allowance from the government which means that we don't have to work."

"Yes, and we can go out and wait in the daily lines while Mother and Hedwig stay home and take care of the babies."

Elsa began to giggle. "Can you imagine if I had to bring Gus with me?"

"I can just see it now. You would be running everywhere"

"We would never even get into a store, let alone actually purchase something." Elsa nearly doubled over with laughter. "I would have to put a leash on him, like a puppy, just to keep track of him."

"Elsa, can you ever forgive me? I'm not angry at you. I never could be," Louisa put her arm around her sister-in-law and hugged her. "I don't know what makes me act so badly sometimes."

"Of course, I forgive you. I don't think any of us in this family could have survived alone."

"Shall we go and see what delights await us this beautiful day?"

"You better hurry or I will get there first." Elsa started skipping down the street.

"Wait for me." Louisa cried out of breath. "Sometimes you make me feel like a schoolgirl. Elsa, you are too much." The girls fell into each other's arms laughing, crying, and holding on for dear life.

Walking on toward town Elsa became aware that it was truly a beautiful day, the sun shining as the big white fluffy clouds drifted aimlessly across the sky creating a never-ending picture on a grand scale.

"I've always loved to watch the clouds and see what pictures I can make from them," Elsa said pointing. "Look there, at that big one over on the left. If you look just right, you can make out a big rabbit. See the ears and the tail. There is even a string of clouds out to one side that looks like whiskers. Do you see it?"

"Yes, and look over there, could that be a silhouette of Otto there in the clouds?" Louisa laughed.

"I do believe you are right. It looks just like Papa." The women continued down the street arm in arm pointing out different cloud formations as well as taking in all the lovely flowers and beautiful green trees that lined the walk.

"You know, you would never realize there was a war going on just looking at this street today." Elsa bent over, picked a bright yellow daisy, and inhaled the heady fragrance. "How can the harsh realities of life be so close and yet so far away?"

"I don't know, but that line up there for bread looks like a harsh reality to me." Louisa pointed at the crowds of people on the street in front of them. "If you take the bread store today, I will see what I can find in the way of some fresh meat for dinner. Shall we meet here at the fountain when we're finished?" Louisa asked.

"That sounds like a good plan."

The lines were already as long as they were every morning as women trying to feed their families fought over the meager quantities of food available on any given day. Elsa was feeling quite pleased with herself as she left the bread store with a nicely baked loaf of rye bread. Papa would really enjoy this. Momma was no longer baking bread at home because they were not able to buy flour. Only the commercial bakeries had flour these days and there was very little of that.

It seemed that each day there was less and less to go around. Some days they could not get bread at all.

Elsa meandered through the square waiting for Louisa, when she heard shouting coming from a group of women who crowded around the statue of Bismarck. She wandered in that direction to see what was causing all the commotion.

A woman dressed in dark brown with the usual white apron was standing on a box next to the statue, shouting and shaking her fist in the air. Elsa stepped closer to hear what she was saying.

"Why do we have to wait in lines every day for the little bit of food that is left for us? The government takes most of what the farmers produce for the soldiers." The woman's voice rose as she continued. "You can see how important families are. We mean nothing at all to the government."

"The farmers are in collusion with the British." Someone in the crowded shouted.

Another voice from the crowd. "I heard the Kaiser is keeping most of it for himself and his friends and not even giving enough to the army, let alone the average citizens like us."

The woman in brown spoke again. "What are we supposed to do? Do not misunderstand me; I want the soldiers to get fed but what about my children, should they go hungry?"

The crowd was openly agreeing with this woman. Elsa herself wondered what she would do if someday she came to the shops and there was no food for Gus. She turned her attention back to the speaker.

"Why do the farmers get to keep so much? I have heard that they are willing to sell to us but the government will not let them.

Someone yelled, "Why should we let the government tell us what to do?"

The crowd was getting more restless.

The woman in brown was waving her arms. "It is not just the government. I ask you, why should farmers get to keep some for themselves and not share it with the rest of us?"

The women in the crowd were becoming agitated now.

"There is enough food out there for all of us, if we just go and get it."

The crowd around Elsa became even more agitated, shouting their approval.

"Just go get it. That is what we need to do. Just go get it." The speaker shrieked.

The women in the crowd took up the chant, "Just go get it. Just go get it."

Elsa spotted Louisa standing off to one side and made her way in that direction. As she got closer, she could see that Louisa had picked up the mantra. She began to wonder what was going on here.

The crowd got quiet again. The woman in the brown dress was speaking once more. "Saturday, we will all go out into the country together and take what we want from the greedy farmers. They owe it to us. We will feed our families. We will just go get it."

Again, the chant erupted from the crowd.

"Ladies, we are sisters." Shouts of approval from the crowd.

"We all have families to feed. Feed them we must." The crowd grew louder.

"Will you join me on Saturday?" Now the crowd was so loud that the speaker could barely be heard. "We leave the square at 5:00 in the morning."

"Just go get it." The women shouted so loud the sound was echoing off the buildings.

By now, Elsa had reached her sister-in-law. She noticed that Louisa's look was one of pure anger as she shouted the mantra at the top of her lungs.

A chill ran down Elsa's back.

Otto pushed his chair away from the table and leaned back, his hands behind his head. "Well, ladies, I must say that was the best meal that we have had in a long time. How did you manage to get such good sausage?" He asked. "And the vegetables from the garden were wonderful. You would never guess we had such severe rationing looking at this table." He looked at Hedwig. "Momma call the neighbors, there is enough left over to feed them all."

"Do not worry, my dear husband, you will see this again for several days, that I can promise you. We will let the neighbors worry about themselves," scolded Hedwig.

Louisa grinned at her own mother Genevieve. "Momma and Hedwig have worked very hard in the gardens to be able to give us these fresh vegetables." she said, clapping her hands in approval. "I don't know how you two amazing ladies manage the children as well as the gardening, cooking and cleaning. Thank you for being such wonderful mothers and grandmothers."

"I know what you mean, Louisa. The whirlwind, Gus and his sidekick, Elsbeth are a full time job. I never knew that little boys could be so lively." Elsa scratched Gus's head and helped him reach another piece of sausage. "He certainly is getting harder to keep track of these days, running every minute like he does. Momma, you and Genevieve must have some kind of magic you work on him just to be able to keep up."

"He is no worse than his uncle was at his age. My only problem is that I am much older than I was when I had to keep up with August."

"Now, Hedwig, you are not getting old." Otto's voice was full of mirth. "You cannot possibly be, because that would mean that I am getting old too."

"Well, Gus does his best trying to keep Genevieve and me young and perhaps more than just a little tired," Hedwig rubbed her head and leaned back in her chair with a grin on her face.

"I agree with you about the tired part," sighed Genevieve. "However, these two beautiful little children give me the will to get up and move each day and keep my mind off my aches and pains and this dreadful war."

Otto took out his pipe and caressed the bowl, "Tell me, ladies, any new gossip in the bread lines today?"

"There was lots of talk about the farmers keeping too much food." Elsa said looking at Louisa. "There was quite a crowd today listening to one woman shout about how unfair everything is and that we should go out into the country and just take the food from the farmers."

"Did you hear this, too, Louisa?" Otto asked concern in his voice.

"There was a lot of talk. Everyone is hungry and unhappy. There is always talk of protest."

"This was different though, Papa," Elsa said. "Louisa, I know you felt it too. Elsa looked straight at Louisa. "I saw it on your face."

Louisa gave Elsa a look full of malice. "I do not know what you are talking about."

Elsa ignored the look. "I don't think these women were from Düsseldorf. They seemed to be there just to incite the crowd." Elsa avoided meeting Louisa's eyes. "It seemed like they were trying to start a riot."

"I think you may be right, Elsa." Otto stood up and began to pace the room. "How serious do you think that this threat is?"

"I think that it is very real."

"And you, Louisa, do you agree with Elsa?"

"I do!"

Otto lay wide-awake beside Hedwig. He could not get the conversation at dinner out of his mind. Ever so gently, he turned over and nudged her. "Are you awake?"

"I wondered how long it would take you to ask me that," She mumbled.

"I think I need to go out to the farm and make sure Adolph and Margried are alright."

"I am not surprised. I worry about them, as well. If what the girls said is true, and I am quite sure there could be some real trouble this weekend."

"That gentle old giant and his wife are getting feeble. They would not be able to save themselves, let alone their crops."

"Otto Kruger, you are a good man. I agree, you should go. Now kiss me one more time and then get some sleep."

Otto leaned over and gently kissed Hedwig. It perpetually amazed him that after all these years he still loved his wife so much. With that thought in his head, he drifted off to sleep.

* * * *

The next morning Otto was up before dawn. It would take him several hours because, with no auto or horses, he would have to walk. He stopped at the door to Hannah's room and pondered whether to wake her or not. He knew how much she loved the old couple and the farm. He would enjoy her company on the long walk, but he let her sleep. He did not want to put her in danger too.

The air was cool and the slight breeze just a bit chilly. The sweater Otto had on felt good now but he knew that soon the sun would be up and it would be much too warm. He walked at a brisk pace, hoping to reach the farm before the main heat of the day. The green fields and smell of clover were exhilarating. Summer had always been a favorite time. Sometimes he wondered if he would not have been a happier man, had he become a farmer. He always loved the countryside and all of its sights, sounds and smells. Last summer helping Adolph plant, nurture and then harvest the crops had been one of the best in his life. It had been so fulfilling to have a hand in the actual feeding of his family.

After about two hours of walking, Otto recognized the landscape was changing. Rolling hills had replaced the fences. The open spaces painted with green and gold fields of corn and wheat. Animals roamed freely and no one seemed to care if the cows or goats were in the road. Several times he had to walk around a grazing cow, who only raised her head as if to say "who are you?" and then went back to eating her breakfast.

There was such peace here; it did not seem possible that anything could ever disturb this lazy summer atmosphere. Yet he knew in his heart that this was just a false sense of security. If the rumors were true, by tomorrow afternoon chaos would replace the peace of today.

Otto rounded a long lazy curve and saw the farm ahead of him just before the sun reached its apex. What he noticed first were beautiful green fields, green, not with crops but rather with grass. This lack of crops did not seem cause for alarm. Adolph was an astute farmer and knew that some fields needed to lie fallow each year to allow the nutrients in the earth to renew. Closer to the house, he came upon a partially plowed field barren of life. Now the hairs on the back of his neck began to tickle. His alarm grew. Finally, the big old house came into view. It looked warm and inviting as always. The front door was open, the chairs were on the porch and the curtains fluttered in the breeze.

He turned up the long drive that led to the barn portion of the house and spied the old farmer standing by the grinding wheel perpetually sharpening one of his tools. Otto let out an audible sigh. Adolph this man, who was like a father to him was alright.

Otto had not realized how much he missed seeing the familiar figure, slightly bent from years of following the plow. He missed his easy smile and keen words of wisdom, his knowledge of the land and his love of country. Yes, it had been a good idea to make this trip today, not just to warn Adolph and Margried about the possible riot this weekend, but for his own piece of mind and wellbeing.

As soon as he was close enough, Otto yelled, "Good morning, Adolph, a fine morning to be alive."

Adolph looked up from his work, "My stars! What brings you so far out in the country on this beautiful week day?" the old man yelled.

"I just thought I would drop by and say gutten tag!" Otto called back as he stepped through the open barn door. "And a fine day it is for a little walk in the country."
The two men embraced and then slapped each other on the back almost embarrassed for their show of affection.

"Otto, it is wonderful to see you. How long has it been since you ventured out into the country."

"I am afraid that it has been much too long."
"What news do you have for me? Everyone is your family is good. Yea?"

"Yes, yes, everyone is fine at home. The children are growing like weeds and it becomes harder each day for their dedicated grandmothers to keep up with them. Hannah is working in the munitions factory and Elsa and Louisa are the ones who stand in the lines every day. Our latest letters from August and Georg indicate that they, too, are staying safe. Even Hannah's friend Paul seems to be safe for the time being. So, all is well."

"That was a very nice litany, and I am sure that Margried will want you to expand on all of those topics you just mentioned. She is very good at getting the details, as I am sure you know. However, you did not mention yourself." The old man looked his friend from head to foot and then in the eye. "How are you doing, and what are you doing out here on a weekday? Should you not be working, driving your trolley?"

"Of course, I should be at my job, but you know how I feel about working for others." Otto looked around the old barn, as if looking for a way out of this question. "All my adult life I have provided for my family by working for myself. I have always been a proud man, a successful businessman, driving and owning my taxi, one of the nicest in the city. I had steady regular customers who would ride only with me." Otto's chest began to swell with pride. "When I stopped in front of the better hotels, customers flocked to my vehicle because it was the finest taxi there. I made a good living all my life and now, because of this war, all of that is gone."

"I fear that sometimes you let your pride get the better of you." The old man knew his friend very well.

"Adolph, you do not understand, I was forced to give up my beautiful vehicle and return to the horses, and, when it became too difficult to feed them, I had to give them up too. I let my family down." He kicked at the dirt floor. "I just wanted to go to the barn and hide there. I could not. Many people depend on me. They could not know how ineffectual I felt. I have never shared this with any of them, not even Hedwig." Otto broke down, realizing his confession.

"I am sure that Hedwig knows how hard all this is for you and is silently supporting you in every way she can," Margried, said. She had unobtrusively entered the barn from the kitchen door when she saw Otto walking up the tree shaded drive.

Otto turned at the sound of her voice.

"Hedwig is a very strong and loving woman who knows you even better than you know yourself." Margried walked to this man she loved like her own son. "You have no need to hide anything from her. She will always be there for you." She wrapped her arms around him as she would have a child.

"Listen to Margried, my boy, She is the wisest woman I know," Adolph praised his wife. Stepping back, Margried cleared her throat and brushed a tear from her eye. "Now come into the house and have something to drink, then tell us why you really came all this way out into the country."

She hooked her arm in Otto's and let him help her into the house. "I am quite sure it is not because you were feeling guilty or because you wanted a day off." She patted his arm. "You have something on your mind that you felt you must tell us today."

* * *

Later in the kitchen, after Otto had given the old couple all details of each of his family members he finally got around to the real reason for his trip. "Yesterday when Louisa and Elsa were in the ration lines they heard very strong talk of women organizing a large gathering to come to the country and loot family farms such as yours. I thought that I must warn you and perhaps help you protect your farm and house."

Adolph put his glass down on the old scared wooden table. "Well, they will not find much on our farm. I am getting too old to do all this farming by myself." He rubbed his back as if to prove his point. "When the government representative came through and said they would be taking ninety percent of everything we grew and leave only ten percent for us, we discussed it and decided that we would plant no crops this year." He looked lovingly at his wife seated across the table. "Margried cannot help like she used to and we knew that it would be just too much for me alone."

Margried picked up the tray of cookies and offered another to each of the men. "We planted a large garden that we are enjoying this summer and will do our best to preserve things for the winter. She set the plate down and took another cookie herself. "We are lucky to have the animals so we have eggs and milk. The two of us do not need much more than that."

Adolph got up and wandered over to the window that looked out toward the road. "We have seen the women that come out each weekend looking for things to buy or steal. It has not been a concern for us. Most of them know us and know that we are old." He laughed a little at that. "They leave us alone."

"I made a sign that we put out each Saturday letting people know that there is nothing here. Show him Adolph." The old man pulled a piece of painted wood from behind the door "No Food Here" painted in red letters.

"Here, have some more tea." Margried picked up the pitcher. " Many of the farmers have signs that say they are willing to share, which really means sell, their crops. I am sure we will be fine. It will likely be no different than any other Saturday."

Otto held out his glass. "I believe it will be worse than usual. The girls said that the organizers already had ten thousand and were trying to get as many as ten thousand more women to go into the country this weekend and not buy or even negotiate." Otto took a drink of his tea. "The plan is to loot anything they can find. I fear this will be a very bad time. With your permission I would like to stay with you and try to help tomorrow."

Margried reached across the table and laid her small gnarled hand on Otto's. "Of course, you can stay. You are always welcome in our home. You are like a son to us and are proving that by the mere fact that you are here and so concerned. Although, I am sure that Adolph and I would be fine if you were not here."

* * * *

The three rose the next morning to gray skies, rain and temperatures much too cold for August. As they looked out of the window, Margried said with a wry smile, "Perhaps this day is God's way of discouraging those who would try to destroy our lives."

"If only that were true. I understand that these women are becoming more desperate each day, and, even more than that, they grow more discouraged with the war and the way the Kaiser is handling it."

"I am glad you are here, Otto." Adolph opened the door to the barn. "From what I am able to read and hear from talking to the surrounding farmers, there is a great deal of discontent with the Kaiser." The wise old man commented.

"It becomes more and more difficult to win a war when the populace does not fully support their government. I have seen it happen too many times in my lifetime."

"You both may be right, but for different reasons." Margried let go of the pump handle where she had been getting water to wash dishes. She subconsciously rubbed her shoulder. "Being a woman, I know that if we feel our families are in danger we will do most anything to protect them. I believe there could be ten thousand women. I would probably join them were I younger and in their position." She began to pick up the big pan full of water.

"Let me get that." Otto gently took the pan from her hands and set it in the sink.

"We women can be very powerful when we believe our families are threatened. Yes, I think that we had better be prepared for some trouble today."

The sounds of shouting and loud banging coming from a distance interrupted their conversation. The sound grew louder and more menacing each minute. Reaching the front porch, the trio saw the first of the throng of women and children that filled the road for as far as they could see back toward the city. They were shouting and banging on pots with wooden spoons. Many carried large cloth bags, already filled. Most marched right past the sign at the end of the lane that proclaimed no crops here. Some, however, seemed to pay no attention to the sign and started up the lane.

Otto left the porch running to head them off, Adolph limping along behind as best he could. "Can you not read the sign? There is nothing here. Old people, who have always supported their country and given it their all, occupy this land. They deserve to be left alone in peace."

"You do not look old to me!" shouted one of the women.

"We just want our share so we can feed our families."

"Can you not see that our children are starving? Give us some of what you have or we will take it all."

Adolph finally caught up with Otto. "The lad is right. We have no crops this year, only a small garden for our own use. There is nothing that we can do to help you."

The group stopped and looked around them, realizing that what they heard was true. There were no fields of anything except grass around them. Slowly they turned around and walked back up the lane to join the others.

Otto spent the rest of the day at the entrance to the lane doing his best to discourage those who would try to gain access to the farm. Adolph and Margried took turns sitting with him. By the evening they had watched a seemingly endless procession of humanity march boldly out into the countryside full of bravado and then straggle back, some with bags overflowing with food and others with very little to show for all their talk of looting and taking what was rightly theirs.

By sundown, the roads were nearly empty and the tired trio felt that they could safely go back to the house. Margried warmed some leftovers for the men to eat and limped off to the comfort of her bed. How glad she was that Otto had been there today. She knew that she and Adolph could never have saved their farm without him.

Much later, Otto sat quietly on the porch, his pipe in his mouth. He had long ago ceased being able to get tobacco, but he still enjoyed the feel of the pipe in his teeth. It was a beautiful evening. The chilly drizzle had stopped in the early afternoon and the sun dried the land. Tonight, the moon was very bright and seemed abnormally close to the earth. The stars were twinkling and just moments ago, he had seen a falling star. Perhaps there would be a meteor shower this evening. How nice to be out in the country on evenings like this.

The turbulence of the day had given way to the solitude and tranquility of this evening. The angry women and their families had all returned to the city, some with plenty, but many with the same concerns facing them tomorrow that provoked the frenzy of the scene today. Yet, now peace prevailed, at least for a short time.

Katydids sang their summer song with the frogs doing their best to sing harmony. There were other animal sounds as well. Occasionally the ringing of a bell around the neck of a cow could be heard as she lowered her head to graze. The sheep let out a random bleat while the nightingales sang their song. Otto leaned his head back and closed his eyes, taking it all in and enjoying just being alive.

He must have fallen asleep because surely he was dreaming. The sound of someone crying crept into his conscience, waking him. Slowly he sat up and listened. The animal sounds where still there, but there was definitely the sound of human crying, as well. Cautiously he left the porch and walked around the corner of the house to where the garden was. There in the garden was a woman, her back bent picking tomatoes from the vines. Quietly he walked up behind her, not wanting to scare her; she might have a weapon of some type. He just wanted to know what she thought she was doing and ask her civilly to leave.

"Ho there, woman, who do you think you are, picking things from a garden that is not yours?" He whispered menacingly near her ear.

The woman jumped then fell to her knees in the dirt and began to cry in earnest, "I came out with the crowd earlier today but there was no food left for me to take. My family is so hungry. I just want to help them."

"So you think that it is alright to steal from old people. Your family is more important than theirs?"

"No, no, I did not know they are old. I just need help for my family. I have four children and they are all hungry. My husband was hurt in the war and is home. His injury healed but he will not get out of bed. I fear that this terrible war has changed his head forever. I have to go to work in the factory every day. My oldest, who is only eight stands in to the bread lines, but she is so young and the others take advantage of her," she sobbed. Getting up from her knees, "I am sorry I will leave now. I never meant to make a hardship for someone else. Please do not hurt me, I will leave now."

"No, wait, what is your name?" Otto was not sure why he asked. She was leaving. He should just let her go. Yet somehow, her story had touched him.

"My name is Hilke. Why do you want to know?"

Otto did not have an answer for her. He just knew that he could not let her go without something for her family. "Here, let me help you get some things for your family. I am sure that Adolph and Margried would not mind sharing some with you and your family." With that, he began helping fill her bag with fresh vegetables from the garden, making sure that they left plenty for the kind old couple who lived on this farm.

Chapter 34
August 1916
Düsseldorf, Germany

Elsa plopped the potato into the pot of cold water, "Momma, have you noticed that Hannah has been acting strange recently?"

"Elsa, please be more careful when you put those potatoes in the in the pot. You are getting water everywhere. I am trying to get these jars ready for canning. I do not want potato water all over them."

"Yes, Momma," she picked up another potato and began to peel it.

"To answer your question, I have noticed that she has been a bit withdrawn, but I think that may be natural for her age."

"Perhaps, but this is different. It seems like she hardly ever talks anymore." Elsa put the potato carefully in the water. "I've been paying attention: at dinner last night she didn't say one single word. That's just not like Hannah."

"I think you worry too much."

"No, Momma, it's more than that. I'm worried, yes, but with real reason. You're just so busy being a grandmother that you haven't noticed." She picked up a carrot and began peeling it.

"I am busy being a grandmother all day because you are off waiting in the lines." Hedwig turned to look at her daughter. "Sometimes I am so tired when dinnertime comes that I can barely walk to the table. Yes, you are right; I have not paid attention to Hannah." The look on Hedwig's face one of anguish.

"Oh, Momma, I didn't mean that you were doing something wrong. Please don't take what I said that way. I only meant..."

"I know what you meant. It is alright." The older woman wiped her face on her big apron as she turned back to the stove. "I will try to do better."

"Perhaps I should try talking to her." Elsa put the carrot in the pot with the potatoes.

"That is a good idea," Hedwig's voice still a little shaky. "I am sure she will tell you if something is bothering her."

Elsa picked another carrot and began peeling. "There, I think this will be the last one. That should be enough for dinner. What else can I do to help you?'

"You could go out into the garden and pick beans and tomatoes for me." Hedwig rubbed her back." Picking is just so hard for me these days." The wear of the times showing on her face. "I am trying to get as much done as I can this afternoon while it is so quiet. Louisa has taken Elsbeth and gone to visit her friend. Genevieve is next door sitting with Frau Higgenbaucher; she has just lost another son and is beside herself."

"I'm not sure how much longer Gus will nap but I will be glad to work in the garden until he wakes up," Elsa got up from the table. "I know, I'll go upstairs and see if Hannah will help me."

"What a good idea. Maybe you can get her to talk to you."

"I'll do my best." Elsa climbed the stairs quietly so as not to wake Gus.

Hannah's door was closed. "Hannah," Elsa quietly called. There was no answer.

"Hannah." She gently called again.

"Go away."

"Hannah, I need your help."

"What do you want?" Hannah asked through the closed door.

"Momma would like us to help pick tomatoes and beans."

"Why didn't Momma ask me?"

"Why would Momma climb the stairs when I could do it for her? Come on now, we really do need your help."

"Oh, alright I'm coming." Hannah opened the door. "I just have to put my shoes on."

"Meet me in the garden. I'll get the baskets."

The sun was shining and the temperature was relatively cool. "I wish the weather would stay this way. It's a beautiful day." Elsa picked a tomato from the laden vine. "I'm afraid it will get hot again soon though."

"It will probably rain again. It seems like all it has done this summer is rain." Hannah put her basket down next to the beans.

"Yes, we've had a lot of rain. Momma is afraid that all the rain will affect the potatoes. She says that potatoes do not like too much rain. They begin to rot right in the ground." Hannah stripped a handful of string beans from the vine. "The wet doesn't seem to have affected the beans."

Elsa stood up and looked at her younger sister who somehow looked older than her eighteen years. "Hannah has something been bothering you?"

"Nothing is bothering me." Hannah declared.

"Are you sure? You just seem very quiet."

"I don't know what you are talking about." Hannah put another handful of beans in the basket, being careful not to look at her sister.

"You just seem different somehow, more distant."

"Nothing is wrong." Hannah's voice sounded defensive.

"I really do think something is bothering you. You're just not my bubbly, always smiling baby sister anymore."

Hannah stood up, dropping the basket on the ground. "What do you expect? We live in a country that is at war. The men we care about are putting their lives in danger every day." Her voice was beginning to rise. "Your own husband, for God's sake, has not been home for nearly two years. Of course I have things that I worry about."

"I still don't think that you are telling me everything. Something is eating at you."

"Elsa, you just can't leave things alone can you?" Hannah threw a handful of beans in the basket with such force that most fell on the ground. "No, you never could. Always in someone else's business. Nothing is wrong with me that enough food on the table, an end to the war and all the men come home safe would not fix."

"Hannah why are you overreacting like this?" Elsa had not expected this kind of reaction.

"Overreacting? look who's talking. You just keep pushing, looking for something that's not there." Hannah walked to the end of the row of beans. "Mind your own business and leave me alone. You don't need me out here." She started toward the house. "You pick the vegetables. I'm sure you'll do a fine job." Hannah was running up the porch stairs now. "Or is this too much hard labor for you?"

"Hannah, what a cruel thing to say."

"Elsa, you have no idea what cruel is. I will trade just one day with you. I will go stand in the lines and you go do my job in the factory." The door slammed and she was gone.

Stunned, Elsa carefully put the basket with tomatoes down and climbed the back steps. What was going on with that child? She was more sure than ever that something serious was bothering Hannah.

Before she could reach the door, it flew open. "What did you say to your sister? She came through here crying like her heart was broken." Hedwig's voice was irate.

"I don't know, Momma. I just asked if something was bothering her and she went off on a tangent. I'm more certain than ever that there really is a problem. I'm going upstairs and try to talk to her."

"Over my dead body you are. You are going to leave her alone."

"No, Momma, I have to talk to her."

"Now is not the time." Momma stood her full five feet tall and moved between Elsa and the kitchen.

"I think now is the time." Elsa insisted. "Now please let me through."

"I have said that this is not the time. And you will respect your mother."

"Why are you doing this? You are treating me like a child. I am thirty-four years old and do not need you telling me what I can and cannot do." Elsa's voice was rising.

"You may be thirty-four but I am fifty-five, and I am your mother. You are living in my house and you will do as I say."

Elsa stood her ground. "Do we really have to have this conversation? Hannah is in some kind of trouble and I want to help her." Elsa realized that was being disrespectful of her mother. She lowered her voice. "Momma, I am really sorry. I should never have yelled at you. Please forgive me."

"Well, I...." Hedwig lowered her own voice. "I do not know what has gotten into me." Hedwig suddenly looked much older than her years as she sank into a chair."

"Momma, I truly believe that something has happened to cause Hannah to act this way." Elsa sat beside her mother and gently rubbed her mother's arm. Something is wrong, I just know it."

"Elsa, perhaps you are right." Hedwig heaved a big sigh. "Please try not to be too hard with her."

* * *

Elsa climbed the steps, stopping midway to consider what to say. After a few minutes she heaved a sigh of resolve and climbed the rest of the steps and walked down the hall to the door to Hannah's room.

"Hannah, I'm sorry for all the things I said. Can we please talk for a few minutes?"

"I don't want to talk to you or anyone else."

Elsa tried the door. It was unlocked. Quietly she opened it to find Hannah sitting on the bed, arms wrapped around her knees, rocking back and forth. The bed groaned as Elsa carefully sat down and laid her hand on Hannah's. Hannah did not pull away. "What is it, darling? I can tell something is terribly wrong."

Hannah did not answer. She just continued to rock. "Is it Paul? Have you and Paul had a falling out?"

"No."

"I know you got a letter from him last week. I brought in the mail." She spied a stack of letters on the little table in the corner of the room. Getting up she walked across the room. "Look, here is that very letter, unopened."

"You have no right to look at my mail." The response sounded half-hearted at best.

"Why haven't you opened this letter?"

"It doesn't matter what it says."

"What do you mean? Of course, it matters. It's from Paul. If you won't open it, I will."

There was no response from Hannah, just rocking.

"This letter says you told Paul not to come visit. He seems very upset by that." Elsa looked from the letter to her sister. "What is going on with you? Why don't you want Paul to visit?" Elsa's feeling of dismay was growing. "Not long ago you ran to the mailbox every day to see if there was a letter from him."

"He wouldn't want to see me if I let him come, not after what happened."

"What are you talking about?" Elsa was back on the bed beside her sister, looking her straight in the eyes this time. "Hannah, talk to me."

"There is nothing left to talk about. What happened, happened and it can't be changed."

"Hannah, you're not making any sense. What happened?"

"Telling you won't change anything. So what's the use?" Hannah stared out the window.

Elsa put her hand on her sister's shoulder. "Maybe telling me will make you feel better.

"Nothing will ever make me feel better," Hannah's voice was barely audible.

"You need to talk."

"I don't know where to begin. It's just too awful."

"You can tell me anything," Elsa's voice was gentle. "I'll do whatever I can to help."

"No one can help me."

"Let me be the judge of that."

Hannah finally looked at her sister. "It all happened at work back in June."

"What happened?"

"I was having a very difficult day, it seemed like I couldn't do anything right. I had made four bad cartridges before lunch."

"So, why is that such a problem?"

"The munitions factory is a terrible place to work. We may not talk or even look at our friends. We are penalized for every mistake we make."

"I have heard other women say those same things." Elsa agreed.

"At lunch time Herr Yeager, he was the floor manager, came over and bothered us; especially me. I made fun of him and that made him mad."

"Probably not a wise thing to do." Elsa said with a nervous laugh.

"I knew better, but I just did not care that day." Hannah stopped and stared out the window again.

After some time, Elsa prompted, "What happened then?"

Hannah slowly turned to look at her sister. "After lunch, I was daydreaming about Paul's latest letter and made another mistake. Herr Yeager saw me putting it in my apron pocket." Now the words seemed to be tumbling out of her mouth. "He came up behind me, grabbed my arm, and made me go to a private room in the back of the building with no windows."

Elsa felt her breath catch. What had this brute done to her baby sister?

"He pushed me up against a table and untied my apron. Then he made me sit in a chair and he tied my hands behind me with my own apron strings." Hannah's voice was full of furor as she told the story.

"How could he do such horrible things to you?" Elsa asked with an air of incredulity.

"That was just the beginning. He unbuttoned my blouse and tore my undergarment. When I tried to kick him, he slapped me on my breast. I just laughed at him and he hit me again so I spit on him."

Now Elsa could barely speak, "Oh my, child, what did he do then?"

"He opened his trousers and exposed himself to me. He rubbed himself on my breasts and...and.." She began to gag and could not go on.

Elsa held Hannah's hands for a long time, said nothing and waited for Hannah to relax so she could go on.

Finally, Hannah got herself under control and began speaking again. "He rubbed my face with his awful thing. He told me to open my mouth but I refused." The gagging started again.

Elsa was having trouble not being sick herself.

"He slapped me again and then forced himself into my mouth. I bit him. HARD! Just about that time, his Onkle, Herr Braun, came in and was very angry. He made Herr Yeager leave and has never let him come back."

Elsa wrapped her arms around her sister. "You poor, brave little girl. How could anyone hurt you like that." She was not sure who was crying the most, Hannah or herself. Finally, she pulled away and sat up staring at her little sister. "What did Herr Braun say to you?"

"He just told me to get dressed and go back to work. And that I was never to speak of this again to anyone."

"And you haven't, have you? I bet you haven't even told Ingrid."

"No, I haven't told Ingrid, and I certainly cannot tell Paul. That's why I can't allow him to come and visit. He must never see me again." The tears were flowing down Hannah's cheeks again. "I will never be with any man. I would be too ashamed."

"Why should you be ashamed? You have done nothing wrong."

"But a man touched me. I had that awful man in my mouth."

"You did what you had to do. I am sure he had planned much worse and you stopped him. You were very brave. Any good and decent man would be proud of what you did."

"I do not believe you. No man will ever want me now."

Elsa took Hannah by the shoulders. "Look at me."

Hannah turned her head away.

"Hannah, look at me now."

Obediently Hannah finally looked at her older sister.

"Listen to what I am telling you." Elsa lowered her voice. "You need to tell Paul what happened and let him decide."

"No, I can't do that. He can never know what happened to me."

"Hannah, do you trust me to tell you the truth?"

After some hesitation Hannah said, "Yes, I trust you.

"You understand that I will only tell what I believe is best for you?"

"Yes ,but I was, and am so very scared."

"I think I can understand how afraid you must have been. I can only begin to guess how you feel now. However, I have a lot more experience with men than you have." Elsa stopped. She wanted to make sure she had the right words. I am your big sister and you need to listen. Everything I have seen of Paul tells me he is a good man. I also believe he loves you."

"That is what he tells me."

"Then, you must explain to him what happened just as you have with me. Let him decide."

"I don't think that I can do that." The tears began to flow down Hannah's cheeks again.

"It will be extremely hard, but you must." Elsa picked up Paul's letter from the side of the bed where she had dropped it. "Here read this letter and then write an answer, explaining why you have been so distant and wait for him to respond."

"What if he never wants to see me again? I do not think I could live with that." Hannah wiped her hand across her face.

"I believe that you will be surprised what he says and does."

"Do you really think so?"

Yes, I do. I would never lie to you."

Hannah cautiously stood up and wrapped her arms around her sister, "Elsa,.... She struggled to gain her composure. "I love you."

There was no need for more words. Elsa wrapped her arms around Hannah.

The mingled tears of the sisters eventually found their way to faded cloth of the bed.

After a long time, Elsa pulled away, laid the letter from Paul on the bed and quietly left the room. She stumbled to the stair and nearly fell before she finally collapsed on the step. She laid her head on her knees and sobbed. It was just not right. How dare that man hurt her sister? If she could get her hands on him she would probably kill him.

How would she ever be able to look at her sister again without seeing that terrible anguish that had played across her face as she told her story? Hannah your story is safe with me. I will never tell anyone. It will always be our secret.

"Elsa, what is wrong?" Momma asked from the kitchen.

"Nothing, Momma. Everything is fine. I'm just tired."

Chapter 35
Early September 1916
Bonn, Germany

"Corporal Ulhman."

Paul looked up from the cemetery plot he was working on when he heard his name called.

"Corporal Ulhman, are you out here?" the disembodied voice called louder.

Paul put down his trowel and stood up, "I'm here in row twenty-three."

"Oh yes, I see you now. You are wanted at the front desk."

"Thank you; please tell them that I'll be there soon." It was late in the afternoon so he made some scribbles on his plat of the grounds, picked up his tools and put them in the cloth bag he had fashioned and slung it over his shoulder.

Paul looked over his handiwork. There, spread out in front of him were twenty-three rows of neat white crosses, twenty to a row, perfectly spaced in relation to the others around it. Each row of crosses was exactly eleven feet from the row in front of it and five from the one on either side. The rows were straight and even, no matter what direction you looked. He had room for exactly fifteen more rows. Only three hundred more fallen comrades in this cemetery. His heart of hearts told him that it would not be enough. Perhaps if the war ended today, but the battle in Verdun, France had been going on since April and showed no signs of ending soon.

This was the second 'holding area' he had turned into a cemetery since being discharged from the hospital. He was sure there would be many more before this war was over.

With one last glance back, he headed for the big stone building in front of him, once a church, now, a hospital. He could smell injury and death as soon as he opened the door, that sickeningly sweet combination of antiseptic, sweat and fear that permeated every hospital in which he had been. Someday this building might be a church again but he doubted that the smell would ever go away.

"Frau Englehardt, someone asked me to stop at your desk today. What can I do for you?"

"Corporal Ulhman, I have a letter for you. I wanted to make sure that you got it before you left for your rooms today. It looks like it might be from someone named Hannah."

Paul cringed at the invasion of his privacy. No one had the right to comment on his mail. "Thank you Frau Englehardt."

"I hope this letter makes your evening a happy one."

Paul left without saying another word. He stuffed the letter in his pocket and began the three-block walk to his room, wondering what Hannah could possibly have to say after her last letter telling him that she did not want to see him. He had written back his disappointment but expected no answer. That had been well over a month ago.

Deciding he was hungry, he entered a little brauhaus. The food here was almost tolerable. Each day they served some kind of stew and watered down beer. At least the food was hot and the beer warm. What more could a man ask?

When he had finished eating he wandered back outside, stopped in a small park and sat staring at the birds. There were a few children playing as their mothers or older siblings keep a close watch. This was almost a happy place. The sun was setting on a beautiful summer day. There should be lovers walking in this charming place. But alas, there were none. All the men were off fighting and the women struggling just to stay alive, feed their families or work in the factories. When would this horror end?

With these dark thoughts in mind, Paul got up and walked the last little bit to his room. The gloom continued as he unlocked his door and entered the miniscule room, only big enough for a bed, chest of drawers, a small table with one straight-backed chair. The walls were bare and the one window faced the wall of the house next door, the space so small that the sun had to squint to get through.

He dropped his tools in the corner and fell to the bed. His body was tired but his mind raced. Cautiously he took Hannah's letter from his pocket, almost as though it would bite him. He held it up but could see nothing out of the ordinary about it. It was too dim in the room to read so he lit the one gas lamp that sat on the chest of drawers by his bed. Eventually, he opened the envelope and carefully extracted the three pages filled with Hannah's familiar scribble. When they had first started corresponding he had a difficult time reading her writing. Over time and many letters, he had gotten used to it and looked forward to some of the silly things she said or the strange way she formed many of her letters. It was uniquely Hannah, part of what drew him to her. He pressed the sheets straight and began reading:

> Dearest Paul,
> This is the most difficult letter that I will ever write. When you have finished reading, you will understand why I told you not to come visit me. You will understand why we must never see each other ever again.

What was she talking about? Frantically he began searching the letter. Words jumped out at him: assaulted, hit, slapped, exposed... He had to stop. He could not get his breath. Something terrible had happened to Hannah. Someone had hurt her. After some time, he was calm enough to think rationally. He went back to the beginning of the letter and read every word.

Then as he read the letter again, anger grew from a small burning coal in the pit of his stomach to a great angry giant that had to come out. He began beating on the bed and walls, screaming at the top of his lungs. How could this have happened to Hannah? His Hannah? A great brute of a man had inflicted himself on the woman he loved. The only thought in his head was that he needed to find this...this...this Herr Yeager and punish him for what he had done. How dare he lay a hand on his Hannah!

He picked up the letter and reread the atrocities; his anger, which had begun to subside, rose again, this time aimed at Hannah. She had assumed that he would not want to see her again. How could she think so little of him? He was pacing the small room. Was she so unsure of his feelings for her that she thought this would make him care for her less? Why would she think that? Why hadn't she told him when this first happened? What was wrong with her? Didn't she love him? He threw himself on the bed, tears of anger and frustration flowing freely.

There was no answer for any of his questions and he felt so helpless. Now he took aim at himself. Getting up he once again he pounded on the wall until his fists ached. He had not been there to protect her. It was all his fault; he should have been there instead of here in Bonn. He could have stopped this from happening.

Eventually sanity began to return to his troubled mind. He walked to the small table took some paper and a pen from a box where he kept his few personal things, moved the lamp to the table and pulled the lone chair to the table as well. He sat staring at the blank paper for a long time. He remembered a cold December night more than two years ago when he had sat just so, trying to decide what to say in an equally important letter. Finally, the words came to him. It was so simple really; there was only one way to answer this letter.

My Most Darling Hannah,
        Where do I begin? The anger that enveloped me as I read your letter nearly drove me insane. Anger at Herr Yeager, anger at you, anger at me, anger at this impossible war and anger at God for letting this happen to you. When my anger subsided, all that was left within me was my overwhelming love for you. Nothing will ever stop my love for you.
        My job is all about death and dying. I do my best to make the final resting place for these men a place of peace and dignity. I say a small prayer for each one as I inscribe his name on a simple white wooden cross. I plant some grass and flowers when I can. With each grave I mark, I understand that my name could be on the next cross.
        So, please, Hannah do not shut me out of your life. I wear your love like a raincoat that protects me from being the next name on a cross.
                                        Yours in love forever,
                                        Paul

        Paul folded the letter and put it in an envelope, blew out the light and was asleep almost before his body reached the bed.

Chapter 36
Late September 1916
Düsseldorf, Germany

"Momma, Momma, Gus haben si gelb blatt," Gus exclaimed running to his mother, waving a fallen maple leaf. The mothers and grandmothers all laughed as the towheaded little boy came running up to them, curls bouncing around his face. Elsa, Hedwig and Genevieve all carried baskets full of apples while Louisa had Elsbeth in her arms.

"Yes, that certainly is beautiful. Now try it in English. I have a yellow leaf."

"Gus habe a yeyo leab." He hugged his mother leg. "See Momma, Gus can do it."

Elsa patted her son on the head, "Yes, you can. Your English is nearly as good as your German. Good boy! Now go see what else you can find this beautiful day."
He beamed at his mother and nearly fell as he ran ahead of the women again.

"Elsa, why do you insist that sweet little boy say everything in English." Louisa frowned, "He is speaking German just like everyone around him."

Elsa stopped and stared at her sister-in-law, "You know very well that Gus is American. He will speak English."

"There you go again, all about being American. Yet, here you are living in Germany with your German parents and family while your husband fights in the German army. That sounds very German to me." Louisa said with an air of self-righteousness.

"How dare you talk like that to me? I don't tell you how to raise you daughter."

Louisa shifted Elsbeth from one hip to the other. "I don't try to make my daughter into something she's not." The little girl began to fuss at her mother's tone.

"What do you know about what I do? You have barely been out of the city of Düsseldorf, let alone out of the country of Germany. You have no right to tell me anything. My son was born in America and is an American citizen." Elsa was angry now.

Hedwig stepped between the two girls. "Elsa, perhaps Louisa is right this time. The Americans seem more and more to be our enemies. Teaching Gus English could be very dangerous for him."

"Momma, not you too!" Elsa could feel the tears forming, "I don't care what any of you say. Gus will speak English when Georg and I take him back to America."

"You see, Elsa, even your own mother agrees with me." Louisa's voice carried a tone of haughtiness. "You are so certain that you are going back to America."

"I am going back to America, Louisa. Not you or anyone else can tell me different."

"It does not look that way to me." Louisa continued to spur her on. "You stand in the bread lines with me every day just trying to survive. When are you going to stop living in a fantasy world and live in the real world, here in Düsseldorf, Germany."

"I do what I have to do." Hands on hips, Elsa stared at Louisa. "Just like you do."

"Well, you need to give up your dreams. You will probably never go back to America. You got lucky and lived in America for a few years, but that was a long time ago." There was just a hint of jealousy in Louisa's voice. "Now you are here so you need to accept that and forget about America."

"No, Never!" The tears stung Elsa's cheeks. "You don't know anything. So don't even try to tell me what to do." Elsa's rage continued to grow. "I hate you!" She stamped her foot. "I will take my son home someday. You just wait. You'll see. I will!" She threw back her weary shoulders and strutted ahead of the other women with as much dignity as she could garner wearing her worn out shoes and patched dress. I will take him home. I am doing the right thing for my son. I know I am.

Hedwig turned to her daughter-in-law. "Do not take what Elsa says to heart. She is just frustrated, as we all are by the situation. She is not really angry at you."

Louisa kept walking. "I know but sometimes the things she says are so hurtful. It's not even the things she says as much as her attitude. She always acts as if she is better than all the rest of us just because she lived in America for a few years." Elsbeth was struggling in her mother's arms, so Louisa put her down.

Genevieve gently put a hand on her daughter's arm. "She is only trying to do what she thinks is best for her son. We may not agree, however, we must allow her to do, as she sees fit for her family."

"But, Momma…"

"Louisa, these are difficult times. You and I are extremely fortunate to be able to live with Hedwig and Otto. Please, darling, try to understand how Elsa must fee…." A racking cough stopped Genevieve.

"Momma, are you alright?" Louisa patted her mother's back.

Hedwig set her basket down and took the one Genevieve was carrying. "Your cough is getting worse," Hedwig sounded worried.

Genevieve seemed unable to stop coughing and was having trouble standing. Louisa gently helped her sit down on a curbstone. Genevieve sat there for some time unable to catch her breath. The coughing finally stopped.

"That was the worst one yet, Momma. I am beginning to believe that there is something wrong."

Unable to speak yet, Genevieve waived off all their offers of help. Unsteadily she got up. "I....am....fi...." She could not go on. The coughing, milder this time began again.

Elsa, stopped when the commotion began and ran back to see what was happening. Louisa looked to be in such distress as she watched her mother, Elsa put her arm around her friend "Oh, Louisa, I didn't mean to hurt you. I don't know what has gotten into me lately. Everything is just so hard. Will our lives ever be as they once were? I wonder if this horrible war will go on forever." The words just seemed to tumble out of Elsa's mouth, "You know I love my family here in Germany, it is just that I am so lonely and homesick. Can you ever forgive me, please?"

Louisa nodded and continued to watch her mother as the second spell subsided.

Hedwig, always the one to bring peace in the family, tried to stir the conversation in a new direction. "Will you look at those two playing in the leaves? I do believe that Gus is growing so fast that he will soon be taller than his mother." That brought a laugh from all the women.

"His long trousers look like lederhosen they are getting so short." Hedwig observed. "I am quite sure that I have some fabric in the attic that would be perfect to make trousers for him"

"That would be wonderful, Momma. My biggest concern for him, though is shoes. He is fast outgrowing what he has. I am not sure what I will do when winter comes. He loves being outside so. I must have something for his feet."

"Frau Higgenbaucher, next door, raised four boys. Perhaps she still has some of their old shoes hidden away somewhere," Hedwig said. "I will make a point to ask her if she can find it in heart to look for a pair."

"Momma, she has lost so much, both Erik and Albert dead in Russia and her other two sons serving in Africa. I do not what to make things harder for her."

"I have known Frieda Higgenbaucher since those boys were babies. I will take her some of these beautiful apples that we have picked from the tree in Genevieve's yard. I expect she will be glad to help with shoes for Gus."

Genevieve, finally able to speak again, "I am surprised that those apples were still there." Her voice became raspier with each word. "I really expected them to be gone."
"I did too," Hedwig agreed. "We are going to enjoy some fine baked apples this evening along with our stew. It will be a real treat to have something sweet."

"Momma, Momma, man." Gus came running, gesturing toward their house.

"Look, Elsa," Louisa pointed, "He's right. There's a man standing by the front door."

"I see what you mean. There is a man in uniform..." Elsa heard her mother gasp. A man in uniform could only mean one thing.

The little group of women stopped, no one wanting to be the first to hear the worst. The man left the steps and began walking toward them. The closer he got, Elsa recognized familiar things about him.

Suddenly she was running. "Georg, Georg." She flew into her husband's arms crying and laughing all at the same time. He picked her up and swung her around. She felt like a schoolgirl again, every care in the world vanished in an instant as the man she loved swept her off her feet.

By the time Georg set her back on her feet, the rest of the group surrounded the couple, all of them talking at the same time.

"Slow down. I can't answer all of your questions at once." Georg pulled his wife closer to his side. "How can one man manage so many beautiful women all at one time? I promise that I will answer all of your questions. Just now, I want to see my wife and son. That child playing over there can't possibly be Gus; he is much too big to be my baby boy."

"Of course, he's Gus; he did not stop growing, just because you went away."

"Do you think that he will remember me?"

Gus looked up at the strange man who had joined this mother and grandmother. Not at all sure that he liked the idea of someone standing close to this mother, he picked up another leaf. "Momma look, Gus hab mor yeyo leab."

"Yes, that is a beautiful leaf and your English is very good." His momma bent down and held out her hands. "Gus, look who has come home to see us. Say hello to your Papa."

Gus gladly allowed his mother to pick him up and he quickly buried his face in the safety of her shoulder.

"Gus, look at your papa. He wants to meet you."

Very slowly he turned his head so one eye peeked out. What was his momma talking about? The man standing there looked nothing like his papa? This man had dark hair on his face and head. His papa had white hair. This was definitely not his papa. "Nein, papa."

"Yes, Gus this is your papa."

"Nein." Gus tucked his face back in Elsa's shoulder. He felt the man touch his leg. He pulled away.

"Gus that is not nice. You are not usually shy around people."

What was she talking about? This was not just any person. She was saying this was his papa. Maybe it would be okay to at least look at this strange man. Cautiously he turned his face toward the man. He is smiling and Momma seems to like him. They are standing very close together.

"Good boy, Gus. See Papa will not hurt you. He wants to meet you."

I wish she would stop calling this man papa. The big man was laughing now and holding out his hands. Maybe it will be alright.

* * *

Georg sat on the ground rolling a ball they had found in the barn, while Gus chased after it and threw it back. Otto sat on the stoop; pipe held gently in his mouth, he caressed the bowl as he had always done. This man has not changed one bit, Georg thought. He has always been and will always be the rock of this family.

The ball hit him in chest and he faked an injury falling back as Gus jumped on him, giggles of delight bubbling forth. Georg could not believe his good fortune at having such a delightful child waiting for him when he came home. He had not even been able to imagine what this child looked like or how his laughter sounded. He would cherish this moment and take all of the sounds, sights and feelings with him as he began his new assignment.

The ball hit him again. He happened to glance up as he fell back on the ground to another round of Gus' laughter. There in the window was Elsa, his beautiful Elsa. His longing for her had become a physical ache as the afternoon and evening had progressed. Now seeing her in the window, he worried he would disappoint her. She was such a beautiful woman; always had been. He was such an ordinary man.

There was nothing outstanding about him, he thought. Yet this beautiful and funny woman had chosen him. Now, after his being gone so long would she still want him, as much as he wanted her?

Many, in fact, most of his friends had found women in the town to spend time with and he was sure they spent much more than just time. Often they asked if he wanted to join them. Always a sister or friend would be glad to spend an evening with him. He always resisted. Sometimes it was very difficult. But when he wanted to give in, he would picture Elsa in his mind and no one else could even begin to compare to her. Therefore, he had been with no other woman since that day he left this house back in the fall of 1914. Now he could barely stand the anticipation. Only this little boy angel sitting on his chest jabbering away kept him from running up the stairs this moment.

Just then, the door opened and Hannah appeared. "Gus, it is time to get ready for bed. You and I are going to have a special time tonight. We are going to have a party, just you and me. Come along now and let's get ready."

Gus jumped off Georg's chest and ran to meet his Tanta. "Party?"

Georg got up slowly from the ground, brushed off his uniform and walked to join Otto on the steps. "I can't believe what a beautiful child he has become. Elsa is doing a good job raising him."

"Yes she is. She is a wonderful mother." Georg could hear the pride in Otto's voice.

"I want to thank you too, Otto, for being his Papa. He needs a man in his life. I can think of no one I would rather have than you taking my place."

"I will never take your place, Georg. I am his grandfather and love him with my heart and soul but will never replace you. Come we will take walk down to Hagen's for a short glass. That will give the women time to get the babies and themselves ready for bed. I am sure that Elsa will need a little extra time this evening."

"Is Hagen's still open? I know that many of the beer gardens have closed because there are no supplies for making beer."

"Hagen's is open, but just barely. I suspect the government officials and owners of the factories have some ways of getting supplies through the blockade. I know that Hagen is not above taking advantage of an opportunity if presented to him. I believe I would do the same, were I in his shoes."

"I expect you are right Otto. I would enjoy a glass of Hagen's finest, even if it does taste like dishwater."

"I have been wondering, Georg, why have you come home now after so long?"

"I need to talk to you about that, Otto. But you must promise me that you will say nothing to Elsa."

Chapter 37
A few minutes earlier
Düsseldorf, Germany

Elsa stood near the window of her room at the top of the house. There, below were her husband and her son. She felt her heart would burst as she watched them playing ball and rolling on the ground together. This was the kind of scene she dreamed about every night. Georg looked so handsome in his uniform. She could hardly believe this man was her husband. How she longed for him. She had long ago pushed all of her physical needs from her mind. She had even given up trying to picture him because it only made her miss him more. Now just looking at him, her feelings of longing were nearly overwhelming.

"Elsa, stop daydreaming and come back to us. He will still be there in a few minutes," Hannah's voice held a hint of jealousy. "This is what Louisa and I have decided. She and Elsbeth are going to sleep in my room while Georg is here and I am going to take Gus downstairs and we will camp-out on the floor there."

"That is not necessary."

"We all know that. This will just make things nicer for you and Georg."

"Gus has never slept with anyone but me. He may not sleep well."

"Don't you worry about that. I will make it a game and I'm sure he'll be fine."

"If you say so." She sounded like a little girl.

"Papa is going to help us move Louisa's bed into this room that way you and Georg can have a bigger bed and no one else will be sleeping on this floor so you have some privacy."

All of the tension from earlier in the afternoon was gone when Louisa said, "I am so jealous, I can hardly stand it. I know that I have seen August since you have seen Georg, but I was so sick I hardly remember. Georg looks wonderful; you are a very lucky woman, Elsa, very lucky."

Elsa knew what they were saying was very true and they were trying to make it as comfortable as possible for Georg and her. Neither comfort nor worry was her main concern now. She wondered, could she be the woman she was before he left? So much had happened. She missed him so much, she was afraid that he would be disappointed in her and yet she could hardly wait for this night to come. She finally turned from the window and looked at her sister. "Thank both of you. You don't have to do this."

"We're not doing it because we have to but because we want to." Hannah closed the curtain. "Now we must get things ready."

"Georg and I will be just fine in the room the way it is."

"No! We both insist that you must have some privacy." Louisa said with longing her voice. "I know you will do the same for me when August comes home,"

"Thank you, I don't know what else to say. This is all just so overwhelming." Elsa took the hands of each of the women beside her. "Thank you, I love you both so much." She looked at her sister-in-law. "Louisa, August will be home soon. He just has to." She hugged her sisters aware of the tears slipping down Louisa's cheek. Soon all three were crying and laughing, the tension of the afternoon long forgotten, these three extraordinary women just glad that they had each other to help them get through the hard times and the good times, as well.

* * *

Genevieve took the dirty dish from Hedwig and plunged it into the warm soapy water. "It is wonderful to have Georg home. The look on Elsa's face almost makes all we have been through worthwhile."

"I am so pleased at how quickly Gus has taken to him." Hedwig cleaned the crumbs off another plate and handed it to Genevieve.

"I only wish that we could all be here together again the way we were before this terrible war."

"Of course we will all be together again. What are you thinking?"

"I know in my heart that we will be. I am not at all sure if it will be in this world or the next."

"Genevieve, how dare you talk like that? All of our boys are coming back and we will be a family again."

"You are right, as usual, Hedwig. However, I am not sure that I will be here to see it happen."

"Just because you have a little cough. It is just a cold and you will be fine soon. I will have Otto get Dr. Ostermann to come by and see you. He will tell you I am right."

"There is no need for the doctor. It is probably nothing, just a little chest cold. Perhaps you could make one of your famous mustard packs for my chest. I feel certain that would resolve my problem," Genevieve said, knowing in her heart that nothing was going to make a difference this time. She knew something was very wrong, she could sense it more than feel it. Nevertheless, she would keep her secret as long as she could. The rest of this family all had too many other worries to be concerned about her. She was an old woman and had lived a good life. When her time came, she would not fight it.

* * *

Later that evening Georg and Elsa were finally alone, each with their own private hopes and fears for this evening. Elsa had found a nightgown she wore on the ship when they came home for a wonderful summer vacation. Somehow, that dream trip had turned into the nightmare they were now living. She had not worn this gown for more than two years and felt very self-conscious.

"You are the most beautiful woman I have ever seen," Georg said as he pulled her to him and gently kissed her forehead. "You have no idea how much I've missed and longed for you. I have dreamed of this moment since the day I left."

"Oh, my love, I've missed you too. Sometimes it hurt so badly that I would cry myself to sleep at night. Every time I look at Gus I see you and all the wonderful times we had together and how we made that perfect child."

After that there was no more talking. Their mutual longing took over and they both discovered that indeed things had changed. Their love and joy in each other increased by a thousand fold.

Finally they lay quietly, still entwined, neither spoke. There were no words. Both knew that they had never been this close before. All they could do was hold on to each other for their very lives depended on it.

* * *

Georg felt like the next few days flew by. Each day filled with laughter and smiles. The routine things persisted. Elsa and Louisa stood in the bread lines each day but Georg came too. Elsa seemed so proud to have him there. Some of her friends resented her and refused to speak. They had lost their men and grief overpowered their happiness for Elsa. Most, though, were ecstatically happy for her and more than a little jealous.

At home, they played with Gus and talked of the future. The nights overflowed with their love. Not once did Elsa question what was coming next. It was as though she knew not to ask. And, Georg did not offer any clues that things were changing.

All too soon, the last day of his leave arrived, and with it the anxiety that Georg had been repressing since his arrival. He must tell Elsa where he had been and where he was going. He knew how dangerous this new assignment was. He also knew that the odds were very strong he would not return.

"Hedwig and Genevieve, you have out done yourselves this evening." Georg stood and bowed to each of the older women. "How you managed to create such a marvelous meal from so little is beyond me."

"Georg, you are making me blush," Hedwig beamed.

"I have been standing in those lines and I know how little food there is. I still think you should not have taken the chicken. She would have continued to give you eggs for a long time." Georg sat down and leaned back in his chair rubbing his satisfied stomach.

"We have several more chickens for eggs. We all wanted to make your last dinner here very special," Hedwig said lovingly.

"I believe we have all just eaten a month's worth of food. Look at what is left of this feast." Georg waved his arms over the table. "Potatoes and kraut. Where you found these vegetables I will never know. The baked apples are enough to make a grown man cry."

"Now I am blushing, too," Genevieve croaked.

"Thank all of you for the memories of these last few days. They will carry me through the next few months ahead wrapped in warmth and smiles of this family."

"Just what is ahead for you in the next few months?" Otto queried.

Georg knew this was coming; he and Otto had planned it that first night down at Hagen's. Otto had sworn to secrecy and had lived up to his promise, just as Georg knew he would.

"Ah, Otto, you have known all along haven't you?"

"Always known what? What are the two of you talking about?" Elsa's voice was full of alarm. "Georg! Papa!" The sound of her voice set Gus to fidgeting.

"It's alright, my darling." Georg smiled at his wife. "I just have a new assignment coming up that's all."

"What new assignment?" Her voice had raised an octave. "Aren't you going back to designing aeroplanes?" Gus was crying now. "What kind of new assignment can you have and why haven't you told me about it?" Her voice now just below hysteria. "Are you going to be in danger?"

Georg put his arm around his wife and took the agitated child from her lap, calming Gus before he began to talk. "You all know that I have been working designing and building aeroplanes since the war began. I have been very fortunate to have this opportunity to do something that I enjoy and have learned so much."

"Have you found it more exciting than the rail yards in America?" Otto wanted to know.

"Yes, very much so. I have had the opportunity to work with some of the greatest designers in the field of aeronautics."

Hedwig seemed confused. "I do not even know what that word means."

"I am sure you do not. It is a word I have only learned about recently. It means the science of flight."

"It sounds very dangerous," said Genevieve.

"Designing these wonderful machines is not dangerous. However, for the past several months I have actually not even been in Germany. I have been working at Anthony Fokker's factory in Holland."

"Holland, you never told me in any of your letters you were not in Germany." Elsa's voice now held a note of anger.

"I have been afforded a great honor to work with this master engineer. I've had opportunities I know I would never have had were it not for this war. Aeronautics is all about the future. These experiences will stand me in very good stead when this conflict is finally over." He paused to let this sink in.

Otto was very impressed. "I read much of this great engineer, Fokker, in the newspapers. His invention the Eindekker-synchronized Spandau machine gun weapon system has made it possible for Germany to begin winning this war in the air."

"I should have known, Otto, that you would recognize Fokker." Georg said with a little awe in his voice at the knowledge of this man.

"The papers say his marvelous invention allows pilots to fire a machine gun through the rotating propeller of the aeroplane and not hit the propeller." Otto paused. "I can almost picture it."

"You're correct, Otto. No one else has this technology. It was a marvel of opportunistic engineering and Fokker became famous as a result."

"Just think, my son-in-law was part of such a great invention." Otto's chest seemed to swell with pride. "Why you are single handedly helping Germany win the war."

"I still do not understand, Georg. This all sounds wonderful, but why do I feel that there is more you are not telling us." Hedwig glanced at her daughter.

"Hedwig, you always were the one who could not take things at face value, rather understood that there was so much more. As usual you are very right." Georg paused, kissed his wife on the cheek and ruffled Gus's hair.

"When I return to duty tomorrow, I will not be going back to Holland. I suspect that Elsa has shared with you from my letters how much I have enjoyed learning to fly these aeroplanes I have helped design. I can think of no greater thrill than flying except perhaps the time I spend with Elsa."

Elsa looked at her husband and then down at her lap. Her face flushed a bright red.

Hannah spoke for the first time, "Why, Elsa, I do believe you are embarrassed."

"Elsa, darling, you should never be embarrassed because of the love of a man. You is my inspiration, what keeps me going day after lonely day. You need never worry that I will stray from your love. However, I am about to embark on a new challenge." Georg paused, gently squeezing Elsa's hand.

"Germany is about to unveil a new design that is a much improved version of the Fokker Eindecker. This new aeroplane is the Albatross D III. This plane is in a class by itself. It's beautiful to look at with its streamlined body and V-strut wheel structure. This is the aeroplane that will keep Germany the king of the skies."

"Otto's voice was full of curiosity, "What does all this have to do with you?"

"Otto, You have read about the former schoolteacher, Oswald Boelcke?

"Yes, of course, He has become quite famous as a pilot."

"You're correct again. He now has devised a plan to form units called Jagdstaffeln. These will be elite squadrons of planes staffed by Germany's best pilots." He stopped, looked Elsa in the eyes, "I have been asked to join one of these units."

There was an almost eerie silence in the room. Finally when no one said anything, Georg continued, "The purpose of these units will be to seek out the enemy and knock them from the skies." Georg's chest seemed to swell with pride. "It is our plan to dominate the skies, not only over Germany, but all of Europe. This is the way the war will be won and I am honored to be chosen to be a part of it."

Otto was the first one to recover from the announcement. "Son, I know that you will make this family and all of Germany proud of you."

"I do not care if you, or Germany, are proud of my husband," Elsa screamed at her father. "I only care if Georg is safe and he certainly will not be safe in a flimsy aeroplane up in the sky with other planes shooting at him."

"Elsa calm down," Georg tried.

"I will not allow it." She turned from her father to Georg, "Do you hear me? I will not allow it." She knocked over her chair, ran up the stairs to their room, slamming the door behind her.

Gus was crying again. He struggled to get down.

"Here, let me take him," Hannah offered. "I'll take him outside"

"I knew what her reaction would be," Georg admitted. "This is why I've waited so long to tell her. Please excuse me while I go and try to calm her. I love you all." Handing Gus to Hannah, he climbed the steps to face his wife.

"Elsa, please open the door." He knocked softly on the wooden panel. "We must talk about this. I love you and I promise that I will come home safely. Please let me talk to you."

After what seemed like an eternity to Georg, Elsa finally opened the door then fell on the bed again, her face to the wall. He sat gently beside her and rubbed her back. She shrugged him off and curled into a tight ball.

"Elsa, please, we must talk about this. I can't leave you like this."

"I will not allow you to do this." She still would not look at him. "You must go back to your nice safe job designing aeroplanes. You WILL NOT fly them again. Do you hear me? Never again!"

"This is what I am being ordered to do. I am in the Army. They tell me what to do." He would never let her know that he had volunteered for this duty and that he knew just how dangerous it was. He understood how poor his odds of surviving were, yet he wanted to do this with his entire being.

"I will be safe, my darling. I have you to come home to, you and little Gus. Who knows, perhaps we have made a new baby these past few days. We certainly have tried hard enough."

Elsa turned over, a little smile on her face. "We have had a good time haven't we?"

"I will do everything in my power to come home to you? I promise that I will be safe. Please, Sweetheart, Leipchen, tell me you understand. I need you to understand." He fell on the bed beside her.

She had a look of sadness and trepidation when she finally reached for him. "I understand, my darling. I will do my best to be strong for you."

As Georg held her he knew in his heart that this might their last night together ever. He was determined to make it a memory to last a lifetime.

Chapter 38
October 1916
The Trenches of Verdun, France

My Dearest Louisa,

    I miss you and our beautiful little daughter more than the mind can even imagine. You are constantly in my thoughts. Only through thoughts of you and our life before this war do I keep my sanity. Many men around me no longer are able to conjure up life before this carnage and their minds leave them. Each day I try, with every fiber of my being, to keep myself whole in mind and body for you.

    I am not sure how much longer I can continue to fight the demons that haunt me. Living in this hell month after month, year after year is enough to turn even God himself into a mindless idiot. Will it ever stop?

    The current offensive has been going on since early July, but then, you know this. I know my father brings the papers home to you every day. He has forever been one who needed to know everything. How I miss that man! He seems so gruff, but under that rough exterior, he is a man of much emotion. Sometimes I think he uses his abruptness to cover up his emotional side. After all, Kruger men must never show any sentiment it might indicate a weakness and make them less of a man.

    I will try to keep my mind focused and not digress into my fantasies of home. Each night the enemy shells us incessantly and in the morning, they send wave after wave of their foot soldiers across no-man's land to attack our defenses. And every day we repulse them. The British do not seem to understand that we have developed a system of trenches that protect us from their shelling.

Is it so hard to believe that after years of living in the trenches, we have adapted to digging and tunneling into the ground very much as rabbits and moles. We have learned to live in the earth, and to use that very earth to protect us from our enemies. As a result, the nightly shelling does not have the effect that our aggressors desire. Each morning we climb out of our holes, turn our sights on their foot soldiers, and retake everything they may have gained during the night.

All of this is not to say that we have no casualties, for they are great. Just yesterday I was at my usual machine gun post. My job was to reload the gun. My partner was operating the gun itself. We were experiencing exceptionally accurate effectiveness when I indicated, with hand gestures, that we needed more ammunition. The sound of battle is much too loud for words. I went down into the trench from the machine gun nest to retrieve the ammunition. When I returned just moments later, I found the gun silent. I looked at my partner to question the reason and there he sat just as I had left him, with only one difference, his face had vanished. Only a bloody mass remained where once his face had been. There had not been a sound from him. He was there and then he was gone. I had no time to mourn his loss, for the guns must continue. I moved him as gently as possible and took up his position. There I sat, in pools of his blood and brought our gun back to life.

Sometimes I fear that this war has turned me into a machine. I am not at all sure that I will ever be able to feel again. I referred to this man as my partner. Of course, I knew his name and probably knew more of him than I do my own family and yet we all try so very hard not to be emotionally attached to those around us for we lose so many each day that to be truly friends would render us all incapable of continuing this effort.

I am sorry my love for the graphic detail of this missive, but I vowed to tell you of my life as it really is.

The enemy continues to try to demoralize us with their relentless onslaught, but they do not know Germans. Just days ago the Brits threw their newest weapon of destruction at us. This massive machine looks very much like a monster from a child's book. It is about twenty-three feet long, thirteen feet wide and sixteen feet high, all made of metal. It crawls along the land on treads and looks much like a giant caterpillar with guns on its back. We have heard the Brits had about fifty of them but only a very few actually made it into battle. Those that did make it onto the battleground are daunting and may be the first weapon that the enemy has thrown at us that can penetrate our defenses.

We have not seen any of these beasts yet at where I am stationed, but I have heard that the giant monsters were able to break through our lines just a few miles from my position.

I am not sure how much longer this kind of carnage can continue. Thousands, perhaps tens of thousands of men are injured or killed each day. It is only by the grace of God that I have not been causality myself, men all around me die every day. Yet somehow, I go on.

I fear that my spirit may sometimes falter. I do my best to keep my mental picture of you and Elsbeth clear but the death and destruction that surround me every minute of every day make it so very hard. I often have to plead with you in my mind just to hang onto the minute particle of sanity that keeps me functioning. Even though I am forced to live like an animal, fleeing underground for my very safety, I do not want to become an animal like so many of the men around me have.

I must put this missive aside for now, as it is once again time for my turn at the front lines. I beg of you to keep me in your thoughts and in your heart. If I am privileged enough to come home to you when all of this is over, I pray that I will still be at least a small piece of the man who left you so many months ago.

All my love,
August

With those last words, August ever so carefully folded the paper in half and then folded it again. He reached for the little leather case that he kept always in his breast pocket. Lovingly he opened the case and for a moment gazed at the picture of Louisa and himself on their wedding day. That happiest of days when the love of his life joined him on this journey. Never did they dream that journey would bring the horrors of separation and war that now engulfed not only them but also an entire nation, nay- the entire world. How had all of this happened? August knew that he would defend his nation to the death, but looking back on the sequence of events that brought about this conflict, he wondered if perhaps so much of this could not have been spared if men had only been more willing to talk and negotiate and less willing to resolve differences with violence. Was all of this necessary?

August placed the letter in the case next to his most recent letter from Louisa. He replaced the folder in his pocket, gently caressing it. He kept these things near his heart always. Sometimes just touching them was enough to conjure up pictures of Louisa and baby Elsbeth, to hear the lovely lilt of Louisa's voice as she sweetly sang Elsbeth to sleep. Oh, how he missed them both.

Slowly he climbed from his burrow, the nest he had lined with dry leaves to help keep him warm. This hole in the ground had become his refuge from the cacophony of war above. It was with grim resolve that he made his way to the front lines. He would do his duty always but as the battle for Somme droned on for so many months, the death toll on each side rising to unimaginable numbers, it became harder with each passing hour to resume his post.

With the sun shining, the beautiful white clouds drifted across the azure blue of the sky on this idyllic fall day. The leaves on what was left of the trees were the brilliant red, orange and gold of autumn. Today seemed the perfect day, as August took his place behind the gun.

The spell was broken, as the hum of machinery from the distance became a more persistent roar of the approaching monsters the enemy had unleashed upon them. August lifted himself up to see over the edge of the trench. What he saw brought his heart to his throat. There, coming directly towards his position, were three of the new British tanks. He watched as the massive guns these behemoths carried came to life. First, he saw the flash of light as the balls left the giant trunks of the metal elephants. It was only later that he heard their sound. He watched, as repeatedly they threw their wrath at his position.

All around him, men were taking action, firing their weapons trying to repel the giants, and yet he stood there watching as if frozen in this position. It was beautiful, all of the light and sound, he could not tear himself away. The sound and light, light and sound surrounded him. It was as though he was watching all of this from above. This strange dance of man and machine throwing light and sound at each other, each trying to best the other. What an extraordinary picture these men were creating. He was sure that he would never in all of his life forget this moment.

Then all was quiet. The sound was gone and all he could see was the light, which seemed to get brighter and brighter, blinding him. It was as though he had become a part of the light. Somewhere in the distance, he thought he heard someone calling his name. He was sure he could hear voices. Perhaps, yes he was sure he could hear Louisa. She was singing that lullaby that he loved so much. "Louisa, where you? I cannot see you."

Then he heard his mother's sweet voice gently chiding him not to taste the bread before dinner. There was his father holding his pipe as he read the newspaper. And Hannah, he could hear the joyous sound of Hannah's laughter. Suddenly it was all gone, the light, the lullaby, his mother and father and even Hannah's laughter. Gone! All that was left was an all-encompassing weight upon his chest. He felt cold, so very cold. He struggled to get his breath. With each passing moment, it became more and more difficult to breath. What was happening? Then he knew. He reached up to touch his heart, to feel one more time the little leather case with Louisa's picture and her last words to him. He was tired, so very tired, he could barely lift his arm.

An eternity passed. At last, with what seemed his last ounce of energy, his fingers groped and finally found that for which they were searching, he saw Louisa, heard her voice one last time, "I'll always love you."

Then, the blackness came and with it release.

"Grandmomma, sad? Tanta Louisa sad too? Everyone sad. Gus be sad too?" Little Gus asked as he climbed into Hedwig's lap. Heartbroken she clasped her grandson, August's namesake, to her chest, kissing his head, his cheek, and his neck. Finally burying her face in the soft silky hair of her grandson, who seemed much too wise for his age. She gently grieved her loss. August's death had torn through the very fabric of the Kruger family, rending a gaping hole that would forever change life.

Hedwig remembered yesterday, the last day of October, such a peaceful day spent enjoying the children's antics until that ominous knock on the door arrived, sending this family reeling into shock and disbelief. She had always felt so privileged and somehow immune, even after Ernst's death, to the fate that had befallen so many others. Now she must face the reality of this war head on with the worst possible results. August, dear wonderful August, was gone.

The loss of her only son was something that Hedwig had feared from the day this war had begun. One by one as each of her friends and neighbors received the news of the loss of a beloved child, she had been the first to bring condolences and offer her strength. When she had received the news of Ernst's death she, herself had descended into that dark and lonely hole within, only to emerge out of the necessity to keep her family together. Now she had lost a child, her first born, her only son. How could she ever survive this? Life did not seem worth living, There seemed no reason to go on. What could possibly bring meaning with her own baby boy gone?

Grief stricken, Louisa collapsed from the weight of the news and Otto had carried her to her bed. Fearing the worst, Otto, called Dr. Ostermann. Genevieve refused to leave Louisa's side.

Hedwig understood that her friend would see her child through this tragedy, even though it was obvious that Genevieve herself was becoming more ill as each day passed. Hedwig also knew Genevieve would give her last breath if only she could save her daughter just one hour of this grief. Even little Elsbeth seemed to sense her mother's distress, for she cried incessantly and would not leave her mother's side.

Hannah, so much like her father, did her best to swallow her grief, keep it to herself. Hedwig heard her last night though, sobbing when she was alone in her bed. Always there for the others, Hannah had already begun to assume the roles of the other women, taking care of the children and doing her best to prepare meals from the meager larder on the shelves.

It was perhaps Elsa's calm dispassionate comment that August could not possibly be gone, the report from the army must have him confused with someone else, that alarmed Hedwig the most. The two had been so close. Elsa had always looked at her brother with almost hero worship.

Even the stoic Otto could not conceal his grief at the loss of their son. He had loved and laughed with this son as a child, and learned to appreciate him as a man. August had been his son and had become his friend. Hedwig knew that this man she loved so much was going to miss his son more that he could even begin to imagine. However, he would not let his emotions control him. The women and children needed him now, perhaps more than ever before, and he would maintain his strength for them.

More than anything, Hedwig knew that she could not allow herself to fall into the dark pit on whose very precipice she teetered. For she knew, even in the depth of her despair, this little boy on her lap, and his beautiful cousin, Elsbeth, August's own daughter, would bring back meaning to her life. These children would soon grow to be the leaders of a new generation who, having endured the overwhelming cataclysm of this war, perhaps would be wise enough to guide their generation in a new direction. Yes, even though all seemed lost at this moment, she must somehow remain strong for them.

"Yes, Gus, Grandmomma is very sad, so are Tanta Louisa and all the grownups. But, you have no need to be sad. Everyone loves you, especially Grandmomma. With your help I will soon be happy again." Hedwig said, holding this darling boy to her heart, all the while knowing that she would never be the same ever again.

"Momma, Momma, Elbeth hurt, Elbeth sad." The pretty little girl rubbed her blue eyes and buried her head in her mother's shoulder.

"I know, Leipchen, your tummy hurts. But Momma has nothing to give you just now."

The wind moaned outside the window. Elsbeth seemed to match its mournful sound as Louisa sat in the big old rocking chair holding both children gently on her lap. "I am sorry," She commented to no one in particular, "Elsbeth just will not cease this endless whimpering. I had hoped that perhaps Gus could cheer her up but he seems only to emulate her, making their cries worse."

"I'm afraid there is nothing any of us can do," Elsa commented. "I tried for hours last night to settle Gus before he finally went to sleep,"

Elsa and Hedwig sat at the big kitchen trestle table pounding dried turnips to make a sort of flour for their latest version of bread. The real flour gone for over a year now, they had become quite adept at making bread from potatoes. Now, even the potatoes were in short supply. The rains last summer and fall had caused the crop to fail. The only food left was the fast dwindling stock of turnips. Each day Elsa went to the cellar for the daily ration. Just today, she had counted what was in each basket and determined that they must cut back to ten turnips per day, if the store was to last the winter.

"Louisa, you must never apologize for Elsbeth. She is hungry," Elsa comforted, "or perhaps tired after all, this daily fare of turnip bread with turnip surprise soup followed by a delicious dessert of turnip crisp is enough to make even a grown woman cry from the sheer monotony, if not bad taste, let alone the lack of nutrition."

"At least the children are still under six years old." Louisa brightened some. "My friend Corrine's son just turned seven and she can no longer buy milk for him unless he gets sick and has a doctor's prescription."

Hannah walked into the kitchen from the back porch. "I am just so glad that we have Momma's chickens in the back because Anna told me that they are only allowed to buy one egg per person in her family every two weeks."

"I think that I miss meat the most," Hedwig joined in. "I think your papa misses a good Hagen brew most of all, but meat would surely be his second choice. He told me last week that he had read in the papers pinned up in the windows in town, that when the war began the stockyards in Berlin were slaughtering 25,000 pigs per week for all that wonderful wurst. Now they were only seeing about 350 pigs per week. Is it any wonder that we are all so hungry? I know we were a very fortunate family before the war, as were most people in Germany, which may only make this depravation worse."

"The things I miss most are the butter and jam," Hannah said wistfully. "The turnip bread might be almost palatable if there were a little butter and maybe some of Momma's wonderful elderberry jam. I can almost taste it now just thinking about it. What a treat that would be, especially if it were on Momma's best rye bread. Just the thought of what we are missing makes me want to cry like the children. When will this war be over, so we can begin to live normal lives again?"

"I certainly do not have the answer to that, but I know Elsbeth is much too small for her age." Louisa said. "I worry she is not growing right because she does not have enough food. I am not sure when this will all end, but I hope it happens soon."

"People are getting so desperate; Paul told me in one of his letters that since he has been sent to Berlin to work on another cemetery, he has actually heard of people trading old potato peelings for fire wood. It seems that for some keeping warm is more important than eating."

"I would trade fire wood for potato peels to have some taste other than turnips. I'm sure I could make something delicious from potato peels." Elsa sighed.

"That is not all; he also said that he had seen a group of men fighting over the carcass of a dead horse in the street. The horse was just skin and bones but it is still meat for starving people. At least Paul is not so hungry. There seems to still be enough food for the army."

The back door slammed and Otto's deep resonant voice joined the conversation as he hugged his wife. "I fear this war will not be over soon and that even the army may run out of food before all is said and done."

"Papa what are you talking about?" Hannah wanted to know.

"It is all the talk in town. Today the United States of America broke all diplomatic relations with Germany. Just proving what every good thinking German knew all along, America is really on the side of the British and French.

Elsa felt a growing sense of alarm, "Papa that cannot be. America is a friend to Germany."

"My dear, Elsa, I am afraid that is not so. The Kaiser did the right thing because he is a monarch of conscience, and tried to end this war. I am sure you remember my telling you back in December he proposed to make peace, but Britain and France could not accept that idea unless it was their own. Somehow, the American President Wilson thought he could negotiate, saying they were neutral in all actions."

"Yes, that is what I am saying." Elsa pounded the table for emphasis. "America would never make war on Germany."

"Just listen my child; the American president wanted us to give specifics of our plans and aims for this war. That would have been the same as treason and the Kaiser refused to go to a conference presided over by Americans. What was the American president's answer to Germany's refusal to attend? War!"

"This cannot be!"

"Oh, but it is true. Now it is time for the German military to unleash the unterseeboot.

"Why are submarines so important, Papa?" Hannah asked.

"You will see now that the Kaiser has signed the documents to allow the navy to show what we can do with this weapon. The rest of the world has seen nothing yet. Germany will never be defeated. NEVER!"

***

Elsa hugged the wall as she wrapped the quilt more tightly around her. Very gingerly, she stretched out her foot to the next step. From years of going up and down these stairs, she knew the next was the one that always made the loudest squeak. It was very late and she did not want to wake the rest of the family, especially the children who seemed to sleep so lightly these days. Carefully, ever so carefully, she made her way down until she was finally standing on the floor. As she walked toward the kitchen, she could see the light from the lamp on the table and she began to feel the warmth of the fire banked in the stove. She moved up behind her father and put her arms around his neck, hugging him with that special love a daughter has for her father.

"Somehow, I knew I would see you tonight." Otto smiled. It had long been his habit to go to bed with his beloved Hedwig and after she fell asleep to get up and come to the kitchen and read in the quiet solitude of the late evening.

"Oh, Papa, I am so confused. I do not know what to think about these latest developments in the war."

"I am sure that your feelings are a confused mix of emotions. I know you love Germany. You grew up here and your family is here. Your husband bravely, and with much allegiance, defends this country every day. However, you made the decision years ago to build your life in a new place, in America, and I know that you love that place also. Although I do not see how anyone could want to live anywhere but Germany, I have always respected your decision and been proud of you for trying to make a better life for yourself and your family. This must be extremely difficult for you."

"Papa, you know that I have never cared much for workings of government. That is for men to worry about. I have always had much more important things to think about, like making a home for my family. Now, I cannot avoid politics. I need to understand what has happened. Throughout this war, I have been able to rationalize my allegiance to both countries. How can I ever choose between them? I always thought that America was neutral and would support Germany. There are so many people in America from Germany, how can they turn against her now. I just do not understand."

"This surely must be difficult for you. I will try to give you some background so perhaps you will better understand." Otto smiled at his daughter. "Before you sit down would you please pour me some more of that hot water from the stove? How I crave a good cup of coffee. The hot water helps warm me, but will never substitute for the aroma and taste of your mother's extra strong boiled coffee."

Elsa got a cup for herself, as well, and brought the big black kettle from the stove, pouring the steaming hot water into both cups. Once again wrapping the quilt tightly around herself, she pulled the chair across from her father and sat down. Knowing that no matter what he told her, she would feel better, for just having this quiet intimate time with this man she loved and respected so very much.

"This break in relations between Germany and America is not surprising to me. When the American President Wilson called for "peace without victory" and a negotiated settlement on his terms that would certainly give America power and prestige over Europe, especially Germany, I knew the Kaiser would never accept."

"What do you mean?"

"Wilhelm has held back Germany's greatest weapon far too long. I think that Supreme Commander Ludendorff was exactly right when he said 'ich pfeife auf Amerika'"

"Papa, why would he say that he did not give a damn about America? It is such a wonderful place."

"You have to understand that he was talking to the American military representative. He was saying that America cannot hurt Germany any more by going to war with her than they have already by supplying Britain and France with munitions and food all these long months. This war has been good for America; it has made them all rich."

"That cannot be right."

"I know, my darling that you do not want to hear these things because you love America. You made a new home and new friends there. However, your husband is fighting to defend Germany, this country, his homeland, not America."

"But, Papa, why are they doing this. I know that all you say is right. Georg is fighting for Germany and I will always love this country, but I still do not understand why America needs to become involved. They are an ocean away and have no reason to be involved at all. Why can they not just stay on their side of the ocean? Surely this will all be over soon and Georg, Gus and I can go back to our home in Toledo."

"I want to show you something." Otto got up and walked to the other room. On a table by his favorite chair sat the hand carved wooden box where he always kept all the paraphernalia needed by an avid pipe smoker. There were always lighters and tampers, two or three special knives just the right shape for a specific pipe bowl, pipe cleaners and polishing cloths, and of course, tobacco of several blends. Now there was no tobacco, it had been gone for many, many months, but this box was still his own very private place. No one else in the house would even dream of touching this precious box.

Elsa could not see what he was doing because it was too dark. In her mind's eye, though, she could see because she had watched him so many times. He would lightly run his hand over the satin finish of the lid, lift it gently, and then his nose would twitch as he inhaled the aroma of tobacco. With almost reverent care, he would lift whatever he was seeking and just as tenderly close the lid.

Elsa watched his form take shape again as he walked back into the dimly lit kitchen.

"I have not even shown this to your mother. I hoped that none of you would ever see this. And yet it was so powerful that I kept it."

He unfolded the paper and on it was a cartoon showing a ship flying the American flag and docked in what was obviously an American port, taking on a load of cargo all labeled ammunition. In the background were three groups of soldiers all wearing German uniforms. The caption read: casualties of this single cargo '30,000 killed, 40,000 seriously wounded, 40,000 lightly wounded."

"What does this mean, Papa?"

"It is my belief that the Americans have prolonged this war. They say they are neutral, but they have been supplying our enemies with food and ammunition since the beginning. Oh, perhaps they tried to sell to us too, but the British blockade has stopped that, and they have supported the blockade by avoiding it. "

"Why?"

"Ever since the sinking of that British ship, Lusitania, where so many American passengers died, they have done their best to stay out of blockaded waters."

"That was nearly two years ago."

"You are correct. Because of the American protests of the sinking of that ship, the Kaiser pulled back on the use of our submarines in an effort to try to make the Americans happy. Yet, look what they do. They make, sell and ship weapons to our enemies. What are we supposed to do, sit by quietly and let them kill us?" His voice was rising, "NO!! I say we..."

"Papa, keep your voice down. You will wake the babies." Elsa patted her father's arm. "I know how strongly you feel. That is why I came to talk with you to help me understand, but it is the middle of the night and we have to try to talk more quietly. Here, let me get you something more to drink." She got up and once again filled the cups with steaming hot water from the kettle on the stove.

"What a wise woman you have grown to be. You often surprise me these days."

"I'm not wise, Papa. I'm just a mother who wants her starving son to sleep through the night. I have no food to give him if he wakes. His time asleep is the only time that his little tummy does not hurt him."

"There, you see, that is what I am talking about. America is one of the reasons that your son is hungry all the time. They will ship food to Britain and France but not us. We would gladly give them our money if they would ship to us."

"Did you not say that they have tried, but cannot get through the British blockade?"

"I did. However, I am not sure how hard they tried. Even after we pulled back on our navel defense so they could continue to trade with us you see what has happened. You said it yourself; your little son's tummy hurts all the time because there is not enough food. I blame that on the Americans as much as I do on the British these days."

"I still do not understand, why now? What has changed to make them do this now?"

"You know that the French have been fighting hard these last few months, and we have lost much of what we won earlier at Verdun."

"Don't say that word, that is where we lost August."

"It is very hard for me too. However, it is a big part of what is happening. Austria, our strongest ally, has run out of food and money. Now that Emperor Franz Joseph has died and his great-nephew, Karl has taken over, we seem to be getting less and less support from them. Karl told Kiser Wilhelm that we are fighting against a new enemy, revolution and that its best ally is starvation. He does not seem willing to help our cause any longer."

"Starvation is certainly a very strong enemy."

"Well, I am glad that Wilhelm ignored Karl and agreed with Field Marshall Hindenburg that we must resume torpedoing of armed merchant ships as soon as possible and without notice.

"How can attacking ships of neutral countries help us win the war?"

"The only way for us to win this war is to stop supplies from getting to Britain, just as they have stopped them from getting to us. They have fought an unfair battle and it is time for us to retaliate."

"Can Germany do that?"

"We have the power to destroy much of the shipping to and from Britain and we need to begin using it. The hold out has always been Chancellor Bethmann-Hollweg and the Kaiser has been reluctant to act without his agreement. Our government is in turmoil over this decision about submarines.

"Why have things changed now?"

"I think that the Chancellor finally gave in because he knew that if he continued to make the Kaiser choose between him and Field Marshall Hindenburg, that the Field Marshall would win, and he would be out. "

"It is always all about politics, is it not?"

"Yes, I am afraid that it is. Hindenburg has said that we need to be prepared to meet the Americans with as much energy and ruthlessness as possible. Now Kaiser Wilhelm has finally signed an agreement and unterseeboot warfare began on February 1st in full force."

"So now that Germany is finally standing up for her rights and showing the rest of the world that she is powerful at sea as well as on land. Perhaps the President Wilson had no choice but to give in and break ties with Germany."

"Leipchen, you may be absolutely right about that. Since the British and French will not listen to the Americans any more than we will, what options did he have left? I do not believe that he is a strong enough leader to declare war against us, though. He wants to just stay over there on his side of the ocean and tell the rest of the world what to do. Now

Germany has told him that we will no longer listen to his banter and are taking action to end this conflict sooner rather than later."

"I surely do not understand how you know all of these things. You are one of the smartest men that I have ever met. Perhaps if you were running the government, we would have been done with this war many years ago."

"There are many more much smarter than me. I am just a humble trolley driver."

Elsa laughed, "You are so much or than that. You are my Papa."

"I am a very lucky man to have you for a daughter."

"Thank you, Papa; I think that I understand a little better now. I am not at all sure how I feel. I still love both of my countries and am quite sure that I will want to go back to America. I also know that I wish all of this to be over soon, tomorrow would not be too soon."

"I doubt your wish will be granted. I too want it all to be over as do, I think, all the parties involved. The problem is that we all want what is best for our country and that is never what is best for the other countries. I fear that we will find no way to compromise so we must win this affair with our minds and our might. This is our war to win and I am sure that it will happen eventually."

The finality of that last statement seemed to signal an end to the conversation. It was very late and Elsa was beginning to feel the need of sleep. She was still conflicted and now more sure then ever that she would never fully understand the world of men and their politics. However, she also knew that this conversation with her father had been good for them both. Otto had had a chance to explain and perhaps vent his feelings about the war and she had been able to share that moment with him.

She often felt that he considered her less important and perhaps less bright than the men in the family. Nevertheless, tonight she knew that he had shared some of his deepest feelings, fears and hopes with her and even though she too now understood that the war would probably continue for some time, she was feeling better about herself than she had in a very long time. She was still very cold and always hungry. Her son would continue to cry because she had no food for him, but at least her father respected her and that was enough for tonight.

Hannah sat on the sofa, the children nestled beside her, all of them wrapped in one of Momma's warmest handmade quilts. "Tanta Hannah, Gus get down and play?"

"No Gus, stay here with us and keep warm." Hannah thought back over the last year. So much had happened. August was gone. America had joined the war. Even though there had been a better harvest last summer, there was still very little food and this winter was so cold. The giant coal-burning furnace in the basement was silent. There was no fuel. Papa had been so proud of that monster when he installed it five years ago. It filled the house with such delightful heat. Now the big old stove in the kitchen that Momma loved so much was the only source of heat for the entire house. Hannah had helped Papa move the furniture to the kitchen so the family could gather and sit in relative comfort in this one room. All of the other rooms were void of family except for the bedrooms at night. And, of course, Genevieve's room.

"Elbeth cold too" the little girl's voice piped up.

"Yes, Liepchen, we are all cold." Hannah pulled both the children closer as she reached down and gently pinched Gus's little leg.

"Tanta Hannah that tickles. Do it some more."

Soon all three of them were laughing together. "We have to be quiet. We do not want to disturb Grandmomma Genevieve. You stay covered and I will get a book to read." Hannah climbed from the warm nest on the sofa and scurried across the cold floor.

"Gus come too."

"No Gus, you stay there. I will be right back. Shall I get the book about Little Red Riding Hood?"

"Yea, Gus's favorite."

"Alright you stay right there and I will be back with the book."

"Gus be the mean wolf."

"Elbeth be riding hood"

"Yes we will all read the story together. Wait for me." Hannah ran up the stairs and then stopped at the door to Genevieve's room. She was now too sick to get out of bed. Dr. Osterman had said that there was a cancer growing in her chest and there was nothing to be done except to try to make her as comfortable as possible. Her breathing became more difficult, it seemed, with each passing hour. She had never been a physically strong woman, but she had always been a tower of strength emotionally. She had endured the loss of her own beloved Friedrich with a grace and dignity that few others ever display. It was only through her strength and support that Louisa had survived the loss of August.

Genevieve guided her back from her grief by modeling just how important it was for her to turn her suffering into love and care for her daughter. Elsbeth must grow up knowing what a wonderful man her father had been. Only Louisa could instill that wonder in her daughter. Hannah was sure that Genevieve was determined to meet her own death with the same grace and dignity she had displayed in her life. Louisa looked up and smiled at Hannah. "Are the children alright?"

"Oh yes, I just came up to get their favorite story, Little Red Riding Hood."

"I am sure that Elsbeth has already announced that she is Riding Hood."

"Of course, and Gus is the wolf."

"Thank you, Hannah. It helps to know you are with Elsbeth right now."

Hannah turned away, going to her own room. There was nothing to say.

Louisa looked back at her mother; she had somehow found the strength to conquer her own demons to care for her mother. She seldom left her side, although there was little to be done anymore to relieve her mother's pain and suffering. The poultices that Hedwig made helped some and the boiling water that she brought so Genevieve could breathe the steaming vapors relived the coughing only temporarily. Louisa knew that the end was very close; her mother was beginning to lapse in and out of awareness. Strangely, those times when she was awake were the worst because breathing was so difficult and the coughing never stopped. She knew she would miss her mother terribly but now she prayed for it all to end. She believed with all her being that Genevieve would soon be with her beloved Friedrich and August too. Oh, how Louisa wished that she too could join them in that place where there are no cares, no grief, or hunger, or cold, just peace, sweet peace.

Genevieve's gentle touch on her daughter's hand brought Louisa back to reality. She looked at her mother and saw a slow smile spread across her face. Louisa felt, rather than saw, Genevieve's hand move almost imperceptibly. She watched her mother's beautiful eyes close and then open one last time as she blinked goodbye. Then she was gone. It had been a long and painful journey to the end. Now it was over; at last she was at peace.

Louisa sat by her mother's side for what could have been minutes or hours. She did not know. Finally, she leaned over her beloved mother, gently kissed the still warm forehead goodbye. A single tear rolled down her cheek and fell on that of her mother as if symbolizing the bond of love they shared would be forever unbroken.

Hedwig stood in the open doorway watching. "She is at peace now. You must let her go." She moved into the room, got down on her knees and gently held Louisa in her arms. "You know that she will always live in your heart along with your dear father and August."

Louisa buried her face in Hedwig's shoulder. "Why did she have to go too? Why are they both gone? They were both so good. It is not fair."

"No, it is not fair. Nothing about this world right now is fair."

"How can you be so strong, Hedwig. I just want to climb into that bed and die with her."

"Yes, I understand, more than you will ever know, but you cannot do that. You must be strong for Elsbeth. You are all she has. I know that she will grow up to be a wonderful woman because she has you for her mother."

"I do not know if I can go on."

"You can and you will. Come, let us go to the kitchen and get you warm. You are so cold your lips are blue. She will be alright now if you leave her for a little while to get warm." Hedwig gently helped Louisa up, this young woman whom she loved as her own, who had lost so much, and led her down the stairs to the warmth of the kitchen.

Hedwig prayed with all her heart and soul that this was the end of their losses. She was not at all sure how much more any of them could manage. This once lively, vibrant and happy home had become like a tomb of cold and despair. She must do what she could to bring back some life to this place and the people she loved so much.

Chapter 42
Early March 1918
Düsseldorf, Germany

Slowly, Hannah realized she was awake. Was it time to get up already? It seemed as if she had just gone to bed? Eventually she opened her eyes and looked out of the window. The sky was black as the coal that had once kept this dear old house as warm as the love that filled it. There were no stars or moon to light her way. She was lost in the darkness of her room or perhaps her mind. Why was she awake? Sleep was so much more peaceful; wakefulness was filled with too much pain.

Pain she refused to admit to herself, let alone anyone else. As she tried to move, she realized what must have awakened her. Her arm was outside the quilt and as she turned to snuggle again in its warmth the sharpness of the pain caused her to gasp. Then the dull ache set in. She knew now, from experience, that it would last for some minutes and then gradually subside until the next time. It seemed these days that all of her joints were like this. The cycle of pain and ache was continuous with little relief. The cold just made it worse. Here she was, not yet twenty years old and she felt what she imagined an old woman must feel. She remembered Genevieve struggling to climb the stairs because her knees pained her so much, now understanding just how painful it must have been for her.

There was also the nearly constant pain in her stomach. That she knew was from hunger. Night was generally the worst for that as well. During the day, she kept busy. There was no time to think of food while at the factory. Between the noise of the machinery and the constant need to make sure that, each assembly was perfect she was able to block out everything else. At home if the hunger became too much she drank water and that would help to relieve the empty feeling.

She had learned though that even water could be her enemy in the fight against the ever-present hunger, too much could make you sick. She was now much more careful than she once had been with water.

She was not alone in her suffering. They were all hungry, not just her family, but also the entire nation. Each day the death toll from starvation seemed to grow higher. The news was full of it. There was not enough food for anyone; it was not just the poor who were dying. The entire nation was under siege because of the blockade. Thousands had died, and millions more were starving.

In the Kruger household, as in most, the children ate first. What was left then was shared between the adults. Hannah knew that her family had been luckier than most and had been able to stave off the hunger longer. Now the chickens were gone, the cellar nearly empty and the lines yielded less and less each day. It did not matter that she earned a wage at the factory; her father brought home his earnings and both Louisa and Elsa had their stipends from the government. All the money in the world was worthless if there was no food to buy.

She looked out the window. Though it was still inky black, she thought she saw the very first rays of light on the horizon, more a dream of the bright warm sun than what was actually there. She lay trying to quiet her mind with thoughts of better times, waiting for what she knew would come.

Then she heard the shuffle of little feet in the hallway. Her door opened ever so quietly and then closed, just as carefully. Again the sound of bare feet on the cold wooden floor. Then she felt the bed sag ever so slightly as Gus climbed in with her. She raised the quilt and he snuggled close to her warm body, his feet, cool from his walk. He laid his head on her shoulder as she wrapped him in her arms. Surprisingly this gesture never hurt when she raised her arm to gather him in. "I love you, Tanta Hannah."

"I love you, too," she whispered back kissing the soft blond curls that brushed her face. She had grown to love this ritual and realized that she must have awakened in anticipation of his arrival. She closed her eyes, knowing now that she could sleep for a little longer.

On the third floor, Elsa listened for the door to open as she heard Gus climb from his bed and make his way in the dark to Hannah's room. He had been doing this for some time now and Elsa knew that it comforted them both. Closing her eyes, she brought up the picture of Georg and Gus on the front lawn playing and laughing as she looked on from the upstairs window. The picture was different somehow.

This was not the lawn in front of the old German house but the lawn behind their darling little house in Toledo. How she missed that house, that town, and that life. As she stared out the window, there were Gus and his father rolling on the grass as the new puppy licked their faces. She looked down at the perfect baby girl she held in her arms and marveled with wonder at the joy life could bring.

Here she was living in her dream house with her handsome husband, who was the envy of all her friends and two marvelous children. Life was perfect. What more she could ask?

She thought they would all take a trip to the zoo today, or better yet, a picnic at the lake. She would make chicken, fried to perfection and a wonderful hot potato salad. Georg could pick some corn from the garden and perhaps some lettuce and carrots. After the lunch was prepared, Georg would pack the shiny black auto that was parked in the garage and they would all drive to Lake Erie for a wonderful warm day at the beach. The children would play in the sand. Gus would dash into the waves and run back to her as the water touched his feet. She could see it all now. What a grand day it would be!

She opened her eyes, hearing the baby crying for her feeding. As she started to get up, she realized that it had all been a dream. Here she was in her little third floor room in the cold house in Germany. It all came flooding back to her. The war, Georg off fighting somewhere, August, her brother and best friend gone forever, the cold, the daily lines, the constant hunger, even the baby crying, Elsbeth in the next room awake and hungry and no food for her.

The horror of this war, of her life, settled in for another day. How had she come to this? Everything had been so perfect. How had that perfection descended into this never-ending nightmare? Surely, it must end soon. Please Lord make it end soon. She knew that she would not go back to sleep, but she closed her eyes, willing the dream to return. At least she could live in her perfect world in her dreams.

Louisa came awake to the cries of Elsbeth. Gently she picked her up and sat in the big old rocking chair. She knew that there was nothing she could do to help the hunger but sometimes rocking would help Elsbeth go back to sleep. With eyes closed, she hummed Lullaby and goodnight, thy mother's delight. Bright angels beside my darling abide, that her mother had sung to her.

How she missed Genevieve. It seemed impossible that she was gone. She had been such a tower of strength. When Friedrich died, Louisa thought her world had ended. Her father was gone, but Genevieve had been there, putting aside her own grief to comfort her daughter. She never left the room, as Louisa nearly died giving life to Elsbeth.

When the news of August's death came, Genevieve already knew that her days were numbered too, but again she never left Louisa's side. She refused to let her stay in bed and wallow in her grief, refused to allow her to neglect her child.

Genevieve knew she must do everything possible to make sure that she lived long enough to see her daughter and granddaughter survived this terrible time.

Louisa fought the demons every day that tried to keep her hiding in bed. It was only her mother's voice constantly in her mind reminding her of her duties and responsibilities that got her up and moving each day. Except for Elsbeth, life was not worth living. Everyone that she had ever loved was gone, her father, her husband and her mother. All of them taken from her. It was not fair that she should suffer so much.

She thanked God every day for August's family. She knew that they loved her and would care for her, all her life if necessary, but it was not the same as having her own family. She felt so alone; it seemed that it was just Elsbeth and her against the world.

Why she had been chosen to walk this road? People were always saying things like "how strong you are," and "You are never given more that you can bear." But, she could not bear all of this. It was just too much.

Now with all the death surrounding her, there was the incessant cold and unrelenting hunger as well. She just wanted it all to end. Sometimes, like this morning, she was sure that it would be so much easier just to put an end to it all. She could put a pillow over Elsbeth's face. It would be warm and soon her crying would stop. She would never have to feel the cold or hunger again. She would never have to know the pain that was all consuming as the result of the death of loved ones.

Yes, it would be better for Elsbeth never to know this world the way she knew it. Carefully she got up and laid the now sleeping child in her bed. She crossed to her own bed and picked up the pillow hugging it to her chest. She pictured August, what a handsome man he had been. His wonderful blond hair and those blue eyes, they were the deepest blue she had ever seen. You could get lost in those eyes and live in happiness forever.

Elsbeth had the same eyes. When she smiled, they were so full of delight that everyone around her smiled too. Those eyes must never know pain. Those beautiful blue eyes must never stop smiling.

Now she was standing in front of the little bed. Gently, she bent down and kissed her daughter on the cheek, so warm and soft, perfection. This child she and August had made was so beautiful, so perfect.

Ever so carefully, she brought the pillow down toward that angelic face. It would be so easy now. Just lay the pillow over her and gently hold it down. She would sleep and never need to wake again. Yes, this was the right thing to do.

"Louisa, what are you doing?" Genevieve cried. "STOP! This is Elsbeth; you must never allow anyone to hurt her."

"That is what I am doing, Mother. I am ending all of her hurt and allowing no more pain."

"Louisa, you must stop."

"But, mother, do you not see what I am doing? I am saving her. We will both join you soon."

"Louisa, it is not your time and not the time of your child. I know that you are in pain. It will get better each day, little by little. Trust me, have I ever told you a lie?"

"No, Mother, you have always been there for me. But now you are gone."

"No, my child, I will always be by your side. Put the pillow down and go back to bed. Let me hold you in my arms."

Reluctantly, Louisa lowered the pillow and walked, as if in a dream back to bed. As she lie down she could feel the soothing comfort of her mother's arms wrap around her. How she wished it were real.

She knew this was all a dream, a nightmare played out in her mind over and over. Her worst fear was that one day she would not hear her mother's voice and then what would happen?

Gently, Hedwig lifted Otto's arm from around her and laid it on the bed. Then, with as little motion as possible, turned over to a more comfortable position. She did not want to disturb this gentle sleeping man next to her. She knew he was truly asleep by his even breathing and occasional snore. How she loved this man. It did not seem possible that one could love someone as much as she loved her husband.

Her mind drifted back over the many years and all they had been through together. He was such a proud man. Being a successful businessman and providing for his family had always been most important to him. Even though he never talked about how difficult it had been to give up the taxi and now be doing a job he had always thought beneath him, she knew how unhappy he was.

These last few years had been the hardest. Losing Ernst and then August had almost destroyed her, but Otto had put aside his own pain and been there for her, held her up when she wanted only to collapse in her pain and grief. He understood and felt her need to be strong for the others, especially Louisa.

That child had been through so much: the loss of her father, before the war, then her husband, and so soon thereafter her mother. Hedwig was sure that she must be in terrible pain, even though she hid it so well. What a good mother she was, taking care of that darling little girl as if there were no cares in this world. Hedwig was sure that Elsbeth would grow up to be a happy and healthy person, with Louisa as her mother.

Elsa too, was a wonderful mother always putting her son first. When she was young, Hedwig had wondered what kind of mother Elsa would turn out to be. She had been so concerned about appearances and how other people perceived things that the thought of her being a mother was very worrying. Now, here she was, in the midst of the worst war this world had ever seen, her husband off fighting, her best friend and brother killed, and yet she found something to laugh about every day. Oft times it was Elsa who made the day bearable, making sure that everyone had a reason to smile. When had this change taken place? Her mother did not know. Had she always been this way and Hedwig just never seen? Surely not, but she thanked the Lord that her daughter had somehow changed into this delightful, confident and loving wife and mother who could find something good even in the worst to times.

Hedwig carefully moved again to get a little more comfortable, her old bones complaining just a little. She had no great pain but she was afraid that as she got older, she too would suffer some of the pain she had seen in her dear friend Genevieve's eyes as she climbed the stairs.

The strange thing was that she was now seeing that look in Hannah's eyes. Oh, she was good at covering it up, but Hedwig knew her daughter and she recognized that something was wrong.

No child so young should have to cover up such pain. She must talk to her about it; try to find out what was the cause. She was so young, not yet twenty. Her bones were still growing. There was so little food, perhaps the hunger was affecting her daughter more than she had realized. Yes, she was sure that must be it. She watched Hannah every day say that she was not hungry and give food to the little ones when she should be eating herself. Did she even realize that she was hurting herself?

She must do something. Hedwig could go without food so much more easily than Hannah could. Spring is upon us, the weather getting warmer; soon the garden would begin to yield life-giving nourishment again. Until then, Hedwig would do something to make sure that Hannah ate more. It hurt her so to see such pain on her daughter's face.

Once again, Hedwig felt Otto's arm surround her waist as he turned over in his sleep. The comfort of that unconscious caress helped ease the worries in her mind and slowly she slipped back into the arms of sleep for just a little longer.

Chapter 43
July 18, 1918
An airfield somewhere
behind the German lines in France

Georg wiped the tears from his eyes as he folded the sheets of paper and laid them on his bed. He had laughed so heartily at Elsa's latest letter detailing the escapades of Gus and his imp of a cousin, Elsbeth that the tears had streamed from his eyes. Elsa had such a way with words. He could just picture Gus in his grandfather's very large shoes stamping around the yard as Elsbeth ran behind him, her miniature white apron flapping in the breeze, trying to catch him and scold him. Gus was so superior in those shoes and Elsbeth such a German wife telling him just what to do and how to do it. How he would have loved to witness these two darling children playing as all children do trying to be like the grown-ups.

Elsa's letters were always entertaining, telling him of all the wonderful things the children were doing and learning. She never failed to include a tale of one of the neighbors or the women in town making it sound as if life were normal and she was just on a short vacation to visit her parents while he was off on a business trip somewhere. Yet, he knew that this wonderful woman he was so proud to call his wife was suffering just as all the other families at home were. But somehow she seemed to always know just what would cheer him and make his days better.

Hopefully, he would be able to show her just how much he appreciated her sacrifices very soon. Germany had attained superiority in the air war, as well as on the ground. If the fighting would just end, and Britain and France accept the fact that the Germans were the superior power, the politicians could end this nightmare.

How wonderful it would be to sit in front of a blazing fire out at the farm with Otto and Adolph and August, rest his soul. He could smell the aromatic smoke from their pipes as they discussed the problems of the world. He knew the four of them could find a solution to this dreadful war, especially Otto and Adolph. Those two amazing men, who had lived such ordinary lives and yet had both experienced so much, seemed to understand the ways, not only of Germany but, of the world. Yes, they could find a compromise and resolution, in ways that the politicians had not yet even considered, ending this insanity and returning some normalcy to the world.

With these thoughts of his wife and family in his mind, George headed for the airfield and this day's mission. The sun shining and the brilliant green of the new leaves were enhanced by the light rain of earlier this morning. The fog had now burned off and the sky was clear of any clouds. It was indeed a perfect day for flying. Georg loved days like this because it seemed he could see forever when he was in the air.

He whistled a delightful little tune as he approached his aeroplane. She was such a beauty. One of the newest on the field, the deep five color lozenge pattern material on the tops of the wings and the lighter color on the underside made his plane stand out from the others on the field, but in the air it was much harder for the enemy to make out the shape and size of his Fokker D-VII. He marveled at the engineering that had gone into this machine to make it the supreme plane in the skies. She was small, smaller than the other fighters, but that made her more maneuverable. The total length of this amazing plane was only 23 feet and the wingspan was only 29 feet. She was light and the powerful Mercedes engine gave her a speed of 120 miles per hour. She was definitely the queen of the skies, and he was very proud to have been chosen one of the first to take her into combat.

His leather jacket zipped, he pulled the goggles down from his helmet and climbed into the open cockpit, ready for whatever today's mission would bring. He had gained a reputation as an ace fighter and was a leader of his Jastra. The other eleven men in his squadron looked up to him for leadership and wisdom as they took to the skies each day. Known for his ability to hunt down the enemy and take them out of the sky, while keeping his fellow fliers and himself safe, Georg enforced the strict code of instructions for engaging the enemy, which he had learned from his good friend Oswald Boelche.

There were just six simple rules the fliers must abide by:

- Always attack from above and dive quickly from the rear at the moment of attack.
- Try to place yourself between the sun and the enemy.
- Never fire your gun until you are within range and you have him squarely within your sights.
- Attack when they least expect it.
- Never turn your back on the enemy.
- Last, but perhaps most important, even after you have damaged him, follow him down until he crashes to be sure he is not trying to deceive you.

Georg's men knew these rules were the basis of their success and understood the necessity of teamwork as well as following the lead of the man in charge.

The twelve planes climbed into the sky, a sight beautiful to behold from below. Their symmetry of formation, perfect, like a flock of giant geese, they seemed to glide on the air currents that would lead them to the front. As they approached the front, Georg stared at the now familiar scene below. There were miles of earthwork, the trenches, where so many men lived and fought and died. Designed to protect the men, they had become a living hell for both sides. Between the trenches was no-man's-land, that area of land, sometimes only a few yards and sometimes miles wide, which separated the two sides, yet belonged to no one.

Today there seemed to be little fighting, the quiet, eerie with anticipation of the next volley of shells. No-man's-land always reminded Georg of a river, the trenches on each side the river banks.

He let his mind wander back to the other rivers in his life. The beautiful Rhine that meanders through Düsseldorf, the lifeline of Germany, carrying all that Germany has to sell to the rest of the world while bringing everything that Germany needs to live, to her people. In his mind he could see the sparkling waters and the barges moving up and down the river almost as if it were alive.

He saw too, that wonderful river back in America, that river near which he and Elsa had settled to make their new life, the Maumee, so important historically to Toledo and Ohio. He pictured the beautiful estates that lined the river's edge as it wound its way to Lake Erie. Oh, how he missed the times he and Elsa had spent wandering along the edge of that river and the beautiful sandy beaches of the great Lake Erie.

But this river below him now, this "river of war" was just the opposite of the other rivers in his life. This was not a river of pleasure and life. No this was a river of hate, revulsion, and never ending death. Shaking his head to clear away these dark thoughts, Georg looked about him and smiled to himself with pride as he saw the beautiful planes of his Jastra flying in perfect formation.

Shortly after they left their own front behind, Georg noticed three British Sopwith Camels flying slightly to the north and above them in the same direction as they were traveling. Using his hand to signal his team he began climbing, the others following his lead. When he had reached an altitude about three hundred feet above the Sopwiths and slightly behind, they dove down at the tails of the English, firing as they went.

Before long, Georg found he had to stop firing and made a sharp curve as the Englishman circled around to meet him head on. They circled to the left and then to the right climbing with each revolution. They soon found themselves at about ten thousand feet. Georg realized that this was a pilot as experienced as he who had no intention of allowing him to get the upper hand.

They continued this waltz in the sky for some time, seeming to get closer and closer each circle they made. As they began descending circles, Georg could see the Englishman's face just as full of determination as his own.

Their dance had taken them back across German lines when the Sopwith began flying in a zigzag pattern making it very difficult for Georg to get him within his sights. Then from out of nowhere, two of his team appeared just above him. He backed off and allowed them to take the lead. Within minutes, they had each fired several rounds and Georg watched as the British plane spiraled toward the ground just a few hundred feet behind the German lines.

Without warning there were two more British planes in the sky cutting Georg and his teammates off from the rest of their squadron. Again the circular climb began; this time there were five of them all moving with such precision that an observer would have thought they had spent many hours in rehearsal preparing for just this one choreographed moment of exactitude in the sky.

Georg had little time to wonder where the rest of his team was. He only knew that he was getting tired of this dance and he needed to make his move. With arm signals to his partners he took a chance and dove toward the tail of one of the Sopwiths. His plane was smaller and faster and the sun was behind him. He knew this was the time to make his move.

He was within fifty feet of the tail of the enemy plane when he began firing.

After only five shots, he quickly pulled up and then dived once more. This time coming even closer as he again squeezed the trigger. He saw the head of the pilot drop forward and the Sopwith began to lose altitude. His instinct was to climb back to safety and let the man fall, but he continued to follow him down.

When the wounded pilot's plane was within one hundred feed of the ground, the nose suddenly arched skyward again and the plane began a sharp vertical climb directly toward the Fokker. Georg was stunned by the sudden reversal. Caught unawares, he was slow to react.

Just as he began to pull up the nose of his plane, he heard the bullets hitting his tail. Then he saw the wing fabric shred and begin to peel off the frame. He never felt the shot that tore through his leg as the plane began its short trip to the ground. Somehow, he was aware enough that he was not going to make a recovery and did his best to guide the plane down onto what had once been a field of wheat.

The landing was rougher than anything he had ever experienced but at least he was down safely. With his plane finally at a stop he began to climb out of the cockpit. It was only then that he looked down and saw the wet spot spreading across his trousers. Still not quite understanding what had happened he tried to stand and found he could not. Then, and only then, did he realize that he was injured.

Suddenly as if from nowhere there was a flash of light and a loud explosion. He heard voices shouting as he slumped in his seat. Closing his eyes, he saw Elsa and Gus sitting on a beach of immaculate white sand that sparkled in the sun like a blanket of diamonds. Behind them the azure blue water shimmered, stretching to the horizon and beyond. Never had he experienced a more peaceful scene. Then all was black.

Chapter 44
July 24, 1918
Dusseldorf, Germany

Hedwig was busy in the kitchen. The scent of summer flowers wafted through the open windows filling the house with their fragrance. This was the time of year the gardens, overflowing with produce, offered promise of full stomachs through the winter sure to come. She bushed a strand of hair off her face and plunged another jar into the scalding water. She savored the quiet as she worked in solitude. The knock on the door took her by surprise.

Who could possibly be at the door? Both Hannah and Otto were at work, Elsa and Louisa had taken the children with them to stand in the morning lines. They had planned to let the little ones play in the park on the way home. Hedwig knew that her friend Frieda, next door had gone to visit her sister and surely all of the other women on the block were already standing in the lines. Dusting off her hands on her apron she made her way to the door. Her breath caught in her throat as she opened the door for there stood a deliveryman with a telegraph.

"Frau Georg Mueller?" he inquired.

"She is not here now. I am her mother."

"I have a message for her. May I leave it with you?"

"Of course you may, I will see that she gets it as soon as she returns." The man handed Hedwig the familiar folded paper, turned and made his way down the steps, on his way to deliver his next message.

Her hand shook as she closed the door and turned back into the house. As if in a trance she walked to the big dining room table and sat down in the first available chair. Staring at the paper in her hand she was sure it contained bad news. It could only be concerning Georg. She knew that Elsa had had a letter from him just yesterday so he must be well. And yet, telegrams were only sent with bad news. It was not a military messenger so he must be alive. What could this all mean?

Laying the paper on the table, she got up from the chair and made her way to the kitchen. Suddenly she felt many years older, the weight of the world on her shoulders. How could she possibly get through another day of this horrible war with her family being torn from her one person at a time? First there was Ernst and then August and Genevieve. The toll that had been taken on Louisa was like losing her as well. Otto was just a shell of the man that he had once been and Hannah moved as if she were an old woman. Elsa seemed to be the only one who still had a reason to go on each day. She always had a smile for everyone and was so wonderful with the children. Hedwig just could not bear to see her world shattered as well.

Going back to the table she picked up the paper and held it to her chest. Part of her felt she should open it so she could prepare Elsa for the bad news. Yet she somehow knew that she must not. Elsa was a grown woman and she must let her deal with this in her own way. Going back to the kitchen she prepared the next jar for the boiling hot water.

Children's laughter instantly filled the house as they burst through the door. "I got here faster than you," Gus cried as he ran through the open back door.

"I have more flowers," Elsbeth retorted. "Grandmomma look what I brought you." She rushed past her cousin to be first in her grandmother's arms. "I picked these just for you. Momma said that you liked yellow ones best so I picked all the yellow ones I could find." She thrust a handful of dandelions at her grandmother.

"I picked some too." Gus pushed his way between his cousin and his grandmother offering the two straggling stems he had brought.

"They are all beautiful and you are so right, yellow is my favorite. Please hold them while I get my fanciest vase to put them in." Hedwig did her best to smile as she spoke to these two darlings who were the light of her life.

"What's wrong, Momma?" Elsa asked, recognizing the strained tone in her mother's voice. "Has something happened?"

Hedwig tried to ignore her daughter and continued talking with the children. "Momma, what is it? What are you not telling me?"

By this time Louisa had come into the house, carrying her packages. She too was alarmed by the look on Hedwig's face. "Hedwig, please what is it?"

Hedwig simply turned, saying nothing, walked to the dining table and pointed at the telegram. Louisa picked it up first, reading the address she silently handed it to Elsa.

Hands shaking and knees wobbling, Elsa sat in the nearest of the big old chairs and stared at the paper. Ever so slowly she opened it:

Frau Georg Mueller, please be informed that Sergeant Major Georg Mueller's plane was forced down behind German lines…

Elsa let out a scream and dropped the paper. "I knew it was bad news. I just knew it," Hedwig said, more to herself than aloud. The glazed look in Elsa's eyes told Hedwig all she needed to know. Her son-in-law was gone too.

At 5 A.M. on November 11, the German and Allied delegations signed the armistice...The ceasefire went into effect at the eleventh hour of the eleventh day of the eleventh month of 1918. The most terrible war in history had finally ended.

World War I a Short History by Michael J. Lyons

Chapter 45
November 11, 1918
Düsseldorf, Germany

The front door slam closed. Georg must be going out for his morning exercise, Hannah thought. He had been home now for nearly a month. The leg wound he suffered was healing well. The scars from the burns to his arms and legs, caused by the crash and explosion of the British Sopwith Camel, would fade but never disappear. A reminder of just how lucky he had been that fateful day.

Hannah and Ingrid, sat cross-legged on Hannah's bed. "I don't know what to think. He's your cousin," Hannah waved sheets of paper above her head. "You've known him all your life. What do you think he means?"

"How should I know. I haven't even read the letter?" Ingrid grabbed for the wrinkled sheets in Hannah's hands. "I only know what you told me at work on Saturday. However, it really must be good for you to be this excited. Let me see what he said,"

"Oh, no you don't! I will read you what he said. The first part is all about the war but I will read that too."

"My Dearest Hannah

It is my most sincere hope that you and all of your family are well. The "Flanders Fever" has taken more men in the last weeks than the war. We are hearing that the fever is as bad in Germany as it is here on the front lines. Death from disease often seems even more horrible than death from the injuries incurred in battle because the agony is so prolonged. I sometimes feel that I will never be able to get away from the sight, smell, and sounds of death. I am a man of the earth pledged and trained to preserve the life that God has given us through the bounty of plant life. Yet, here I am dealing with death every hour of every day. I know that I should not complain because I am not on the front lines. I dwell in relative safety away from the barrage of terror with which most of the men must deal continually. Still all this death is almost more than a man can endure. I do what I can to make their final resting place a place of solace and peace, but I am afraid that I can do little to make them beautiful; there is neither time nor money. I can only say a small prayer for each as I lay them in the ground."

"Oh! Hannah that all sounds so terrible. How do you suppose all those men manage to survive from day to day? This war is so terrible!"

"Georg says that he thinks it will be over soon. It's wonderful to have him home. Elsa is so happy; she spends her whole day singing. Little Gus tells everyone he sees that his Papa is home. Moreover, he won't take off Georg's cap. He even sleeps with it on. Georg walks with a bit of a limp but other than that, he seems to be doing very well. He says that he'll have to return as soon as he's completely recovered."

"Has Georg said anything about Wilhelm?"

"Both he and Papa say with Wilhelm II's abdication and the formation of a republic just two days ago, the news of the terrible defeats each day from France and all the unrest here at home, our new leaders must find a way to end all of this very soon."

"I certainly hope so. I just want everyone to come home."

"I want that too, especially Paul. Let me read you the rest of his letter. This is the part that I was telling you about"

Enough of this talk of death. When I get so low, I do my best to turn my thoughts to brighter things. You are always the first thought that comes to my mind. I picture you sitting under our favorite tree at Hagen Brau. You are dressed in your American clothes and are the loveliest woman I have ever seen. Then I remember our first kiss. I can see your eyes, as blue as a summer sky and so full of wonder. I smell your scent that reminds me of the most beautiful rose in the entire Palace garden. Finally, your lips, I feel their softness that welcomes me and I taste the magic that only you can give me. That magic that surrounds you keeps me warm and I know your love will bring me home.

"Hannah, he writes so beautifully. I had no idea he was such a poetic man. He was always different from his brothers, so quiet and sort of artistic, but I don't think that I ever realized just what he was really like."

"I'm sure that I bring out the best in him," Hannah laughed.

"Listen to you. When did you get so confident about men?"

"I'm not confident about all men, just this man.

"Well, read me the rest of it. I can hardly wait to hear what he says next."

When this war is over, and I can only hope that it will be soon, I do not know how soon they will let us all come home. I may be one of the last as I am sure I will be required to do all that I can to take care of the last of those to make this dreadful warn-torn land their final resting place. When I do get home, you are the first person that I want to see. The dream of holding you in my arms again keeps me eagerly waiting each next day. I close my eyes and I see us in our own home. I rise and go to work each day while you make our home the welcoming place I know it will be. Then, when I come home each night you are there waiting just for me. Perhaps before too long we will be blessed with the laughter of children to fill our home. In my dreams, our life is perfect, you and me together for the rest of our lives, living and loving, filling each new day with joy.

This is what I see for us. I can only pray that you feel this way too.

Yours forever
with love,
Paul

"Hannah, you're so lucky. Has he ever talked like that before?"

"Not like this, talking about home and and…and…and babies." It's just a little frightening."

"I do believe that he's asking you to marry him. With all that beautiful prose, I 'm surprised that he doesn't just ask you. It's almost as if he's assuming that you'll be married."

"When I first read this letter I felt the same way. How dare he make such assumptions? Then as I reread it I thought that maybe he is just telling me about his dreams. My dilemma is what do I say back to him? I really don't know what to say? Help me, Ingrid, you know him so well."

"I'm not sure I know him at all anymore. He may be my cousin but it sounds to me that you know him a lot better than me these days."

Blushing, Hannah laughed. "Ingrid! I have never done anything but kiss him and that seems like a lifetime ago. We were so very young then and so many things have happened since then. He talks about coming home and having this perfect life and I don't know if life will ever be anything close to perfect ever again.

"I understand how you feel." Ingrid got off the bed and began pacing the room. "You're right, life will never be as it was. But we can still be happy and look to the future."

Hannah got a dreamy look on her face immediately followed by a frown, "Oh, how I wish that we could go back to 1914 and that wonderful summer just before the war. Now that was perfect. We were so young and naïve. We had everything that young girls could wish for; school, friends, family, youth and most of all innocence. It has only been four years but a lifetime has passed."

"I know what you mean. Here we are. We have been working in the factory for three years now. Every day the same drudgery and when we are home there is the constant worry about where our next meal will come from. Even more than that, there is the constant fear that someone will knock on our door with a telegram or you will get the dreaded envelope with a black boarder." Ingrid walked to the window. "Oh, how I hate those envelopes. These past months there has been so much death here at home with the influenza. I do not think that I know a single family who has not lost someone. These last four years truly have been a living hell.

"Just look at us," Hannah said. "Only a few minutes ago we were laughing so hard that we were crying with glee and now here we are talking about war and death. It just seems to permeate everything. No matter how happy we are, we cannot get away from its strangle hold on seemingly all of life." Hannah's voice rose to almost shouting in her anger at the war's toll on their lives.

"Well, perhaps it is up to us to try to make a difference. I know if I were in charge of the government, I would stop this war right now. Today!!!" Ingrid agreed with her friend.

"What is that noise? It sounds like church bells ringing. Do you hear it?"

"Yes. Wait, there is another church, can you hear them?" It's only eleven o'clock in the morning and it's a Monday. Why are there church bells ringing?" Ingrid wondered.

"Listen, there are more. They seem to be ringing all over the city. Something must be happening. What's going on?" Hannah yelled as she jumped off the bed and headed down the stairs with Ingrid on her heels.

"What is all the ruckus about? Does anyone know?" Hannah cried as the girls headed for the door. "Has something happened?"

"Is Düsseldorf being attacked?" Ingrid asked as she nearly flew out the door. "What is going on?"

"We're not sure. Georg has gone down the street to try to find out," Elsa tried to hold the struggling Gus very close to her. "You cannot follow Papa right now. He'll be right back. I promise."

People were pouring from their houses into the streets as the commotion just continued to grow. The symphony of church bells had now been joined by sirens and horns on the few autos still left on the road as well as the blast of the tugs horns on the river and those at the factories.. It seemed that everything capable of making a loud noise was vying for a part in the impromptu, chaotic orchestra of this Monday morning. Hannah wondered what could possibly be the meaning.

"Here comes Georg. Maybe he found out something." Hedwig said, wringing her hands in her apron.

Running as fast as his injured leg will allow him; Georg made his way up the street through the crowd. "THE WAR HAS ENDED! THE WAR HAS ENDED!!" He shouted at the top of his lungs.

"What did he say? Elsa asked. "I couldn't hear him."

"I think he said something about the war," Louisa grabbed up Elsbeth to keep her from running into the crowd.

"HE SAID THE WAR HAS ENDED!" Hannah shouted at the top of her voice. "IT IS OVER!" she looked back at her family waiting on the steps as she and Ingrid ran down to join the hullabaloo in the streets.

Epilogue
July 1919
Bremerhavan, Germany

Climbing on the bench and stretching just as far as her 5 feet 2 inches would allow, Hannah waved one more time. She could just see the very top of the smokestack of the disappearing ship. It seemed like such a giant just a few minutes before, she was sure she would be able to watch it for hours. Now as the horizon swallowed the last of it, reality began to set in. They were gone. Georg, Elsa and Gus were on their way back to America. What had started out as a wonderful summer vacation five years ago had finally come to an end. She would miss them terribly, yet she knew how much Elsa was looking forward to getting back to her old life. Would it ever be the same? Somehow, Hannah doubted it.

"Sit down, Hannah. You will just make yourself even sadder." Paul reached out his hand to help her down, then sat down beside her. "They are gone. You have to recognize that. You will see them again. I promise if it is the last thing I ever do."

Hannah leaned her head on her husband's chest as he pulled her close. She felt his heart beating and knew in her very soul that he would keep his promise. She closed her eyes and allowed herself to feel the strength and love that radiated from him.

So many things had happened since that day back in November when the bells rang tolling the end of the war. It was only eight months ago and yet it seemed a lifetime. She had felt for so long that the war would go on forever and then almost with no warning it was over and life changed again. Their little family had endured much in that big house, Momma worked so hard to make a home. Because of her, they had gotten through all the trials, disappointments and even some joys together. Now there was no one left in the big house but Momma and Papa.

As soon as the weather began to get nice, Louisa and little Elsbeth had moved back to Genevieve's house. Papa and Georg spent months doing repairs because the house had been empty for nearly five years. They fixed all the broken windows and pipes. Miraculously it appeared that all of the furniture was still here. The women had gone each summer, even after Genevieve's death, planted a garden, and spent some time in the house nearly every day, hoping that people would realize that it was still a beloved home and part of a family.

Louisa said that it was time to get on with her life. Her friend Corrine had lost her husband, as well, and the two of them were running a boarding house. Corrine and her son, who was now nine years old, helped Louisa with the cooking and cleaning. Together they served two meals a day for the four men who each had a room on the second or third floor.

These were men who had come home from the war to find that they no longer had families, most having been lost to starvation or the horrible flu epidemic last year. Louisa actually had room for at least two more people and she felt sure that she would be able to fill the house and make a reasonable living that way. She brought Elsbeth to see Momma several mornings a week and Momma watched her while Louisa did her marketing. Momma seemed to look forward to those mornings with more anticipation each week.

In March, they celebrated Gus's fifth birthday. He had been such a tiny baby when they arrived from America. Now he was going to go to school in the fall. How could that be possible? Hannah had watched him learn to walk and talk. Elsa was such a good mother who never gave up her dream of returning to America. She was so proud of the fact that Gus was an American citizen and had made certain that he learned to speak English.

Hannah had listened and played along as he was learning. However, she had to admit that Gus was certainly better at that strange foreign language, than was she. He often carried on a conversation with either his mother or father using both languages as if they were one. Hannah was sure that he would easily adjust to his new home in Toledo.

In April, Paul came home and before she had had time to think she was getting married. It had been a small wedding in their home. Only the family had been there and, of course, Ingrid and her family. She was Paul's cousin, after all. One of Paul's brothers had been able to attend. The best surprise had been Greta. She and her family had just arrived back in Düsseldorf from Bonn.

After the wedding, Paul and Hannah had moved to the farm. Adolph and Margried were having difficulties taking care of the all the responsibilities and had encouraged the young folk to join them. Paul was able to take over most of the actual duties of the farm yet somehow allowing Adolph to believe that he was still in charge. Margried had had another difficult winter and appreciated all of Hannah's help cooking and taking care of the house.

The men often sat in the evenings and discussed the war and all of it ramifications. Where Germany was headed in the future? When and how would the economy rebound? Both seemed sure that there would never be another war like the one just fought.

Not long before their wedding Papa had given up his position on the trolley and begun driving his taxi. Being his own boss again seemed to breathe new life into his old bones. Hannah knew that he would never get over the loss of August and the sacrifices that all of them had had to make. At least he was back doing what he loved and that was something.

"Come, darling, it is time that we start back." Paul brought Hannah out of her reverie. "Your Papa will need his wonderful auto in the morning and I promised him that we would get it back all in one piece." He gently held her hand and helped her up. Slowly they walked back to the place where they had left their vehicle.

"I am just going to miss them so very much. I got very used to having them all here over these last five years." Hannah sighed, tears forming in the corners of her eyes. "I'm certain that I could never have survived those terrible times that were insinuated upon us all without little Gus's daily antics and Elsa's wonderful sense of humor."

"I know, my darling, I am going to miss them too. I will especially miss that gleam in Georg's eye each time he looks at, or speaks about little Gus." Paul's voice had a wistful quality.

Slowly a smile began to spread across Hannah's face and her cheeks started to glow with warmth she felt each time she looked at this man she loved so very much. "I have a feeling that you may be having a gleam in your own eye next spring," she laughed as she threw her arms around his neck.

ABOUT THE AUTHOR

Penelope Ohmann Lindblom is a retired teacher and tutor for students with special needs. She lives in Monroe, North Carolina with her husband Charles Lindblom. They have four children and ten grandchildren.

Penelope enjoys reading, writing, traveling and singing when she is not working helping children learn to read.

Made in the USA
Charleston, SC
27 May 2015